GYPSY OF THE SEA

HELEN DEAN BREWER

LOST COAST PRESS
Fort Bragg
California

To my husband Charlie
Love Always

BOOK I

ONE

Sophia hadn't seen Vanessa in years when she saw her in Cambridge. Traveling in Boston for a week, Sophia bumped into her in Harvard Square on a Saturday afternoon. To Sophia's surprise, Vanessa hadn't changed. One would have expected lots of transformations, considering that Vanessa was very impulsive — she moved with the flow and mood of things, quickly adjusted to her surroundings. They greeted each other politely, and asked the usual questions two friends ask who have had a falling out and haven't spoken to one another since. Neither harbored hard feelings — the reason they hadn't spoken had become meaningless during the hiatus.

They decided to go to lunch and catch up on each other's lives. Vanessa suggested the Bombay Restaurant. Sophia had heard of it, the restaurant on the second floor of a renovated mansion right in the center of town, and agreed. They sat at a small table against the window overlooking the street. A waiter greeted them. Vanessa ordered water, and Sophia asked for a Bloody Mary.

"You're still drinking your Bloody Marys?"

"Oh, yeah. You know I've always loved Bloody Marys," she said, stirring her drink. "So, how's everything? Are you still living in the North End?"

"Yep. Signed another lease for my apartment just a few weeks ago. I like the neighborhood, but it has gotten too expensive for

3

me to buy anything, so rent it is. Everything else is going well. I'm still working at the nonprofit organization. We just got back from a trip through Spain. The kids on the trip this year were great; they completely fell in love with the country."

Vanessa and Sophia weren't always this distant with one another. They'd become very close three years earlier, after having met at the Flying Pig Youth Hostel in Amsterdam. It was located in the center of the city, just two blocks from the train station and right near the Red Light District. Sophia got off the train from Paris and walked straight to the hostel. She dropped her pack near the front door and walked down the narrow hallway to the reception desk. A guy in his early twenties with dirty blonde dreadlocks was sitting behind the desk, smoking a joint and watching a football game on the TV, which was precariously positioned on a filing cabinet. He had his feet propped up on a wooden stool and was leaning back casually in his chair.

"Hey, how's it going? Do you have any beds?"

The guy turned around in his chair, exhaled a puff of smoke, and smiled at her. He was wearing an Adam Ant T-shirt.

"Yeah, we do. Is it just you?"

"Just me. How much is it a night?"

"Twenty-five guilders. How many nights do you want to stay?"

"I don't know. We'll see."

Sophia paid him for the first night and gave him her passport for collateral, then grabbed her backpack and walked past the stoned guests who lingered in the hallway discussing current events from their perspective. Sophia turned around and asked the guy, "Hey, where can I find some good puff?"

"Everywhere," he replied with a long, drawn-out laugh.

Sophia nodded, fully understanding what he meant, and climbed the stairs that led to her room. She knocked on the door before opening it, but no one answered. There were four beds in the small, clean room — two were bunk beds — and one bathroom. She leaned her backpack against the wall and collapsed onto a bed to nap.

She slept for hours.

It was dusk when Sophia awoke. Remembering where she was and feeling hungry, she showered and decided to go down to the lobby to see whether anyone was hanging out and if they had plans to go out for the night. A group of backpackers sat on the couch drinking Heinekens and talking. Sophia approached them.

"Hey, what's going on? I'm Sophia. Have you guys been staying here awhile?"

The blonde one turned toward her. With an Australian accent, he said, "Hey, what's up? I'm Andy. This is my friend Marc and his friend Monique. And this one," he said, pointing, "might be your relative — she's from the States too — this is Vanessa."

"How did you know I'm American?"

"Your accent. You Americans talk with flat vowels."

"Oh, I thought you figured it was because I'm not wearing dark socks with my sneakers; I thought maybe that could have thrown you off."

"No, it's your accent." Andy smiled.

"Nice to meet you, Sophia," Vanessa said. "Where are you from?"

Sophia told her.

"And you?"

Vanessa told her.

On the way to the Greenhouse, in the Red Light District, they decided to get something to eat. Monique spoke so little that Sophia asked Vanessa about her. Vanessa said that Monique was from Nice and didn't talk much because she couldn't speak English very well. Vanessa told her that she had met Marc the other day, spending her holiday in Amsterdam, lingering on the Aussie's arm and trying to converse with him in his limited French, which he was teaching himself out of a pocket-sized language book. She wouldn't attempt to speak English; she would rather have him thumb through his book and look up the exact word he was trying to express.

By the end of the evening, Andy was completely stoned, so Sophia and Vanessa ended up talking the whole night — forming a bond between two American girls traveling through Europe alone. Vanessa told Sophia she had just graduated from college on the East Coast and was reflecting on what she wanted to do with her life. She used the word "reflecting" to explain her decision to travel to Europe before going home to get 'a real job,' as it was defined back in the States. Vanessa's indecisiveness amused Sophia — she liked that Vanessa wasn't a structured, mundane girl who had her life planned out to the moment she expected to retire. She found such people boring.

They spent a lot of time together during the remaining days that they were in Amsterdam, and then decided to travel together for a while, moving on to Budapest and then to Brasov. They thought it would be a thrill to linger in Count Dracula's castle.

"Well, that's great," Vanessa said. "I'm glad everything is working out for you."

"So, how's everything with you, Sophia?"

She knew what Vanessa was getting at. The little inquiry that can have so many implications — the strength of this seemingly innocent question could stop the motion of the air. The moment she saw Vanessa reading a magazine at the newspaper stand in Harvard Square, Sophia had known that this question had been on her friend's mind since the war. Sophia had spotted Vanessa at the stand, and touched her arm, wondering if it really was her old friend, and Vanessa had looked up, a surprised expression on her face, then a look of inquiry, curiosity. Sophia noticed that Vanessa quickly stopped herself from asking right away how everything had turned out with the guy she had met at the end of her trip in Europe.

It was inevitable that the question would arise, and Sophia would have to tell Vanessa something. There was no hiding now; she felt exposed—a feeling like a vacuum inside her chest—and had to surrender to the question, at least for now. She tried to swallow the lump in her throat, but it was as if a rock had lodged there. Sophia hadn't talked about Abraham since she had last seen him in Albania about a year ago. She didn't want to talk to anyone about it because she didn't know where she could possibly begin. So much inside her was unsaid, and now she was feeling this vacuum.

"Everything is very good," Sophia said. I'm doing graduate work in history out in California. I'll be finished with classes next year, and then, of course, comes my dissertation, so I'm going to be in California for the next few years."

"What do you want to do afterward? Do you have anything in mind?"

"I'd like to teach at a university—we'll see what happens."

"Look at you, the studious one!" Vanessa said. "I knew you had it in you."

Vanessa quickly changed the subject.

"And what ever happened to that guy Abraham you met when visiting family? The one you told me about. Remember when you and I split up after traveling together for a little while and you went to Albania? Are you still keeping in touch with him—if you possibly can, that is?"

Sophia took a deep breath and ran her finger around the rim of her glass. She looked down at the people on the sidewalk below, walking toward the university. "The last time I saw or spoke to Abraham was in Albania. It was great meeting him, of course, but you know how limited that kind of thing can be..." Sophia looked down at the table and fumbled with her napkin as she spoke. "He joined the KLA and fought in Kosovo last year."

"He what?"

"He joined the Kosovo Liberation Army and fought in Kosovo."

"He did?"

"Yes," Sophia replied, emphasizing the "s."

"You never told me that he did that. How do you know?"

"Well, he told me before he left."

"You never told me any of this. What happened?"

"He never came back from that war, as far as I know, from what I've been told." She could feel her voice become weak as she spoke the words "that war." It angered her that she had to distinguish it as that war. There were so many wars in the Balkans.

"Good God, Sophia! I'm so sorry to hear that."

Sophia hoped Vanessa didn't notice her eyes becoming watery. Sophia hadn't talked about Abraham in awhile, so she never became emotional about him; she didn't know if it was because she was hurt or frustrated or both. She was surprised to find herself reacting this way, to know that it was still bothering her. Sophia turned away to hide her eyes. If only Vanessa knew what happened, she thought. The whole story, not the part I casually tell everyone.

"There's a lot more to it than what I'm telling you, and I'd rather not talk about it—probably never will. I think of it as just an episode in my life that's probably better left alone."

Vanessa looked at her, and Sophia looked back, confused, not knowing what her friend was thinking. Vanessa might have been remembering the time when they'd had a falling out and Sophia had left things unsaid. Or maybe she was thinking it was foolish of Sophia to keep it all inside. It didn't matter, though—Sophia really felt she didn't need anyone to talk to.

"Well, how was visiting with your family?" Vanessa said, changing the subject. "Did you have a good time?"

"Oh, that was great. I'm glad I went there to meet my relatives, the ones on my father's side whom I've never met. That was an experience all in itself. I'd like to go back someday."

"Good, I'm glad," Vanessa said. She stared at Sophia again for a moment, knowing that Sophia's story wasn't making sense; it was contradictory and had holes in it, but she could see that Sophia didn't want to talk. "You know, Sophia, it's not healthy to hold things in. You should really let it out. From what I could tell from your emails after we got home from Europe, you were completely into this guy. What really happened?"

Sophia felt ashamed and betrayed. She hurt, felt like a failure. She wanted to take all these feelings and hurl them away, couldn't believe she was still so affected, that her emotions could resurface from just a simple conversation with an old friend. She wanted to lock them up and forget them until she was ready to remember—when she was too old to feel anymore.

"Thanks, Vanessa, but like I said, it's probably better left alone. I'd have to create enough room inside myself to think about what I did and what I experienced, but I'd rather just move on. I went to Albania to visit my family, to take the trip I was supposed to take with my father. These are the memories I'd like to keep."

"Why don't you write it down? Write down everything you want to say about your trip to Albania—the good and the bad—everything, all the stories, all the lies, all the truths. Just for you. I'm sure that will help."

"Vanessa, I wouldn't know where to start."

"Start at the beginning. It's as simple as that. When you're finished, I'd like to read it—if you don't mind, that is."

"I'll think about it when I get home later this week. But if I write this, Vanessa, I'm going to write it in the third person."

"Why?"

"Because I'm not that person anymore."

From the beginning, Sophia said to herself, then spoke into the air, "For all sad words of tongue or pen, the saddest are these: 'It might have been.' I think that quote is appropriate here. Do you know who said that? I forgot, but I haven't forgotten the quote. Maybe I will begin my memoir." She laughed as she said this—sounded amusing to her for some reason.

"Good. Oh, here comes our food. It's really great to see you again, Sophia."

"It's nice to see you, too, Vanessa," she replied as she placed a napkin on her lap.

Two

There were so many things Sophia might never understand because it wasn't her war. These wars would never be her wars. Her world was so different from theirs that the things they fought for were meaningless to Americans. But to them they were something to live and to die for. If not, a man couldn't hold his face up to his children without being overwhelmed by shame. History lingered in the air in their part of the world; it was their identity, and they remembered it. They remembered what happened to their people and their culture as if it had happened yesterday.

In this part of the world people spoke in the past tense, thought in the past tense, breathed in the past tense.

Where she came from, history had become more an assimilation of cultures, a perfected process of mixing people from all over the world and molding them, like an assembly line that placed people on a moving belt, stripped them of their clothing, and put on appropriate American clothing. Moving on to the next station, it combed their hair in an American style, and, last and most important, it pulled out their tongues and replaced them with new ones, tongues that had no accents or lisps, and with a little practice could speak English. This was how America liked its immigrants. And this new image, this new identity, this new definition of themselves defined them. It was not they who had created this. No one knew anymore who had. It became part of the American culture and remained that way. No one would change it because no one really wanted to.

But this part of the world, this part where Sophia was venturing, was different. When another culture tried to mold them, people remembered, and they didn't like it.

On the morning she would drive to Albania, Sophia said goodbye to her family in Greece. She was leaving to visit other relatives, their relatives too, yet they didn't want to see her go. They were so happy their American cousin had came to visit, but to go to *that country* was another matter. They remembered when they too had lived in Albania, just over the border in a village tucked away in the southernmost part of the country. It was hidden from the world, and no one had ever heard of it unless their own heritage originated there, or they just happened to be studying the history of the Ottoman Empire or Greece or Yugoslavia or World War II.

It existed within a milieu of medieval rites — a synthesis of pagan and Muslim and Christian ideas, an outlandish oddity right in the middle of Europe. A cultural uniqueness endured in those mountains. There was something distinctly unusual about the country, and she wanted to see it for herself. But as odd as the representations she heard might be, Sophia was looking forward to visiting her relatives, the smell of morning air, the intimacy of country life, and the isolation in the mountains. Yet her relatives reminded her of a life of struggle that she could only possibly imagine while listening to the stories they occasionally told.

"In this pocket of the world, after the Great War people became Albanian nationally, but culturally they were Greek, and this most definitely affected their lives," she would hear herself explain to friends. "Wars sometimes do that, switch borders, and the people aren't told they're being switched. It's similar to the war between Texas and Mexico, when the Mexicans who lived in the Southwest suddenly became Americans, but couldn't speak English, and were Catholics, not Protestants. Different eras, different people, same problems."

Kosta had sent a letter to the family, announcing that he was bringing Sophia to visit. When they received the letter, they passed it around the entire village and told their world that she was coming, that she would arrive in the next couple of weeks, making this trip without her father.

Her father's mind had never wandered very far from his birthplace. He talked about his life in Albania, and wanted her to see where he had come from, what he had been exposed to.

But his time had run out before he could show her his village.

Once they left Border Control and got past the lines of cars waiting to cross into Greece, they entered Albania, drove down the main road, and then headed off to the right onto a road that few people ever traveled. This would take them to three Greek villages, the farthest being the one they were going to. They drove through the first small town, where people sitting on their doorsteps watching the day go by abruptly stared at them as their car passed, wondering who this foreigner was and what she was doing here. They looked at her with wonder, like she was an alien from another world, and most shocking, was traveling with one of their own.

Kosta stopped the car so they could buy bottled water for their trip into the mountains. An old man, his face weather-beaten and his eyes watery and deep blue, was sitting on a beat-up wooden chair against the wall of the town's cafe. He held his cane in his right hand and a soggy cigar in the other. Assuming the man was the owner, Sophia got out and approached him to ask if he sold bottled water. He looked at her as if she were a mystery, as though he'd never before seen another human before. She walked up the steps and stood in front of him. His eyes had never left her face as she walked toward him. She smiled and pointed toward the counter behind him, and spoke to him in Greek.

"Excuse me, do you sell bottled water—the non-carbonated kind?"

"Where are you from?"
"I'm from America."
"Where in America?"
"Chicago."
"Oh, Michael Jordan, Chicago Bulls!"
She laughed. "Is that all you've heard about Chicago?"
"Al Capone, bang, bang!"

They arrived just before dark as the dirt road climbed toward a broad stretch of land. A boy ran to the car, waving his arms in the air and yelling to anyone that they had arrived. He came to the driver's side and clung to the car door as Kosta drove slowly toward the cluster of homes.

"Papa, you finally came back! Is this my cousin from America?" the boy asked.

Vangelli looked at her and whispered something in his father's ear. "Yes, son," Kosta replied, "this is your cousin Sophia from America."

"Hal-lo, hal-lo!" he showed Sophia the little English he'd learned.

Vangelli ran away toward the village just ahead, wanting to be the first to tell everyone that she had arrived. People came out of their homes and looked out to the only road that connected them to the rest of the world. They wanted to see who this foreigner was — the stranger they had only heard about.

That stretch of land Sophia had seen from a distance became a farm as they drove near. A few weeds and crops defined it, and a run-down tractor sat in the grass. It was faded red and dusty — a playground for the kids. The air tasted crisp and it cooled her lungs. *Mountain air provides a cleanser for the human body, a purifier for the soul.* As the car crawled along, Sophia slumped back in the seat, letting the night air captivate her.

Old, she first thought, staring out the window. Everything looked old and worn and tired. The stone cottages looked exhausted, like they had been through a lot and had witnessed too much. She felt like she had just stepped backward in time, to a place time had forgotten, as though history had decided to make a defining mark during a certain epoch and happened to pick this, a medieval one.

Just above a valley, the houses seemed to be placed randomly on the mountainside. They were of brown and gray wood and stone, and had small window openings with no panes of glass. Animals lurked in the yards, fenced in by flimsy wire that the men had cut down from the newly placed telephone poles installed by the government. The villagers were in agreement that everyone they knew or needed to know was within either shouting or walking distance.

A path made of rocks, pressed into the ground from years of being trod upon, led to the village. At the valley's edge stood an Orthodox Church. Abandoned now, though much used in the past, it had been a part of their existence in one way or another since time immemorial. Wrapped around the church was a rusted iron fence, its large front gate secured by a padlocked chain. The broken windows, the weeds crawling all over the landscape, the layer of dust that had spread itself over the entire church, had been left this way. It was partially destroyed and entirely shut down in 1967, when the president at the time banned all religion, and was never rebuilt or used after that. They had become used to the idea of not going to church, perhaps praying from inside their homes and then looking out their windows at the church. *If we could have, God, we would have.* Sophia was fixated on the church. Isolated and old, it seemed lonely. How much the village had been neglected by the world, marching to its own beat.

She watched the village become larger as Kosta drove up and stopped at the plaza, yet her first impression remained intact. People gathered around the car. Sophia looked out the window as they scrutinized her. She felt microscopically observed. "Going to Albania was an encounter with time, a very interesting trip," Sophia would say later when people asked about it.

They put their hands on the car — touched it, gazing with wonder at who was inside. A few men, sitting on the stone wall that wrapped around the plaza, abruptly stopped their conversations to look. Rarely did people visit their village, and if there was a visitor, it was never a foreign one.

Sophia hopped out of the car and they approached her with wide-eyed smiles, reaching to touch her hands and kiss her.

"We're so happy you made it, that you didn't forget about us. I'm Penelope, your aunt." She reached up toward Sophia's face, clasping both of her hands, kissing both of her cheeks. Penelope was dressed in black and wore black stockings and black shoes — her father had passed away ten years ago.

As Kosta opened the trunk to get out her backpack, Sophia talked and hugged and kissed this family, her family. They didn't want to let her go, kept holding on to her, the first one to visit them since her father had left fifty years ago.

Kosta introduced Sophia to the rest of the family. "You already met my son Vangelli." Kosta pointed to a girl in the back of the group. "This is my daughter, Athina, and this," he explained, gesturing toward the young man standing next to Athina, "is Stavro, another cousin of yours."

Sophia walked up to them. "Good. I have found you."

"Good you have made it," Athina said, kissing both of her cheeks.

Athina was a vibrant girl, full of life. She was about Sophia's age, maybe a little younger. She stared at Sophia, and smiled and held onto her hand as they talked.

"How was the drive? Was it okay?" she asked, still smiling.

"Yes, it was fine. A little bumpy."

"Of course," she laughed. "The roads that lead to the mountains aren't that good. We don't have too many visitors. A bus comes once a week, but sometimes, if it breaks down, no one comes until it gets fixed. And that could take more than a month. It's good you came with a car. The bus is old." Athina pointed to a thoroughly run-down bus next to the plaza. Sophia thought it couldn't run even if someone tried, and had just been left there because no one knew what to do with it.

Stavro shuffled his feet in the dirt and looked on as they talked. He didn't quite know what to say, so he reached into his pocket for a pack of cigarettes, took one out and lit it.

"Hey, Stavro, aren't you going to greet your cousin? You know how far I've traveled just to see you?" said Sophia.

He smiled shyly and approached to hug her. "Good you have made it."

"Good to have found you."

"Let's go into the house and get settled. I'll make some coffee," Kosta said, lifting Sophia's backpack and walking up the path to their home. Stavro grabbed the backpack from him. "Let me take this, Kosta."

Penelope walked with Kosta, Vangelli squeezing past them, running up the path. Athina and Stavro followed, and Sophia walked alone behind everyone. The villagers waved at them and smiled at Sophia as they passed, greeting and welcoming her — this foreigner who had traveled halfway around the world to visit them. Even though she didn't know them, she was still visiting them. Whatever happened here happened to the entire village.

Tired and sluggish, Sophia tuned out the voices ahead of her as they chatted about how everyone was doing. The sounds of crickets in the grass were magnified, the mountain air chilled her skin. She turned around and looked up at the sky. The bright moon hung high above the mountains, illuminating the village. Other than the sun, she thought, the moon was the only thing that had shed light on this village for a long time. She turned and followed her family to the tiny, brightly-lit house at the top of the hill.

Stavro opened the door and put the backpack down against the wall. Everyone followed inside, quickly filling the room. The living room smelled damp and old, as if it had been stored in an attic for memory's sake. A small table sat in the center of the room; the chairs around it didn't match. It was worn, generously used for all occasions, particularly for afternoon talks and coffee. A big chair sat in the far corner of the room. Next to it, against the wall, was a brown couch, above which a photograph of the village hung, slightly crooked, a thin layer of dust on its frame. The paint on the walls was chipped and rough. Beyond the living room were two small bedrooms. One had a full-size bed with a trunk at its foot, over which lay a white lace cloth. A mirror hung near the single closet. The other bedroom had two small beds, one at either side of the room, with a nightstand between them. The bed farthest from the door had a very concave mattress. A small stack of outdated magazines lay next to it, famous European singers and actors on the covers.

"That's the room where you'll be sleeping, Sophia," she heard Athina say from behind. "I'll be sleeping in there with you," she said, pointing to the room with two beds. "It's going to be so much fun. I'm so happy you're here," she said, hugging her.

"I'm very happy that I'm here too, really," Sophia said, and let go.

The one large window looked onto the front porch and down the hill. On the window ledge, a statue of the Virgin Mary looked in. She seemed to have been placed there strategically, perfectly, placed to see what is.

Though the room seemed neglected, it felt used and welcoming.

Places like these aren't on a map until someone comes along and puts them there with their thumb. Who are these people? How would we class them in the big scheme of things? For centuries, they have lived in barbarian fiefdoms, controlled by their own rules and laws, their foundation lying in the customs and traditions of their culture. Isolated from the rest of the world, partially because of topography, partially because of politics, they were perceived as a lost society defined by feral forces.

Then, along comes a man who feels their pain and tells them he understands and empathizes with them and their feelings of suppression. He is one of them. The people embrace him because he instills hope in them. He studies their habits of mind and embraces them. This is the way it is, then, and the people believe in it and have faith in it, and they force themselves to love it. And they do, for a time, until they can't lie to themselves any longer.

The forces that precipitate spiritual exhaustion are among the most powerful in the world.

They eat away and deteriorate a society swiftly and methodically, penetrating its people to their core. They may try to shake off this delusion and free themselves. Some make it and some don't; some have loved ones who don't make it. And they're remembered.

But in the end the people regain their spirituality and acquire a new sense of hope, one more tangible and less elusive. The dictator falls, and social unrest is uncapped and let loose. The dictator dies, perhaps, or is forced to leave, but his crony-infested regime remains intact. Nothing has changed, really, except the names. The people have released themselves from their government's relentless corruption and try to replenish their spirits, but after a fifty-year hiatus, nothing has changed. The same shams are implemented, the same ploys used to persuade people to believe in the administration. And the cycle recurs continually.

Hope can eat away a person's soul and compassion. In the end, when everything has been devoured, hope remains, even though there is no solution in the future, no remedy to fix all that has been lost. Hope builds itself up again, and the people's spirituality lingers in the air. And the government senses this and embraces it. It wants its people to believe in it once again, and have faith in it and trust it and love it. And the government has a grandiose vision to help its people partake in the great capitalism of the world. *You too can become wealthy and live in a beautiful country.* And the people's hope swells, moved by these fantastic words. They feel it and want to taste it and love it. They want to know what it's like to be wealthy and live in a beautiful land, and have people envy them. They listen to the words and have hope in them. *Invest your money in the Federal Reserve and you too can receive a lot of interest on your money.* The people are drawn to this and can't ignore it, and little by little they begin to take the money from underneath their beds and put it in the federal bank because they want to believe. The promise is fulfilled for a month, or two months, or three; and the people believe it, and have faith, and hope again. Everyone is happily becoming wealthy, receiving the interest they were promised for four months, five months, or six months, perhaps a year. Until one day, in the middle of the afternoon, the bank accounts disappear somehow, as if the wind had blown them away. And the people's faith deflates in the moment and their hope just shriveled up.

It is truly astonishing how a country's body politic can be moved by one man's passion.

THREE

"Your father was a strong boy, we remember that about him. One time, someone made a bet with him that he couldn't lift a horse on his back. The man challenged him to lift the horse for just a few seconds. It wasn't a big horse, just a pony, but still, it was *a pony*. Your father accepted, shook the man's hand, and stood on a tree stump. The pony was brought over, and he just grabbed its front legs and lifted. I tell you, if I didn't see if for myself I wouldn't believe it. That story is still told here in the village. Everyone remembers Nonta, the boy who lifted a pony on his back."

This was what they told Sophia as she sat in the living room drinking coffee with her newly acquired family. They remembered her father when he was young, strong, and vibrant, when he was able to do anything, feared nothing, and challenged everything. But they didn't know him when he was old and sick, tired and weak and scared.

Her father's strength dripped out of his body the last days he was alive. The doctors wanted to release him from the hospital so he could spend his last days in his world, in his comfort, in his awareness. They said they couldn't do anything more to stop the cancer from spreading. Her brother pushed the wheelchair to the front door and carried their father up to his bedroom, where he would spend the remainder of his life; he never left his bed until he closed his eyes for the last time.

She remembered coming home from class one day and going up to his bedroom to talk. She knocked on the door before she entered, slowly opening the door, anxious to see how he looked. These days frightened her. He was weakening and becoming frailer. The lump of his body under the covers looked small, but somehow his mind was still alert. When she walked into the bedroom, he lay, half-asleep, rearranging the memories in his head, which ones were the most important, which had become petty, organizing what was important and crucial these days, though time had lost all meaning. It didn't matter what time of day it was—he slipped into and out of sleep whenever his body felt like it. Through these last days, however, he always asked her how her day was, and if anything new was happening in her life.

He still wanted to be a part of it—and she would let him.

She talked with him as if nothing were wrong, hoping to keep his spirits up, but she did it mostly for herself. It was a time in her life when she needed normalcy, and she always got this from him. When she told him about a paper she was writing for class, he would listen attentively, his mind a great contradiction compared to his body. He would ask questions and she would answer in great detail.

The day after he was released from the hospital, he asked her to open the drawer of his nightstand and take out a small jewelry box. She took out the box and opened it. Inside was a gold pocket watch with black Roman numerals. The watch had been passed along over the generations, had been in the family forever. He told Sophia that it had been given to him when he was a boy, during World War Two, and he wanted her to have it.

Sophia thanked her father and put the watch in her pocket. She promised him she would take care of it and pass it on—maybe to a child of her own when she started a family. She changed the subject then, telling him about the paper she was writing for her Russian History class. The topic she had chosen was the Bolshevik

Revolution. Halfway through their conversation, when his mind began to tire, her father asked if they could continue talking later in the evening. Earlier, she had noticed him drifting in and out, his eyes closing for a longer time and then slowly opening again, but she had persisted. She finally gave up and told him she would bring him dinner in a few hours. "Rest well," she said, then walked out of her father's bedroom and shut the door behind her.

She leaned against the door and slumped to the floor, burying her face in her hands, crying softly.

Sophia's parents would occasionally visit her at college. They came one weekend in October and took her out to dinner that evening. They sat at a table toward the back of the restaurant, drinking a bottle of wine her father had ordered. Her mother was the one to ask if she had found anyone yet, someone she could bring home to the family and announce that this was the man she was planning to marry.

William came to mind, but Sophia quickly pushed the thought aside. How could she possibly tell her parents that she was thinking of her professor? What would they say? "What do you mean, you're dating a married man? You are not dating this man; he's just using you, plain and simple." She would deny it, telling her mother she didn't know the whole story and how it had come about. She would defend her relationship with William and tell her parents that he was in love with her and she with him, and that if he weren't married, things would look more respectable. "Trust me. I know what I feel and I know how he feels," she would say to them, and her mother would scoff and her father would smile, perhaps wanting to believe her. But this would never happen. She would never tell her parents about a relationship that involved complex explanations. For them, love and life and marriage were simple — people were what made these things more complex and confusing.

"No, I haven't found anyone yet. I've got time."

"You don't have that much time. When I was your age—"

"I was already married with two kids," Sophia finished her mother's sentence for her. "I know, Ma. You always tell me this story. But I'm not you. I'm doing other things with my life right now."

"Well, you better hurry up. You're not a little girl anymore."

"And I'm not that old, either."

"You're looking older. You're starting to get a little heavier. I guess your metabolism is slowing down. And your eyes, they look tired, and around the corners they're starting to get wrink—"

"Ma, don't start with me tonight," Sophia said, staring her mother down.

This was a typical conversation between the two of them, but Sophia tried filtering out what her mother was saying. Her father looked out the window when her mother went off on this humiliating tangent; acting as though he weren't listening, focusing his attention on something very interesting outside. Sophia tried changing the subject to avoid another unnecessary argument about something she and her mother could never agree upon.

She continually told herself that the way William made love to her proved that he was in love with her, the way he grabbed the back of her hair and pulled her close, the look on his face. She didn't need to convince anyone about what they felt for each other. No one would be able to understand, anyway; no one would be able to realize that it was more than a professor/student relationship. It could be something more if circumstances were different, if certain people weren't in the way. And she enjoyed the fact that no one knew of the relationship. It was their secret, and she didn't have to defend it to anyone. She could relish it as much as she wished, and think about yesterday afternoon as much as she liked. Locked in the vault of her mind, it was hers. And his. She could protect it from the outside world, protect herself from being misunderstood and perhaps looked down upon. She would remind herself of this, would become lost in it at times, and it would help her confirm her belief.

Leaving his office to go home to her apartment, Sophia would feel happy, and this was what was most important to her. A man she deeply admired and was attracted to was making love to *her*. She wouldn't always be able to keep this secret life separate from the real world in which she lived. It was something that had no existence outside his office and his mind and hers. It was as if she were two people — a dichotomy of two experiences, two exposures to the world.

But after leaving his office, she felt content in her own home, alone. William reassured her that he would try to make things different for them one day. If he could. And he would tell her that they would see each other soon, and make love again, and share each other again.

For now, this was enough for her.

We carried with us what we could find among the ash and soot and torched wood that used to be our home. Somehow, I found old photos of my father and put them in my shirt pocket as my mother rummaged through the pile, looking for anything we could use to rebuild our home once the war was over and the Germans had left. She looked away every time she began crying again. The Nazis had made her cry.

After our village was burned down, the villagers lived in the valley below for weeks before they could rebuild their homes. Ours was built quickly because my brothers and I built it together, and then helped the older people with their homes. We built the stone cottages as they were before — in the exact same locations on the hill. We wanted everything to be the same as before the war started. We wanted to forget this memory — it was difficult, but we tried.

I recall the first night in the fields, lying on blankets in the grass, looking up at the stars. We didn't know what else they were planning to do to us, whether they were going to come back and terrorize us again in another way. I didn't know how their minds worked, what they were capable of. The images that raced through my head were horrific. Every night, I would hear my mother crying, her face in the grass, trying to muffle the sounds of her grief. She had become exhausted, her self-sufficiency stripped from her by what the soldiers had done to our village. She had lost all that had sustained her, everything she needed to provide for her family. I'm certain she thought of my father, wondered what he was doing in Constantinople at this very moment that our family was in the fields, left with nothing because of this war. And he, he was in Turkey, working for us, he told my mother before he left ten years ago. I had never seen my mother like this — it frightened me. I was afraid to look at her, too scared to see what I had never seen before. She didn't say anything to us; she just cried. We sat in the fields looking into the darkness, sometimes looking at my mother. Her back was turned toward us in the night, her shoulders shaking each time she let her pain out. We left her alone; we didn't want to bother her in her moments of release.

During the day, we would go back to our village and rebuild, and at night we would hide in the fields, looking for the soldiers, looking at the stars. Occasionally, I would hear an old man humming, lying on a blanket in the fields, entertaining himself with a song. But the song was always melancholy, a nostalgic tune that defined the moment we were in. It was a song, though, and it broke the silence that persisted around us. This is how life was for weeks; this is what we did. We didn't eat much, either. We managed to find some vegetables and bread, but everything else was gone.

Every night my brothers and I took turns in the fields around the place where we slept, looking out to see if any soldiers were coming, carrying rifles across our chests. The other men did this too, protecting the women.

I was twelve years old.

Sophia gently knocked on her father's bedroom door, waiting outside until she heard his voice. Her father woke up from his nap and answered his daughter's knock.

"Yes."

"Pop, it's me. Can I come in? I brought you your dinner."

"Yes, Sophia, please, come in my dear."

FOUR

The next morning, Sophia awoke with the sun shining in her eyes. She reached for the glass of water that sat at the edge of the bed, her mouth dry from the ouzo-soaked dinner they had eaten late last night. Yawning, she stretched her body on the narrow bed and lay on her back for a few minutes, studying the cracked ceiling.

She heard footsteps outside the bedroom door. She was alone in the room; Athina's bed was already made. She heard whispers in the kitchen, suggesting that everyone wasn't up just yet. She lay there a bit longer, trying to get a grasp on everything that was foreign and mountain and village and peasant. She pulled the thin blanket up, covering herself to her chin. The blanket smelled of mothballs, as if it had been stored in a trunk for a hundred years. It was too short to cover her from head to toe, and her feet stuck out at the foot of the bed. She noticed how dirty they had gotten in just one day. Darkened by dust and dirt, and bright white on top where her sandal straps wrapped themselves around her feet.

Sophia took another drink and raised herself to the edge of the bed. She pulled back her hair and walked into the kitchen where Athina, Kosta, Vangelli, and Penelope sat drinking coffee.

"Good morning, Sophia. Did you have a good sleep?" Kosta asked as he got up from his chair and motioned for her to sit.

"Yes, thanks. Has everyone been up long?" she sat down in the empty chair.

"I just woke up a little while ago," said Athina.

"Would you like some coffee, Sophia?" Penelope asked her.

"That would be great, thanks. Hey, Vangelli, good morning."

He let out a small laugh and touched the top of her head. "Good morning to you. Did you have a good rest?"

"Yeah, it was fine."

Sophia asked Kosta what they had planned to do today. He told her that in this part of the world, things weren't really planned, they just move along. Penelope made another pot of coffee on the open stove in the corner of the room. The smell filled the air and gave Sophia the jolt she needed. "How far is the monastery Agios Sarandas from here? Is it still there?"

"How do you know about Agios Sarandas?" asked Athina.

"My father mentioned it to me a few years back."

"It's still there, said Kosta. "Hasn't been rebuilt since the war. It's no more than an hour's walk from here."

"It hasn't been touched?"

"Nope, not since the war," Vangelli chimed in.

"How would you know, you're only ten!" said Athina.

"Oh, I know! I know everything about this land."

"Yeah, Vangelli, tell us more lies," said Athina.

"Does anybody ever go there?" asked Sophia.

"Sometimes people take a walk out there. Shepherds who sleep there during their travels tell us that nothing really has changed. Nobody bothers with it anymore, they leave it alone," said Kosta.

"What ever happened to the monks who lived there? Did some move to another monastery?"

"They were executed. Some fled to another village. The president at the time believed that religion corrupted people's thoughts and wouldn't allow them to think clearly."

"What happened to everything inside the church—the icons and relics?"

"Probably destroyed in the fire. They set the church on fire, but it wasn't completely destroyed." Kosta said this matter-of-factly, as if this was simply what was to be expected. It seemed he knew more than what he was telling her, yet for some reason didn't want to say. Perhaps the conversation was taking him back several decades, to stories he had heard of things that happened before he was born.

Sophia took the last sip of her coffee and set the cup upside down on the saucer. "So who's the fortuneteller in this house?"

"I think that would be Mama," answered Kosta.

"'Well, are you going to tell us our fortunes, Penelope?'"

"You know about fortunetelling?"

"Of course I do. I'm Greek aren't I?"

"Greek? You're not a Greek, you're an American! You were born in America. You live in America."

"So? You live here in Albania. Are you Albanian or Greek?" asked Sophia.

"Ah, that's a very complex question. We don't want to discuss that so early in the morning. But you, you're an American in our eyes," Penelope smiled.

Kosta said that people had made life-changing decisions based solely on what a fortuneteller told them, finding the answers in the coffee grounds in the bottom of their cup. Going along with what they believed was their fate, they would sell their flock of sheep, move out of the village, or move into a relative's home because theirs would be struck by lightning sometime soon. Kosta said that his friend George Baros' home was never struck by lightning, even though the fortuneteller said it would be. Mr. Baros moved his family back to their home after living at his brother's house — fourteen people in all — for a couple of months. His wife told him that she would leave him if he didn't move the family back to their own home. He believed her.

Penelope sat down next to Sophia and examined her coffee cup. Vangelli crowded in, trying to look over his mother's shoulder to get a glimpse of Sophia's future. Kosta sat back and crossed his legs, pulled a pack of cigarettes from his shirt pocket, and offered one to Sophia.

"No, thanks. I don't smoke."

"Okay, let's see what the future holds for Sophia," Penelope said as she held the cup close to her face. "I see a sudden change in your life. Something soon."

"Yeah, well, I'm here!"

"It seems that you have lived a happy and full life, and will continue to do so."

"That's good."

"You said you don't have a boyfriend back home. Is that right?" Penelope looked at Sophia.

"Yes, that's right."

"Well, it seems to me that's going to change very soon," Penelope said with a slight smile in her eyes.

"Oh, yeah?" Sophia laughed, scanning everyone's faces.

"Maybe you'll find an Albanian boy and get married. Maybe you'll decide to live here," Athina said.

"I don't know about that—"

"Oh, yes. It says it right here. You're going to fall in love soon. Look at this," Penelope showed the cup to Sophia. "You see this shape right here?" pointing with her pinkie. "It looks like the shape of a heart. And see this line, how it goes through the heart? This means love. You're going to fall in love in the near future."

"How do you know it will be soon?"

"Because the line is short. If it were longer, love is further away."

"We're going to find a nice Chatista boy for you and get you married. You're going to end up living here!" Kosta said, laughing, as he blew out a puff of smoke.

"Maybe," Sophia said going along with the game. "So what's Athina's fate?"

Athina passed her cup to her mother. She studied it very hard, knitting her eyebrows as she found some insight, then tilted her head to the left for a moment, summing up her thoughts in her mind. "You're on a road to self-discovery."

"What?" Athina was genuinely confused.

"Self-discovery. You're in search of something. Something that means much to you, but you don't know exactly what. You'll find the answer to something that has bothered you for some time. Is anything bothering you?"

"What's that something?" Vangelli asked.

"I don't think anything's bothering me."

"I can't really tell," Penelope said. "But it may be something that happened to you when you were younger, something you've carried with you all of your life. Are you sure there's nothing bothering you?"

"Come on, don't trouble them with these games," said Kosta as he crushed his cigarette butt between his finger and the ashtray.

"What, Pa? This is fun. 'Self-discovery,'" Athina said, pondering. A feeling of importance swept over her face.

"Don't believe any of this. It's all superstition."

"No, it's not," said Penelope. "Things really come true from this."

"How about that time George Baros moved his wife and six kids to his brother's house because their neighbor, Maria, told him his house would be struck by lightning? That never happened."

"Oh, I remember that. When you walked by the house you could hear the wives fighting."

"Vangelli!" Kosta said with a look that silenced him.

"Why would anyone listen to old Maria?" Penelope asked. "She's senile."

"And you'll be too if you keep on believing this fortunetelling that you do," said Kosta, and kissed her cheek.

"Can we take a walk to the monastery today? Sophia asked, changing the subject. "Would you want to do that?"

"Yeah, that would be fine. Vangelli, do you want to go?"

"I'll go!"

"I'll bet Stavro will come too. Vangelli, tell Stavro we're going to the monastery today. Tell him he should come."

Vangelli ran out the door. They could hear him squeal as he ran down the path to Stavro's house. Sophia got up and put her coffee cup on the counter.

"Leave it, we got it," said Athina. She took the cup from Sophia and carried all their cups to her mother to wash in a bucket on the counter.

Kosta got up and walked toward the back door. "I'm going to get the eggs from the coop so we can boil them. You like eggs, don't you, Sophia?" he asked as he shut the door behind him.

The monastery sat between two large mountains about an hour's walk from the village. Vangelli led the way, running ahead of everyone until Kosta shouted for him to wait for everyone to catch up. No one lived in this part of the world, and rarely did anyone pass through other than shepherds traveling from one valley to another. The trail that led to the monastery extended across the top of a hill and down to the front entrance of the church. Seen from above, the monastery looked like it had been placed in the bottom of a grassland bowl, like it didn't belong there. There was the bush and the rock and the trees—nature—and then the monastery, a seemingly contradiction. Except when a bishop traveling by mule through the mountains would stop to visit, there was no contact with the outside world.

To be His servant in this world—to obey His words, to obey His beliefs, to obey His spirit—guarantees a prosperous life hereafter. They wake up thinking of God, they eat thinking of God, they sleep dreaming of God, to find a sense of purpose, an explanation for the way they are, helps preserve their sanity—their sense of being. What type of fulfillment do they receive when they live in the mountains and pray to God? If there is an answer, there is justification for their lives, a justification attached to thought, intellect, and spirit.

Sophia wondered whether the monks who had lived here had ever questioned God's existence. Solitude can make people act in strange ways. Alienated from the world, surrounded only by other monks, their vision becomes mirrored. In monotonous isolation, religion evolves in its own rhythm — a continual encounter without the secular world. The religious must have used passages from the Bible to help explain their lives. She knew that any passage could be taken out of context and applied to virtually anything.

How could a certain passage from a religious text help explain the condition of people's lives all around the globe?

"You see, Sophia," Kosta said, gesturing toward Athina and Stavro, "we don't have everything here. We don't have much, so we focus our lives on our culture and the beliefs we learned when we were young. This is all we know. When you're isolated as much as we have been, things really don't change that much for us. I mean, we're not influenced by the outside, and when people live in a village their entire lives, well, this adds another layer to their isolation."

Sophia looked toward the mountains. "I think I understand you."

"What are you two talking about?" Athina prodded.

"We're talking about your country," Sophia said.

"What about our country?"

"How things are here."

"And how are they? How do you think they are?"

"Things seem simple, but actually they're not."

"What do you mean?" asked Athina.

"Well, if someone were to come here and see how you live, they would think you have a simple life, an easy one. But really you have so much more to worry about—things we take for granted or can't even comprehend. We just don't worry about certain things."

"So what do Americans worry about?"

"Having a nice car and a big house…and how they're going to pay for those things, of course."

Sophia spent her first days in the village observing. She replied when spoken to, but took no initiative to start a conversation with anyone. She wanted to know the secrets of the village, what made it tick, what made the people laugh and cry, what they ate, whether they ever went to the nearest city for a visit, how they dreamed in the mountains.

But the village thought Sophia had gone into a sort of culture shock. They thought she couldn't adjust to the mountain life. Her aloofness compelled them to question her, that she wasn't going to survive her time here or desperately wanted to go back home. They stared at her and she at them, thinking entirely different things. She was fascinated by their movements, the expressions on their faces, the way they slaughtered a lamb for dinner in the open field. These things were foreign to her, even alien.

They observed her, too, but not as discreetly as she. The common courtesy of not staring at a person had never made it here. They stared at her unrelentingly, to the point that when she walked by they would turn their heads and continue staring. In complete isolation, a person will stare at anything out of the ordinary, just to get a glimpse of something novel.

And maybe understand it.

FIVE

Sophia's father was sitting at his desk. Stacks of papers and letters were spread all over, along with a pile of old photographs. He had been sifting through his things all morning and was about to start putting them away when Sophia walked into the room and sat on the couch facing him.

"Hey, Pop, what are you doing?"

"Just going through some of my things," he said, looking at a photograph. "Do you want to see me when I was a little boy? If you can't tell, I'm the one on the right" He leaned over his desk and gave her the photo, in which two young boys stood near a tree, both of them wearing knee-length shorts and dirty T-shirts, their hair cut short to the scalp.

"How old were you here? You look about eight," she said, laughing. "You have a very serious look on your face, too serious for your age." She paused for a moment. "Pop, who's the boy next to you?"

"That's my friend Arseni. We grew up together. He lived at the end of the village, down the path from our house. We always used to play together. Yeah," he sighed, "he was my good friend. I think I've must have been around ten or eleven in that picture. Just a few years younger than you are now."

"When was the last time you spoke with him?"

"When I left Albania. Yes, it was 1945. He stayed behind in

Chatista, because his mother was sick and he didn't want to leave her. He was married at the time too. He said he would meet us in Ioannia in a few weeks, but we never heard from him."

Sophia stared at the photograph. "Do you know what ever happened to him? Do you know if he's still alive, Pop?"

"I think he is. One of your aunts who lives in the village mentioned him in a letter a couple of years back, but I haven't contacted him."

"Why not?"

"I don't know. I just don't know. It's not that I haven't had time. It's one of those things that you just let go," he said, looking up into the air.

"Why would you let it go like that?"

"Your aunt said in one of her letters that Arseni's life has been very rough for quite some time, and that people question his state of mind. I left the village shortly after his wedding — he married very young, when he was still a teenager. The marriage was an arrangement, but he fell in love with her easily enough. His wife passed away shortly after they were married. From what your aunt has told me, he never really recovered from her death."

"How did she die? Do you know what had happened?"

"Yes. Yes, I do," he said uneasily. "When Enver Hoxha came to power and the communists took control of the government, they came to the village and told us of the changes that were going to happen. The way we farmed, the food that was to be distributed to us and how much, the traditions that we lived with forever, were all about to change. They disrupted the lifestyle we had been living for centuries. Some people obeyed their orders for the sake of obeying, and others tried to defend their way of life — everyone's way of life. From what I've been told after I left, Arseni tried to defend the village's way of life."

"And?"

"Well, Arseni was one of the people who stood up to them," he began. "He spoke out to the soldiers and told them that the people of Chatista could take care of themselves, and he gave himself as an example. From what I've heard, he really defended himself and the others, pointing out that Chatista was self-sufficient and didn't need help. That was when one of the soldiers asked him who was his family, whom did he have to provide for. Arseni pointed to his wife, who was standing next to him, and said, 'This is my family.'

He paused for a moment.

"Well, what happened, Pop?"

"We shouldn't talk about this, sweetheart. Not now," he said.

Sophia understood that her father didn't want to continue. "Who told you this story?"

"One of the men who was there escaped Albania shortly thereafter. He knew we were in Ioannia, and found us and told us what had happened."

"Dad, your mother was there after the communists came, wasn't she? What happened to her?"

"That's a whole other story, Sophia, one that we should discuss some other time," he said softly.

Sophia sat on the couch looking at her father, taking in the story he had just told her. War and governments and soldiers were something completely foreign to her life. Her father was a book, a history book that she could read and try to experience. "Why wouldn't they just let the people live their lives like they had? I mean, if that was what they wanted, the communists should've just let them be."

"This was the government's way of controlling people and the economy."

"How long was Enver Hoxha in power?"

"He came to power after World War Two, late 1945, and remained until he died in 1985. Communism lasted in Albania for a few more years after his death, but it was faltering, and it collapsed a few years later."

"What happened to the government then?"

"When communism couldn't hold up its mask any longer, then came democracy — democracy as *they* defined it. When a people are oppressed for such a long time, and then get a taste of freedom, a sense of democracy, they begin to go overboard. They'd never known what it felt like to have an opinion, to make decisions for themselves. This can also be very destructive, as bad as that might sound. They get a feeling of having so many choices, and there's nothing wrong with that, but people sometimes make bad choices — there's a fine line between democracy and anarchy. Democracy did come to Albania in name and in theory, but not in practice. The government basically just changed its name and continued to run the country its own way."

"Can it do that?"

"A government can do whatever it pleases — remember that. But what would anyone expect from a people who have been twisted and turned for half a century? Old attitudes die very, very slowly; people feel comfortable with only what they know. The people were focused on survival, and they relied only on themselves to survive. They thought about what they had to do to get money that day to provide for their family that week. They couldn't count on anyone — not their government and not the world — to come to their aid. It was a very selfish society, but when you don't know any other way, what are you supposed to do?

"In life sometimes, human consciousness, a sort of empathy for society, is lacking. It's a vicious cycle that no one can really stop. Many people don't understand that there is, paradoxically, a certain commonality among all of us, even though there are wars. This commonality exists all over the world, and it should breed a solid sense of human consciousness — but it doesn't. People don't see how they could make things better by acting honestly and compassionately toward others..."

Sophia gazed at the photograph of her father and Arseni, which was still in her hand, studying their faces. They had stories in them, narratives behind the eyes.

Her father was staring at the back of the photograph.

He went on to explain the invasion by the Italian army, building the new Roman Empire, Mussolini's decision to make a bridge to the Balkans—Ciano's vision, perhaps. He told her how the Italians arrived at the port of Durres in 1939 and captured Tirana, controlling the country's economy and military and how they arrived in Albania, kicked out King Zog, and wanted to make their way into Greece.

All the while the Germans had watched.

The Italians promised to help them become more self-sufficient, build roads and schools—completely redo the nation's infrastructure. They would build railroads and help make the country a bit more "modern." Some were loyal to the Italians, and others, they questioned the courtesy of a foreigner. Those who were loyal were eager to become more modern; to be like the Italians, a power in Europe, to create a body politic, a constitution, perhaps, that the people could embrace. The Kanun was old; it was outdated. That was their vision, their dream—but not for the Italians.

The Italians wanted another coastline, "a fifth coast," was what they said. They looked across the Adriatic Sea for footing in the Balkans, to be a little more east—part of a New Roman Empire. Some saw this in the Italians quickly. It was known that these people across the Adriatic were misanthropes—quick to be discontented. But the Italians thought of ways around this, and they stayed in Albania for some time. They created a fictitious government that consisted of puppets, and believed their new subjects were tolerating this. Ciano believed he could make it go on, and this newly acquired land would be Italy's forever.

When a man's personal mission becomes his passion, his rationality begins to slowly diminish.

But there came a point when the Italian troops couldn't maintain order any longer—unskilled at it, perhaps. Their subjects became more concerned, more questioning of the Italians' intentions. But the

Italian government had what it wanted at this point. The Albanian Federal Bank was located in Rome.

The Germans were keeping their eye on the Albanian/Italian situation, and broadcast their opinion to the Italians whenever they saw fit. They told the Fascists what to do and when to do it. Most of the time they would listen because their choices, their strength, were becoming increasingly limited, but at the same time, they felt the German threat on their necks. Hitler and his Nazis were lurking around the corner, waiting to see what was to happen.

Her father had been playing at a friend's house when the Germans came to Chatista. They were much stealthier than the Italians, creeping through the mountains like snakes. The villagers heard that the Germans were coming to secure the border to Greece, and they waited until they saw the tall, blonde soldiers make their way into their homes. The villagers knew what to expect of them — they had gone through this routine with the Italians.

The soldiers stayed in Chatista for several weeks, making themselves comfortable in people's homes, eating dinner with families, sleeping in their beds. The women went into the mountains and brought extra water containers with them to wash their uniforms, scrubbed the dirt from their pants, and hung them to dry next to their children's clothes. They accommodated them as best as they could to prevent any commotion and anger among them. He remembered three soldiers, including one officer, who stayed with them in their home. His mother cooked their meals while they sat on the front porch, smoking their cigarettes and resting their feet on the table. Sometimes they would ask for specific dishes — a luxury that they began to expect. The language barrier was never a problem: when they wanted to eat chicken, they would point to the chicken coop in the backyard. When they wanted steak, they would point to one of the cows in the field.

When the soldiers left for a few hours during the day for their duties, his mother cleaned the room they slept in, and prepared their next meal when they returned. She treated them as if they were her own, her family. The soldiers enjoyed Albanian hospitality—they told her so. She told them that she wasn't Albanian, she was Greek. "Whatever," they would say to her each time she tried to correct them.

It was near the end of the war when the Germans had come to Chatista. The soldiers looked tired and worn, as if they had given up fighting because they realized that it was becoming useless, perhaps meaningless. Their injuries were beginning to scar them, their memories were becoming embedded in their bodies. They lost sight of what they were fighting for and tortured people just for the sake of torture sometimes, not necessarily as a means to an end. It was at this point that the goal had been lost. The direction of the war had been misguided. Time was running out, and they needed to get as much terror into the enemy as they could before the nation's leaders called for surrender and peace.

One day, her father went down to the pond for a swim with Arseni and found several soldiers swimming. They walked to the other edge of the pond to avoid the soldiers and stood there watching them. The Germans swam and played around with each other, smoking cigarettes and lying on the grass under the sun as if they didn't have a care in the world. The boys watched from behind the trees for a few minutes, wanting to swim in *their* pond. They felt displaced. This pond was something that was theirs, and they had lost it to the Germans. It was at this moment that he knew Albania had been lost. This was before he had been living in the fields for weeks.

"Did I ever tell you the story of how I was almost taken away by an eagle? Arseni was with me when it happened," her father said, still staring at the back of the photograph.

Sophia started laughing. "No, you never told me, Pa. Somehow, I think I would remember a story like that."

"When I was a young boy, about five or six years old, Arseni and I were swimming in the pond at the edge of our village, at the bottom of the hill. After we finished, we lay in the grass, drying off. There was an eagle flying over our heads, way up in the sky. It kept on circling above, watching us. Then, all of a sudden, it swooped down and grabbed my hand, right here." He showed Sophia where the eagle had clawed his right hand, near the thumb. "The eagle gripped me with its claws and was trying to lift me off the ground. I grabbed a tree branch, trying to hold on so the eagle couldn't lift me off the ground. Arseni was standing next to me, swinging at the eagle with a stick, trying to make it let go."

"Was anyone else around to help you?"

"No, it was just the two of us. I don't think anyone was even near us. So, we were fighting with the eagle and all the time I'm crying for my life. The eagle was trying to lift me and then drop me when it was in the air, and then take me to its nest."

"How did you get away?"

"After a couple of minutes of fighting with it, the eagle gave up and let go of my hand. I still have a scar from its claw—look." Her father reached out his hand to let Sophia look at the scar between his index finger and thumb. "Yeah, we were really scared. After the eagle let me go we ran up the hill to my mother's house, yelling. I ran into the house crying; my hand was bleeding. I think Arseni was more shocked than I was. I have a lot of memories of my old friend Arseni. I often wonder how he's doing when I think of the times we had together."

Sophia looked at the photograph one last time before giving it back to her father. "Maybe one day we could go to Albania. Do you ever want to go back?"

"Yes. I think I'd like to go back one of these days. I don't know if much has changed."

"I'm sure a lot has changed since you were there. It's probably a whole different world from what you remember."

"I don't know about that."

"Pop, when you left Albania, how old were you?"

"Sixteen."

"Why didn't your mother leave with you?"

"She didn't want to."

"Why?"

"Because most of the older people wouldn't leave their homes, even if their lives were in danger. Their life is here," he said, pointing to the floor, "even if life is bad, it's still here." But when we were kids, your uncles and me, we never looked back. We couldn't, because there was nothing to look back to, besides our family. But I have some regrets about leaving. About leaving when I did."

"What do you regret about leaving?"

"I regret that I never went back to see my family again, and my friends. But we couldn't go back; nobody could've gone back even if they wanted to. I also regret that I left my mother behind. She went through a lot after we left. She was exposed to a lot. It kills me to think about what happened to her, and I can only imagine the pain she went through. I will always regret that I never saw my mother again."

"If you were older, I mean much older, as old as your mother, would you have left when you did?"

"Probably not."

"Pop, what happened?" she asked again.

She wanted him to tell her right then what had happened and how it happened. She wanted him to give everything to her and not leave anything out. He was confessing a lot to her, felt the need to confess what he had been feeling for a long time.

A burden on his memory, a light to his soul. With a look in his eyes, he began his story.

Six

We counted the soldiers while we hid in the brush in the middle of the night. There were two near the stone wall that wrapped around the plaza near the valley and another four at the top of the hill. Illuminated by the moon, their silhouettes betrayed their presence. Their rifles lay comfortably in their hands. The two near the plaza walked back and forth, wondering if there would be anything to do tonight, anything to shoot at. After a few moments, one of them placed his gun against the wall and sat on the ledge. He reached into his pocket and pulled out a pack of cigarettes. He moved his hand slowly toward his face, put the cigarette in his mouth, and lit a match.

That face. I remember seeing the face of a loyal soldier.

His distinctive nose protruded and his thick, dark eyebrows had a life of their own. I clearly remember his eyes and how they looked in the match's flame. The look in them that told a story that was not similar to mine, but similar to the enemy's.

"Steve, didn't you say there were eight soldiers guarding this area?" Steve was looking into the night, scanning its darkness. He was lying on his stomach, watching the soldiers' every step. We were so close to the two by the plaza that we were able to hear them talk. And there were the four at the top of the hill overlooking all of Chatista, witnessing all from above.

"Yeah, there are eight, but I only see six. We can't leave until we know where the other two are."

We were nervous, all of us—Demetri, Alexi, Steve, and me. We didn't know what was to come of this, and we really didn't know what we were doing. We were young and scared, had a vague idea of what would happen to us if we got caught. Three weeks earlier a man had been caught trying to escape Albania; the soldiers took him back to his village and tied him up like a wild animal. They broke both of his legs in front of the entire village and threw him at his house.

The communists had begun guarding this area a few months ago because they said it was a strategic region—the floor of the Balkans. It lies at the bottom of mountainous region, tucked away and forgotten. But this land had become occupied by different political regimes and struggled with something we had no concept of, so it was our time to go. My brothers and I wanted to leave this country. Somehow, we knew how our lives would be and wanted no part of it. Strangely, our mother wanted us to leave, too. She knew and we knew that this would probably be the last night we'd ever be in the same land, and the next time we saw her would be in the heavens. But we never talked like this to each other. It was never said aloud, but I think we knew.

As we lay anxiously on the ground a little past midnight, we started to wonder if tonight would be our night to escape. We heard that to cross over to Greece from our village would take about three hours, that is, if you didn't get lost in the mountains.

We have nothing. I remember I kept repeating this in my head. *We have nothing. We have nothing. We have nothing.* I missed my mother. I wanted to tell her one more time how much I loved her and tell her that she did well in raising us. We knew she needed us, but she knew that we needed a better life more. She never left the village, but I guess she knew in her heart that there had to be a better life than this for her sons. I felt in my pocket for my father's watch that my mother had given me before we left our house. I remembered the last thing my mother said to me in our kitchen: "Nonta, I want to give you something before you boys leave tonight. I want you to have this because I think you're the one to find deep meaning in many things." She pulled her weathered hand out of the pocket of her dress and placed a gold pocket watch in my hand. "This is your father's watch. He gave it to me before he left for Constantinople to work. Take the watch, my son, and remember your father's story, and ours, always."

I took the watch and looked up at my mother. Her eyes were filled with tears. As she blinked several times to rid herself of the blur, the tears ran down her cheeks. I didn't want to remember my mother's face like this. I took the handkerchief from my pocket and gently rubbed her cheeks and asked her to smile for me. She listened and stroked my hands.

"Oh, Nonta, how can I explain this to you?" she said in a whisper, worried that a soldier would hear her in our home. "How can I help my sons understand why I won't leave and why I want you boys to go? You must understand that times have not been easy for us, and I don't think they will be soon. They're taking a stronger hold on the country, and they're beginning to bother us villagers now, telling us how to live our lives. I saw many bad things during the war thirty years ago. I don't want my sons to experience what I've seen."

"I love you, Mama." I didn't know what else to say to her.

My mother walked into my arms and cried into my shoulder. I placed my hand on the back of her head. I didn't want to leave her alone. How could I do this to her? I wanted to stay home and help her, be a son for her, tell her it would be all right. But I knew it wasn't true. Nothing was all right. My mother wanted more for us.

"Mama, I'll always keep Pa's watch and remember why you're giving it to me. I know you don't want it to stay here, you want it away from all of this."

She looked up at me, her eyes red. I told her to stop crying and not let anyone see her like this. "Come on, Mama, it'll be all right." I reassured her that we'd be okay and that she could get help from our neighbors. She knew this, but I knew I had to tell her again.

"Remember, Nonta, take care of each other and watch out for one another. Tell Alexi not to bite his nails, and make sure Steve doesn't lose his temper with anyone. You don't know what kinds of people are out there. Be careful of anyone you talk to."

She took my face into her hands and looked at me one last time. Her fingers stroked my cheeks and moved to my forehead. She gently kissed my face where her fingers had been. I looked down at my mother and told her that we'd be all right.

But I didn't know who 'we' was.

"I love you, my son. Remember what I told you, and remember why you are leaving Albania."

Yes, I would remember.

I stepped out of my home and walked down the hill toward the pond. I could feel my mother's stare, her eyes glued to my back as we began our journey. I didn't look back. I didn't look back to anything.

The last I heard about my mother was that she had been captured by the communists and forced into a camp because she let her sons leave the country. They kept her in the camp for five years. Five years. The same amount of time we hadn't heard from our father when we left.

After we counted the soldiers, we crept through the valley toward the mountains that would lead us out of Albania. We didn't know how long it would take, we didn't know if we'd get lost. What we did know was that we had to get to Greece before sunrise. The moon lit the valley, casting giant shadows of what was in the grass. Everything seemed larger to me — the trees seemed to tower over us in the dark, their shadows stretching out in the night. Steve led the way and we followed closely behind him, with Demetri following his every step. The brush, dried by the summer sun, crunched underfoot as we made our way along the lightly beaten path that others had taken in recent months.

Keeping step behind our group, I walked hypnotically, my mind fixed on my surroundings, keeping a steady, methodical pace to push my brothers quickly, yet quietly enough to get over the border. I knew that if we didn't make it across tonight, our chances of going back to our village or making it into Greece later were slim. We had nothing with us — no clothes and only a little food that would last us about a day, if that. We would be trapped in the mountains, not knowing where to turn or when, and paralyzed by fear. A shepherd would find our remains and understand what had happened to us. . . .

We had been walking for a couple of hours when I heard a branch snap not far behind me. It made a loud cracking sound, as if a heavy weight suddenly rested itself upon it. I quickly stopped, frozen in the moment, listening for anything. My brothers kept walking ahead, oblivious of what I was hearing and thinking. Suddenly, the quiet that surrounded me was too quiet for my comfort. The loud noise of a branch breaking, and now dead silence. I looked around in the darkness, but I couldn't see anything except for the shadows that the moon had given me. Something didn't feel right; the night seemed to close in on us as I waited for anything to give light on what I feared most. I waited a moment longer. Nothing. I decided to catch up with them, climbing up the path ahead of me.

As we continued to walk I heard another noise behind me. I stopped and this time heard shrubs crunching, footsteps moving slowly, creeping up from a short distance. I looked up at the moon and saw the top of the mountain, how close we were to the other side. *Just over the top of that mountain,* I said to myself. I ran up to Steve and whispered to him what I had heard.

"I think someone's following us. I heard footsteps from behind."

We stood together listening. The sound of footsteps was slowly moving closer and closer, and then more were coming from the right. Steve motioned to us to follow his lead and we started to run up the narrow path. We heard shouting from behind, telling us to stop or be shot. We kept going, not trusting the voices in the darkness. The footsteps chased us for a little while and then we were being shot at. I held my ears when their rifles went off, jerking my head down after every shot — the crackling of the rifle controlling my movements. We kept running faster up the mountain, and that's when Demetri tripped and fell to the ground, crying. Alexi tried pulling him up, but Demetri wouldn't move.

"Come on, Demetri! Come on, get up! They're going to kill us if you don't get up!" Alexi yelled in his ear, tugging his hands free from a tree stump.

"No, no, no! I don't want to get up! I'm scared. I want to go home. Take me home!" Demetri cried, gripping the tree.

I helped Alexi pry Demetri's hands from the tree and pushed him along up the path. Demetri continued to cry as he ran. Steve was running ahead, leading the way. He saw a cave ahead and ran into it. We practically fell on top of each other when all of us ran in, shuffling ourselves in the blackness, stumbling through the rocks. We tried to keep quiet, standing anxiously, listening to the noise of the rifles outside. I could hear my heart pounding in my chest, the noise throbbing through my body. My legs shook from fear. I was so scared that I felt like I was experiencing this moment outside of my body.

I hope we get out of here. I hope we make it out of here alive.

I reached into my pocket and grabbed my father's watch, making sure I still had it. Holding it in my hand and feeling it tick, I tried to slow my breathing, tried to get my heartbeat in rhythm with the watch.

We stood still, listening to the voices and their guns firing at random, the soldiers checking to see if we were hiding in the bush. We could hear them clearly. "They're very close, they're going to find us," Alexi whispered. Steve put his hand over Demetri's mouth and told him to stop crying. I stood at the mouth of the cave. I could see three soldiers walking a short distance away from us.

"Come on, they probably ran off this way. How many did you see, Ali?" we heard one of them say.

"A few of them. I saw them run this way up the path," he said, pointing to the trail we had taken.

"Forget about them. I don't want to waste my time. Let those damn Greeks go back where they belong. We don't need their kind here, anyway," said another, and started back down the trail toward our village. "Hey, Ali, stick your head in that cave. See if there's anything in there."

The soldier moved closer to us and I could see him looking into the cave as he walked toward the opening. My heart jumped and I could hear Demetri's muffled squealing under Steve's hand. Standing stiffly, we waited there; I slipped my father's watch back into my pocket.

The soldier took a step into the cave and waved his flashlight into the darkness. I remember the expression on his face when he saw us. He was taken aback at seeing four young boys huddled there. He looked at our skinny bodies and our dirty, ragged clothes. He peered into our faces one by one, recording the images he saw, wondering what to do with us. We were petrified, shaking as we stood there. We heard the soldiers outside ask if there was anything in the cave. He paused for a moment and then moved backwards out of the cave. "No, there's nothing in here," he said, looking at us, stepping slowly outside and turning off his flashlight.

Half an hour later, when the world was quiet again, I poked my head out of the cave. All was clear, and we could keep going. Demetri said he was too tired to go on, he wouldn't be able to make it. Using his belt, Steve tied Demetri's wrists together, then turned his back to him and pulled Demetri's arms over his head and down around his neck. "Jump on my back," Steve said to him. "I'll carry you."

We started running up the trail toward Greece again — chasing the moon as the darkness chased us. I led the way this time, my father's watch in my hand.

When my boys ran down the path from our home, the mountain seemed impossibly large; it looked as though it intended to swallow them whole. They zigzagged through the valley, following that secret path known to only a few. They knew where to run — to the left for a few meters, then to the right, and when you get to the crooked olive tree that looks like an outstretched hand, run straight up to the heavens until you reach the other side. That mountain was either my sons' enemy or their guardian, depending on the outcome.

A mother lets her children go hoping that they won't forget her, and won't forget where they came from. A mother hopes she can teach her children the values that she was taught, and let them pass those values on in other lands. A mother who must let her children go is tormented. To live in a world that compels a mother to make such choices is frightful.

The Fascists rushed in and then the Nazis. Mussolini wanted to make this land a part of his burgeoning "New Roman Empire," and the Nazis wanted to take over the world. But the communists were gaining momentum; at the end of World War Two they took control of the country. "Thank you," I guess, is the politest thing one could say. The communists made their mark on this soil with an addition to the topography — cement shells dotted the countryside. The communists made Albania their world, and stayed for a long time — never left, really.

A mother protects her sons even more than her daughters. They are the ones who will carry the family name, provide for their family, and take care of their mother when she becomes frail. She wants to make certain that she'll be all right when she becomes old. She wants to see them grow big and strong, and in time, return to where they came from. And she wants to be proud of them.

Governments won't allow sons who flee the country to return. They keep such men — disloyal, unpatriotic, corrupted by the outside world, contaminated, worthless — at bay. Governments have restrictions for men like these, who don't believe in the regime and its propaganda. There is order and everyone must obey.

We don't want tainted men. You will do as you're told and not question us. We are in power. We control you. We will make sure you and your family are provided for. You don't know what's good for you. We know what's good for you. You are impressed with what's on the outside, but you have everything here. Why did you leave? Your definition of freedom is wrong. You have liberty here. You have a free mind here. You don't have to think. We do your thinking for you. That's what a government is for — the Provider.

So men like these can return only at their peril. They might be humiliated in front of the loyal, patriotic, worthy citizens who stayed in the country and obeyed the propaganda. They might be tortured. They might be shot. Still, some wait until the right changes have been made, until power has changed hands, and then they return to where they came from. That is, if they can remember where they came from.

My sons, all teenagers, left our home through the mountains. Did they know that this was how it would be? How did they know what no one else knew? They left in the middle of the night. They kissed me goodbye and left. They said they would be back soon.

They knew they were lying to me.

Secrets wander through villages, shifting, and swaying slowly through the homes. And when a secret is told, it becomes a story. The story fills the night air around a family porch, teasing young men when they meet at night to socialize in the plaza, burdening farmers as they move the soil, and filling young girls with dreams of, perhaps, leaving the village and even becoming a little independent. "The Bayas boys left Chatista, did you hear? They went a few nights ago over the mountain to Greece. They are gone. What will happen to their mother? What will she do? She let her sons go."

Moving and growing, such stories stretch themselves across the village and lie like a veil over the community, and everyone is contaminated because that suffocating veil touches everyone. Some push the story, repeating it to another too loudly, too boldly, too enviously. Eventually, a soldier hears; the story angers him, chokes him. *Where is their loyalty, patriotism, worthiness?* And the soldier tells his officer, and the story provokes him. *Who are these boys? Who is their family?* And the officer moves swiftly and defiantly through the village, his rifle in his hands. His soldiers follow on his heels, moving quickly up the paths to the home at the top of the hill. Families look on, dreading the worst, feeling guilty for having told the secret too loudly, boasting that they knew it, wanting to see if their neighbor knew, too.

The villagers shelter their children, rushing them inside their homes, trying to protect them from the soldiers—The Providers. The officer reaches the house at the top of the hill, strides through the front door, and orders his soldiers to grab the woman who is hiding in the closet. They wrap their hands around her arms, drag her out of her home, and carry her down the path to the bottom of the hill where a military truck awaits, the driver smoking a cigarette.

A grin on his face.

The woman screams, asking the village for help, asking God for help, but the villagers do not move and there is no God in communism. To subdue her, a soldier strikes her on the side of the head with his rifle butt. They toss her into the back of the truck, and the officer tells the driver to take her away. The village looks on, wondering what will happen to her. *Where are they taking her, the mother who let her sons go for a chance to taste freedom, to not forget the land they came from is being taken away by the government that is protecting them, providing for them, making decisions for them?* As the military truck heads north on the road into the mountains, the officer turns around and looks at the villagers. They abruptly go back to their sitting and farming and playing and sleeping and eating and cleaning.

It is a summer afternoon and the sun is high and bright. A slight breeze fills the air. The village doesn't see the mother again, the mother who let her boys go, who allowed them to escape, for five years.

Forced not to recall, they cannot forget.

The communists swept through the land and got the support they were in search of. The intellectuals who lived in the cities were forced to hush their voices. Many were locked in prisons for years, and their families felt the burden of being related to a dissident, an anti-government instigator. Their reputations, too, were contaminated with the poison of free thought, this contamination lasting sometimes for generations. Men who had jobs in intellectual circles were forced into physical labor—everyone needed to assist in the production of food and goods and the construction of government housing blocks. People were treated like machines—the art of mechanics.

Initially, many farmers gave the communists their unconditional support because there was a chance that a change could arise in their farming conditions. The communists confiscated the large plots of land owned by the beys, redistributing them to the peasants. The former powerful landowners at once felt what it was like to be powerless.

The peasants had hope.

But within two decades the land was taken away from the peasants and became collectivized. They were forced to work on collective farms and grow only the crops that were assigned to them. Government officials would come to the villages and take all that was grown, tossing the food in the truck beds, the villagers looking on hopelessly. The first to receive were those in the cities. The fruits of the farmers' hard work were taken away and distributed to the rest of the country by the officials who grew lazy in office. But they had no choice. The president's hold on the country was tight and brutal, the consequences of insubordination fatal. No one had a hand in his own destiny.

The land was silent.

In 1967 the sweeping decision was made to ban religion. Mosques and churches were razed—hundreds of buildings gone, and the history they stored wiped out. Even cemeteries, with their religious motifs, were destroyed. The people realized that Hoxha was a dictator who was destroying the culture, their very existence. He tried to control everything in their lives, and he succeeded, because the people trusted him.

They had hope.

But he wanted even more reform, so, after breaking ties with Khrushchev's Soviet Union, he created an alliance with China, believing that its communist ideology was purer because it disdained religion, a view he greatly admired. But this alliance lasted only a short time—he began to think China was impure as well, influenced by cordial relations with the West. He decided to isolate Albania, believing that the country could become a self-sufficient socialist republic model. Albania's doors were completely closed to the outside world, its windows clamped shut.

The country fell into the abyss of time, falling backward as the rest of the world tried to shake off the Second World War and move forward. Isolated, Albania couldn't gauge its progress. It believed its momentum was on par with the rest of the world, but the country fell further and further back. It reached the point where catching up seemed impossible. All the backwardness of the Ottoman Empire, the brutal force of the Soviet Union, and the paranoia of China were merged in this one country.

And then the dictator died.

His stronghold on the nation was released. His appointed successor, Ramiz Alia, took over office in the Communist Party until communism gave way to the Democratic Party in 1991. Communism wasn't working, but the Democratic Party was filled with men who were very similar to the communists, merely under a different party name, so the old propaganda hung on in the nation.

The wind wasn't strong enough just yet to blow the dust away.

BOOK II

SEVEN

There is a pattern in the cracking paint on the ceiling. If you're looking up from the bed next to the door, it moves more toward the left than the right. If you're on the other bed, the pattern moves toward the right, extending itself all the way to the window, trying to escape. The paint used to be whole, a single entity, but now it's broken up into tiny regions that have claimed their independence. Some are smaller than others, suggesting a homogeneous ethnicity. Some are larger; the cracks made certain that these regions stretched over the smaller ones, pushing them out of the way.

Other cracks began to emerge within the smaller regions, and the paint within these regions became weak; even tinier cracks begin to form within, making them smaller, tribal-like, their borders too weakened to hold them together. Somehow, the larger areas stayed intact a little longer, perhaps because they were held together by large, solid borders, or because they were solid from within. When the smaller areas of paint became too weak, tiny sections began to break off and fall onto the floor. They chip away continually because they can't hold together any longer — they become tired, exhausted. But there are too many factions, too many distinctions within the larger regions of paint. It is only a matter of time before the world sees how the paint on the ceiling will ultimately play out.

They too might lose their existence and become like the smaller regions, because cracks might emerge and form within them. And they could fall from the larger picture of the region, the larger pattern on the ceiling.

"Why did you leave your country at the time you did?" Sophia asked her father one day.

"I left because we had to."

"But you're not answering my question, Pa. Why did you leave then?"

"We had to leave because there was nothing for us to do in our country. Nothing was offered to us. It was our time."

Her father slept during the day, his eyes wide at night, looking at the darkness that surrounded him, the walls that illuminated the night hung over him. He thought of his life in the country of his birth, the one he left so long ago, the village that he was raised in, lived in, and left. He remembered the look on his mother's face when he said goodbye to her in the middle of the night, the forced smile that crossed her face as he hugged her and told her he loved her, then followed his brothers down the path into the valley.

Sophia would talk to her father during the middle of the night, to help him exorcise the thoughts that lingered in his mind. Sorting through them, he remembered running across the border into Greece in 1945, how he and his brothers ran to a police station because they didn't know where else to go. He remembered the look on the face of the officer who stood behind the desk as they walked through the front door. Four dirty, frightened, and confused boys coming into the station, begging for help by the look on their faces, the youngest one crying because he was so tired and scared. The policeman helped them — simply because they were young and bewildered. Her father remembered sitting on a wooden bench against the wall of one of the rooms in the station with his brothers, eating bread that the police had given them, thinking of his mother.

And what was to become of her.

"Please don't do this! Don't do this to me! I have sons!" she pleaded. "I have boys. Boys your age," she then said quietly. "Please, don't do this to me!"

She screamed and cried as the young soldier ripped at her clothing, exposing her chest, scratching her skin, grabbing her arms. He looked at her with contempt, freeing the power that had come over him. He let it all slip out of his skin, porous to the hate, the anger, the rage that suffocated him.

He pushed her down to the ground. She hit her head on the concrete floor and let out a yelp. He slapped her across the face to quiet her. He pulled apart her legs.

She begged him again not to touch her, to not do what he had planned to do. She looked over his shoulder as he lay on top of her, unbuckling his pants.

She begged him to leave her alone, watching the other soldiers watch her.

"Please! I beg you to stop this. Please! I beg of you!"

She looked in his eyes and knew what he was thinking, what he wanted. She asked him a final time.

"Please! Don't do this! I have sons. I have boys…your age…My sons are your age…I have four boys…"

He hit her with the butt of his gun. He told her to shut up or he'd kill her. This was all he said to her.

She surrendered to the moment, closing her eyes as she felt his hands ripping the front of her dress.

Sophia poured herself a cup of water from the plastic container in the kitchen and sat outside on the porch before the house awoke. Sitting on a chair that leaned against the house, she looked out into the valley below. A woman walked toward the village, leading a mule that carried several containers of water on its back. A few farmers were already in the fields. The village was gradually waking up, slowly gaining speed. The great paradox, she thought, was how much work is needed to maintain a village, yet a sense of sleepiness surrounds it. It takes a lot of energy to create this aura of leisure. In her veins she had the blood that creates villages such as this, the genes that define the mindset of those who live here. She looked at the stone houses around her and wondered how people could possibly live like this, so isolated from the rest of the world, yet, in a way, part of a bigger picture that they helped define. She didn't know whether to feel sympathy for them, which would imply that they needed help. If people have been living like this forever, why would they need anyone's sympathy now? Wasn't this just the way things worked in the world?

She tried to imagine how she would get along had she been born in the mountains of this country. Would she have the same thoughts she did now? Would she already have been married, with several children to look after? It felt odd, thinking of the things that would have molded her, yet being aware enough to analyze them. Would she have been analyzing these thoughts if she were born here, or would she have a different mindset?

Deciding to go for a walk, Sophia headed down the path toward the pond. She knew she would be alone so early in the morning, before the village kids ran down the hill and jumped into the water. The decision to walk to the pond this morning led her to meet Abraham for the first time. He was fishing when she walked around a bush and saw him there.

"Oh, my God! You scared me," she said, putting her hand to her chest. "I'm sorry," she said, and turned to walk back up the path.

"No, it's okay. You can stay if you'd like. I'm just finishing my catch," he said.

Sophia knew that it wasn't appropriate to speak to him at the pond, alone, at this time of day. It wasn't as if she had bumped into him here when the village was awake. But she liked the sound of his voice. She thought it would be all right to talk with him for just a minute.

"Are you visiting here?" he asked her.

"Yes, I have family who live in the village."

"Who's your family?"

She told him.

"Hmm," he sighed and looked down. He was friends with Stavro, and told her this. "How long are you staying?"

"I'm not quite sure. Probably several weeks."

Their conversation continued this way for a few more moments, and then she decided that it wasn't appropriate to stand here talking with him, a young man she didn't know and wasn't related to. She noticed that he was looking at her closely—her eyes, her arms, and her legs. For some reason it didn't bother her that he was glancing at her body. She took his interest as a compliment because she thought he was good-looking. But it was his voice to which Sophia was particularly attracted. It had a calmness that was mesmerizing; she felt she could sit and listen to his voice all day.

Yet she cut short their conversation and said goodbye to him and began to walk back to the house.

"You know," he said abruptly, and she turned around, "I fish here pretty much every morning. You can come and visit me anytime you like."

She walked back down the path a little toward him and stood arms akimbo. "What's your name, by the way?"

"My name is Abraham."

"Abraham," she said into the air. "That's not a common Greek name. Do you always invite people to watch you fish in the morning, Abraham?"

"No, I don't," he said, quickly looking down into the pond. He thought he might have been too forward with his invitation. "I didn't mean it that way. I just meant that if you wanted to talk, here's a good place. It's quiet, and not many people are around this time of day, that's all. It was nothing more than that. I'm sorry if I offended you."

"I wasn't offended, Abraham. I was just asking."

He looked at her and smiled.

Sophia smiled back at him and said, "Well, maybe I'll visit you here one morning," then turned and continued up the path to the village.

Sophia didn't tell anyone about speaking to a guy named Abraham who was fishing in the pond. She knew she had to be quiet about this sort of thing in the village, and thought it best to keep it a secret. This wasn't difficult for her. She often kept things to herself — her thoughts, her feelings, her encounters with others — if she felt even slightly attracted to someone. Her friends couldn't understand this about her, how she could possibly hold things inside and not want to tell anyone. Yet her friends considered trustworthiness her finest attribute, a trait that compared to none.

By the time Sophia got back to the house Penelope was awake, but said nothing of her coming back in so early in the morning. She didn't ask, so Sophia never told her where she had been.

The following day she decided to go back to the pond to see if Abraham was fishing. It didn't matter, she thought — completely harmless if she went for a little walk and happened to follow the steps she had taken the other day. He probably wouldn't even be there. He was just making small talk with his friend's cousin, a visiting stranger. That's all it was, she said to herself. But as she walked down the path toward the pond, she felt a tingling in her stomach. She remembered his voice and how soothing it was. He could have said anything, talked about anything, and she would have been drawn by the way the words sounded coming out of his mouth.

Nervousness swarmed her for a moment. How foolish that she was trying to see this Abraham, whom she happened to meet by chance. *He probably told me to come by whenever I wanted just to be nice. But what if he's there? What am I going to say to him? I have to say something more, not just the small talk one makes when first meeting someone.*

Sophia walked slowly toward the pond, acting like she wasn't hoping to see Abraham again, though this morning she had put on a little makeup and brushed her teeth before stepping out of the house. She put on a nicer shirt, too, not the one she'd worn to bed the night before. She came around the bush and peeked over to where Abraham had stood the day before, but no one was there. She walked to the edge of the pond and stood exactly where he had.

She was alone.

At that moment she realized how foolish she was to believe he would be here this morning, or any morning. Standing there alone, Sophia felt vulnerable and exposed, as if she had been tricked into believing he would be there. She quickly turned around to walk away from the microscope she felt she was under. As she came around the bush, she saw Abraham walking down the path toward the pond, his smile coming toward her. She felt a flutter in her stomach and smiled back at him and, not thinking, walked back to where they had stood yesterday morning.

"You're not fishing today?"

"No, I fish occasionally, not every morning."

"But you told me yesterday that you fish here every morning."

"I said that hoping you would want to come back to meet me here," he said.

"So this was your ploy to get me to here?" she asked.

"Maybe."

"And you remembered me."

"Of course."

Hearing this made her heart beat faster and she blushed. She tried not to think the thoughts she shouldn't be having about a guy she had just met at the edge of a pond. But he kept staring at her and smiling, looking in her eyes and focusing on her face, mesmerized. She stared back, thinking they were about the same age; he could've been a year younger. They talked for a while. *What if someone sees me standing here, talking with this Abraham, whom I'm not related to? I could easily disgrace my family by just standing here with him.*

Two boys ran down the hill and jumped into the water, screaming. They splashed around until they saw Sophia and Abraham standing there, and then started to giggle, saying something in Albanian that Sophia couldn't understand. Abraham turned to them and spoke, his hand gesturing at the hill. They replied, and he then pointed toward the other side of the pond. The boys obliged this time, swimming to the other side.

"Are you sure it's all right if we talk here?" she asked him.

"I'm not quite sure."

Sophia said nothing, but realized that it felt stupid standing there and having to worry about what two young boys thought, and what they were saying in a language she didn't understand. She grew impatient and decided that this wasn't right, that if she wanted to talk with him when other people were around, she would.

"Well, it was nice talking with you again," she said and started up the path.

"Wait. We can meet somewhere else if you want. I mean, if you'd like. I know a place."

She wondered if she should take this Abraham seriously now, certain now how people would really think of it. This guy, her cousin's friend, who was asking to meet her somewhere else, what would people say about this?

"Where is this place?" she asked.

"The schoolhouse. We could meet tonight in the old schoolhouse. It's over there, at the edge of the village," he said, pointing with his thumb over his shoulder. "We could be there and no one would see us."

Sophia knew what he meant by this, and it seemed completely

harmless. He couldn't sit down in the plaza and talk with her even for a few minutes while the entire village looked on. Still, she had to ask. "Why would you want to meet me in the schoolhouse late at night?"

"To talk with you. Just talk."

Looking at him, Sophia couldn't help smiling because he was trying to find a way to meet with her, and at a place where she might feel comfortable. She agreed to meet him early the next morning, when everyone would still be asleep. What made her say yes was his voice, the way he said "just talk." The words fell from his lips and floated in the air in front of her. She watched his lips when he said goodbye to her at the edge of the pond.

And thought about how she would like to kiss them.

Sophia lay awake that night, making sure everyone in the house was asleep. After an hour, all became quiet except for Athina's light snoring. As Sophia lifted herself onto her elbows, Athina shifted on her bed, making it creak. Sophia walked quietly past Athina and grabbed her shoes as she made her way out of the bedroom. Slipping past Vangelli, who slept on the living room floor, she saw that his mouth was open wide, as if he were waiting for someone to pour water down his throat. Sophia tiptoed over Vangelli's legs and he rolled over on his stomach. She grabbed the blanket he had thrown off of himself and tucked it under her arm, then sneaked out the front door and through the yard. The roosters were awake, shuffling when she passed. She opened the gate, making sure it didn't screech too loudly, latched it shut, and made her way down the path to the bottom of the village. The moon shone on her as she walked past the sleeping homes.

Abraham had told her to meet him at the bottom of the hill. She searched, but couldn't find him. He was waiting for her behind a large oak tree off to the side of the plaza. He sat against its heavy trunk, smoking a cigarette, carelessly flicking the ashes on his pants as he rested his arms on his knees. Abraham spotted Sophia walking toward him. He took a last puff of his cigarette, tossed it into the bush, raised up, and jumped over the stone wall.

"You made it," he said, a big smile on his face.

"Of course, though I didn't think I was going to be able to — everyone wouldn't go to bed. But as soon as they did, I snuck out of the house."

"Let me take this." Abraham took the blanket from her and tossed it over his shoulder. He jumped back over the stone wall and helped Sophia climb over. He took her by the hand and led her through the tall grass toward the place where he had been fishing when they first met. At the pond's edge Abraham took the blanket and flipped off his shoes.

"I thought we were supposed to go to the schoolhouse tonight so no one would find us," Sophia said, as she followed his lead and took off her shoes.

"It's a warm night. I thought it would be nice for us sit out here if you don't mind. Do you mind?"

Sophia sat on the blanket. He sat next to her, very close, feeling her arm against his own as he leaned his weight on the palms of his hands behind him.

"Do you hear the crickets? They're very loud here in the mountains. Sometimes too loud."

"They wake me up sometimes during the night. I'm not used to them," she said. "Are you a light sleeper?"

"I have to be," Abraham replied.

"Why is that?"

"In our village, anything can come up to your window during the night and attack you."

Sophia laughed. "You sound so dramatic. Is that what you worry about when you sleep?"

"Sometimes."

"What else do you think about?"

"Oh, a lot of things,"

"Like what?" Sophia laughed.

He looked away. "I don't know."

"You don't want to tell me?"

Abraham shifted and looked at her. *She is so beautiful. How could I have found such a beautiful girl?* Sophia looked at him inquisitively, studying his face as she waited for him to speak, not knowing what he was thinking. She thought her laughter might have offended him.

"Tell me, Sophia, what is it like in America?"

"What's it like? I wouldn't even know where to start."

Abraham moved closer, turning his body toward hers. "I mean, is it anything like it is here?"

"Oh, no. It's nothing like here."

"Tell me, then."

"Well, Americans have a lot of freedom to do as they please. It's not like here, where people are always being watched by neighbors. I say this because here we are in the middle of the night meeting each other. You and I can't have a conversation alone without people thinking, well, certain things. In America, people generally go about their own business, and there's not much of a community effort like you have here in a village. I mean, people help each other, but they aren't as considerate and helpful as they are here."

"How do you mean?"

"There's a sense of obligation here to help each other in time of need. It's a little more important here. People don't usually help each other build a house in America, let's say, like they do here. People do that as their job and get paid for it. They won't do it for nothing, just for the goodness in them."

"Why not, to help a neighbor?"

"Most people in America don't talk to their neighbors. They don't even really know who their neighbors are."

"What do you mean they don't know who they are?" Abraham looked at her shocked.

"Most people don't know their neighbors, especially in cities. People just go about their lives and don't talk to their neighbors, probably because they feel like they don't need anything from them. *I don't need my neighbor to help me build my home, and I don't need my neighbor to help me feed my family.* Everything is bought in one way or another."

"Sophia, what does freedom feel like?"

"It feels like having a lot of choices."

"It would be nice to become an American," Abraham said. He turned away from her and lay down on the blanket, looking up at the deep sky. "And feel its greatness."

They talked awhile longer, slightly brushing arms as they shifted on the blanket. Abraham made her laugh and she smiled at him. He asked if she would like to meet with him again in the middle of the night. This time, they would meet at the schoolhouse because they would have more privacy than sitting out in the open by the pond. She said she would like that.

Sophia noticed the sky beginning to lighten just a little and looked at her watch—it was five A.M. Abraham helped her fold the blanket, and told her it was his pleasure meeting with her, and that he looked forward to seeing her again. He kissed her softly on the cheek and carried the blanket for her. He walked ahead of her, so that he could distract anyone who might be walking down the path and Sophia could hide if she needed to. And so it was, the first time they met during the middle of the night.

Smoking his morning pipe on his front porch, Old Man Arseni watched them walk up the hill into the cluster of homes.

Sophia felt giddy as she lay in bed the following evening, placing her watch on the floor next to the bed to make sure she was able to see when it was time to go. She couldn't believe she was doing this again, meeting Abraham in the middle of the night, meeting him because she was attracted by the sound of his voice. This was what had lured her, made her surrender to doing such a foolish thing, sneaking out in the middle of the night to meet with Abraham. She expected nothing more than to meet with him and talk. Yet her curiosity was about him, this Abraham who was fishing at the pond one morning, and made her feel she had to put her watch near the bed to track the time. His boldness intrigued her; that he felt it was all right to talk with her and smile at her and ask if he could meet her in the middle of the night. She had seen the schoolhouse before, knew exactly where it was and how to get there. She just hoped no one would see her walk down to the edge of the village.

Sophia waited in the schoolhouse for Abraham. She had gotten there a little earlier than they had planned, when it was safe for her to slip out of the house. She didn't want to miss this chance to see him again. Her watch showed 1:20 A.M. *He should be here in a few minutes.*

Sophia sat down on the blanket near the window and lit the three candles she had found in the kitchen earlier that day. She looked around the room, at the candles, at herself, and suddenly felt foolish. *What am I doing here? I'm meeting a guy I don't know — I don't even know who he really is.* Her thoughts twisted and her surroundings suddenly felt surreal, like she was in a dream, and didn't belong there. She blew out the candles and folded the blanket, and was about to walk back home when she heard the door slowly creak open. Her heart stopped as she waited in the dark for the person to come in, feeling more and more overwhelmed. But she saw Abraham standing right in front of the door, keeping it open, letting the moonlight shine in.

"Are you leaving?" he asked her.

"Uh, yes. I mean, no. No, I'm not leaving."

"If you want to leave, you can," he said to her as he walked into the schoolhouse.

"Well, I didn't think you were coming."

He looked at his watch. "I'm only two minutes late. Did you wait too long?" he said, smiling at her.

Sophia smiled at him, feeling a little embarrassed. She laid the blanket on the floor and lit the candles again. They sat next to each other.

First the small, meaningless talk, then Sophia started to talk a little about her life at home, more about her travels in Europe and here to the village. Abraham asked about her father. Hesitantly, she told Abraham about his death and how they were supposed to travel to the village together, that it would have been his first time back since 1945. Somehow all of this slipped out—she never thought that she would confide in Abraham this way.

She tried to change the subject. She told him that she had been in school practically her whole life, since she was five, and this amazed him. "How? How can you go to school for so long? What are they teaching you for so long?"

She told him that this was normal in America, and that many people went to school for several more years than she had. She moved two candles closer to her, used a rock to scratch a crude map of America on the concrete floor, and made an X where she lived. She told him how large America was and how many people lived there, how she lived by herself, owned a car, and drove it to see her family.

"You live alone?" he asked.

"Yes. My mother's house isn't near my school, so I have an apartment that I live in by myself."

"What do people say about that, about a girl living by herself?"

"Nothing. It's very common for a girl at university to do just that."

He watched her. A candle blew out and she got up to light it. *How beautiful is this girl. This is how I envision the perfect girl, what a perfect girl ought to be.* They were in the same room, but in worlds of their own, making sure everything was in place and everything was perfect. But everything was defined in two different ways. Abraham was trying to figure out if he should do what he wanted to do. The night, the moment, seemed perfect, but he was afraid, afraid of frightening her, envisioned her running out of the schoolhouse, waking the entire village.

For a moment, Sophia forgot about him as she fixed the candles. Then he moved slowly toward her and stood behind her. Sensing him, she stopped what she was doing and quickly turned around. He was standing right near her, his hands clasped behind his back, smiling into her.

Abraham's closeness startled her and she stepped back. This made him want her more. He moved closer, wrapped his arms around her, and held her, nuzzling his chin into her neck. He stayed there until he felt her calm, and began to kiss her neck, running his hands down her back. He moved her against a table and kissed her, feeling her body near his. She felt him against her and pressed herself to him. He lifted her onto the table, kissing her, pulling at her jeans. He held her tightly against himself, breathing into her ear. He kissed her face, her head, her neck, her chest. Slowly moving on top of her, he spread her legs slightly apart with his knees. Sophia pulled at his belt and loosened it, lowered his zipper, and slowly pulled his pants halfway down his legs. She felt his breathing in her ear as she pulled him close, her hands clenching his back. They held one another until he lay soft inside her.

Abraham looked at her and laughed and smiled and carefully lowered her to the floor. He lay next to her, feeling the chill on his damp skin. He stroked her hair and held her as she rested her head on his arm. Her face had a slight smile as she lay with her eyes closed.

"Are you okay?" he asked.

"Yeah. Are you?"

"I'm fine, just fine."

Abraham awoke a few hours later. The candles had burnt down to their ends. He looked out the window and saw the horizon transform from thick black to bright orange. He gently awoke Sophia and kissed her. They dressed, folded the blanket, and walked out of the schoolhouse. He walked her to the bottom of the path to Kosta's house. He smiled at her and she smiled at him. Sophia walked up the path, opened the gate, and slowly opened the front door and crept inside. Abraham turned around and walked toward the orange sky.

Sophia let her mind wander back to America and the life she had left behind for a short time. She realized that when she went back to the States, back to her life, she would be a completely different person. She wouldn't be able to recognize herself. Her friends would think that she lost herself somewhere along the way.

She thought about William, about the time they were in his office one Thursday afternoon, discussing the lecture he planned for class that week, but not really listening to one another. Other things were floating in their minds, like the last time Sophia had stopped by his office for help. She invented casual excuses to come by and ask him a question about the lecture he had just given, and he would answer politely, as if this were really what she had stopped by for. He understood why she would knock softly on his door, walk shyly into his office, and ask silly questions. Then he became the pursuer; he had been waiting for this moment too. He got what he wanted—maybe.

The first time they were together was awkward for both of them. After class one day, Sophia said she needed help and asked if she could drop in later that afternoon. But after asking, she kept looking at him, longer than a person normally would. After telling her that a drop-in visit would be fine, he looked away; then, realizing she was still staring at him, turned to her again. She gave him a quick smile, and then turned and walked away.

She was in his office by 5:30 that afternoon, when the other professors had already gone for the day. Instead of sitting in one of the wooden chairs directly in front of his desk, she placed herself strategically on the couch that faced his desk from behind the chairs. She sat at one end and got a bit more comfortable by adjusting her hips in a slow, upward motion, looking at him from the corner of her eye.

That afternoon, when they had finished making love, they looked at each other, searching for answers in what had just happened so suddenly. Though Sophia had planned it to happen just as it did, and William had probably imagined it, perhaps even obsessed over it, this was something that had come from nothing — a slight glance in the classroom, a suggestion to meet after class — and had now reached its peak. She thought that no more would come of it. He was to be her thesis advisor, and she a graduate student.

Their subsequent meetings and their lovemaking in his office remained exciting for Sophia; the curiosity of it, the mystery of the unknown, never diminishing. Yet, there were still secrets left to be unfolded, there was still that anticipation. When she walked into his office to discuss her thesis, she would close the door and make sure it was locked, and they both knew how the meeting would end. She would be on his desk, her feet resting on the arms of his leather chair, the books on his desk pushed just slightly closer to the edge.

Afterward, when he stood back from her, he would try to act the professor, suddenly aware of his improper behavior. Sometimes he would gaze at her with a professorial look, one that didn't fit the moment, and Sophia would laugh at him for this contradiction of acts. She thought it was cute that he would quickly pull up his pants and begin to answer the questions she had asked when she first walked in, the questions she had thought of moments before asking them. As if he felt he had to make things right by giving her this as well.

Their affair continued through most of her last year in college. Sophia never told anyone about what was happening between her and William; it was theirs. She enjoyed her time with him, however limited it might be, and knew that it would be over once she completed her thesis and graduated. They had nothing in common outside this relationship. They were from different worlds, different generations. She had her life and her friends; he had his life — and his wife.

It would have been very awkward, if not impossible, to have a deeper relationship, one that would require dinner dates and introductions.

Some people enjoy relationships at arm's length. Claustrophobia surrounds them, suffocates them, when they feel they are getting too close, a distance measured not in location, but in emotion. They want to feel no attachment to what is before them. It is theirs for the moment and nothing can be expected other than what is just now. The element of surprise is what really intrigues them—the unexpected phone call, or visit, or touch on the shoulder, the lingering thoughts that accompany all of these. They seek the thrill of it, an exciting diversion within life's routine, but with no mandatory phone calls, no drives expected after a long day at work, trying to stay alert yet all the while thinking of sleep.

This, in essence, was Sophia's relationship with William. Neither expected anything out of it, and neither ever pushed for more, because the other could always put a stop to it with a simple reminder that this was a professor/student relationship and that's all. But Sophia liked the way their connection had evolved. She enjoyed her freedom, yet enjoyed knowing what to expect during their meetings. She was content that he wanted her, and it didn't matter that it might be the only way he wanted her—a woman to meet with and lift on top of his desk. She knew he enjoyed their scenario. He would tell her he wanted her, and say things that he dreamt, perhaps, of saying to his wife; going through the motions of what he would need to do to get his marriage back on track; to find a rhythm that, if it went smoothly with Sophia, might go even half as smoothly with his wife. Maybe he was practicing on Sophia. And she would let him. Yet she wanted to believe that their passion for each other was not merely a convenience, but a real attraction between people, an episode of meaning in their lives, a secret never told. And she wanted him all the more because of this.

While he made love to her, he would whisper how wonderful she felt and how much he cared for her. Sophia would let him carry on and hold him, but she never completely believed; she always thought of it as something that slipped off his tongue in the moment, yet she would listen. And she would say such things to him, but was always cautious, always conscious of her thoughts so they wouldn't slip out of her mouth. It might have been fear of what she would say — something that might frighten him away, and maybe scare her, too.

One time, they were on the couch and he was on top of her. After he was finished, he lay motionless, relaxed, contented. His face was turned away, and she heard the word "love." When he looked at her a few moments later, she pretended to be asleep.

EIGHT

The village had experienced a harsh winter, so Mother Nature was a little gentler with them in the spring. During the month of March there was an epidemic of diarrhea; in pajamas and untied shoes, everyone ran out of their homes to the outhouses. It didn't matter that it was frigid cold—if nature insisted they go, then they must. A few boys from the village traveled to Gjirokastra to find a doctor. He arrived a week later and handed out the appropriate medicines to those who desperately needed them. Sophia arrived shortly after the epidemic ended, and heard everyone's stories along with the details of how they handled their particular cases. They were looking for sympathy and insight from their visitor, a suggestion perhaps.

By the end of March, winter left them alone and the village began to thaw itself. The mountain air was again scented with myrtle, and the sun warmed it. It was the season to plant crops to store for the following winter, to ration them when the village was blanketed in snow again.

Kosta got an early start the morning of the first of April. By the look of the sun and the feel of the breeze on his skin, he knew it was going to be warm that day. Late the night before, when the world was asleep, Kosta had quietly taken his plow out to the field and set a piece of bread next to it on the soil.

He awoke the next morning and made his way to the field after breakfast, Vangelli following close behind with a shovel over his shoulder. Kosta walked anxiously toward the plow to see if the bread was still there.

"Ah, the piece of bread is still here. Look Vangelli, the bread is still here," he said to his son in relief. "We will have a good harvest this year."

"Sophia, I want to tell you something."

"What is it, Pop?"

"You have to listen closely; my voice is becoming weak and tired, but I know what I'm saying. Listen to me, please."

"Pop, I'm listening."

She waited for her father to speak as he collected his thoughts. In the days before he passed, her father told her that he forgave the world for all the hardships he had experienced, all the pain he had been subjected to, all the frustration. He was focusing upon the last moments he would have.

"I believe God has made me suffer in order to bring a pleasant life for my children."

Life drifted out of Sophia. "Don't say that, Pop. You know you didn't have a bad life," she said, trying to prevent the conversation from descending into darkness.

"Yes, I strongly believe this. I believe that I suffered so you would never have to."

Sophia started to cry. "Pop, your believing you suffered for us, this is too great a burden for me to hear."

There was a brief silence between them. "You've given us a good life," she told him.

"You are my favorite, too. I always worry about you, how you'll manage in life." He stopped for a moment to retrieve his voice. "I wish everyone had treated me the way you have."

"Everyone has treated you well. Don't think of these things now."

"These are the thoughts that now travel through my head, Sophia."

Late one evening they sat around the kitchen table. Kosta and Vangelli had just gotten back from their trip to the neighboring village. Penelope was in the kitchen cooking three chickens from the yard, and set the table with potatoes, vegetables, bread, and cheese. Athina was at a friend's house and was not going to have dinner with the rest of them, Penelope had said. Sophia came in from the back porch, where she had been reading a book that she picked up just before coming to Europe. It was about a girl going back to her roots, her heritage, and a voyage of self-discovery. Sophia thought it was a good time to ask about the old man she had seen, the one who lived at the edge of the village.

"Who's that man who sits outside on his porch all day? Sophia asked Kosta. "The man who lives near the pond."

"Which house are you talking about?"

"The one that's sort of small, gray stone."

"That's Arseni. We call him Old Man Arseni here in the village."

Arseni, Arseni, Sophia repeated in her head. Where have I heard that name before? I know I've heard the name. "Was he a friend of my father's?"

"They grew up together in the village. I'm sure they were friends. Why do you ask?"

"I remember the name Arseni. I remember my father talking about him a few years back. My father told me stories about him. That is, if the man who lives at the edge of the village and my father's friend are one and the same." She thought for a moment. "I may visit with him after dinner."

"You don't want to go over there — that man is crazy," Vangelli said, with his mouth full of food.

"Vangelli! Don't talk like that about other people. How would you like it if someone spoke like that about you?" Penelope chided.

"Well, he is, everyone knows that. We see him walking around in the fields by himself like he's lost. Sometimes when we go to the valley to play we see him, but we run away because we don't want to talk to him. He looks really weird."

"Looking 'weird' doesn't mean he's crazy, does it?" Sophia asked.

"He's crazy. I've heard the stories about him. I know what made him crazy. When he was younger, his wife was kill—

"Vangelli! That's enough, I said. We are not to discuss this any longer. I don't want you to ever speak of him this way again," said Penelope.

Sophia raised her eyes from her plate and stared at her, then looked at Vangelli, who had tapped Sophia's knee under the table to get her attention. "He's really, really crazy," he mouthed to her.

Sophia nodded. Penelope looked at Vangelli, and he went back to eating his dinner.

After dinner Sophia excused herself from the table and said she was going for a walk down to the plaza. She said she wouldn't be gone long, grabbed her sweater, and walked out the front door.

She took the path toward the edge of the village, the house closest to the border. Old Man Arseni wasn't on his porch, and Sophia wondered if she should go back home and try some other time. She walked a bit closer to the front of the house and noticed a lit lantern on a table inside. She decided to walk up to the front door and knock, just to say hello.

Sophia knocked twice before hearing noises inside. She waited to see if he would answer. After a few minutes, she knocked again, then gave up and walked down the steps. Then, for no reason, she turned around. Someone looked at her through the curtains and then quickly closed them.

She walked away.

"Have you met my cousin yet?"

"No, I haven't."

"She's from America. I'll introduce you to her sometime. I have yet to see her today; she's probably at my uncle's house."

"How long is she staying here?"

"I don't know. She's starting school soon. I'm not sure exactly when. You'll have to meet her, she's really nice," said Stavro, pulling out his cigarettes and offering them to Abraham and Yanni.

"Has she ever been here before?" asked Yanni.

"No. I have a lot of family who live in America," Stavro said, trying to impress his friends. "But they've never come here."

"Where do they live in America? New York?" asked Yanni.

"No, not New York."

"Who's that?"

Stavro and Abraham turned around to see. It was Sophia. She was walking toward them.

"Hey, Stavro," she said.

"I was just talking about you. I was asking them if they'd met you yet," he said, gesturing to Yanni and Abraham.

Yanni was staring at her. She was used to this by now because stares were so common here.

"Hello."

Yanni and Abraham nodded.

"Where were you?" asked Stavro.

"Just went for a walk down by the pond. I have to work off all this food I've been eating since I've been here. I'm starting to gain weight."

They didn't know if they should laugh at this so they just sat in silence.

"So, how long are you staying here?" Yanni asked her.

"I don't know. It depends. If I like it a lot, then I'll stay a while longer," she said, glancing at Abraham.

"You should stay," Yanni said. It's nice here when the weather gets warmer."

"Perhaps I will. It was nice meeting both of you. Stavro, I'm going back to Kosta's house. Are you going to be there later?"

"Yeah, I'll stop by."

She walked away and the three of them were alone.

"That's the cousin you were talking about?"

"Leave it alone, Yanni. Remember, she's my cousin, and she's only going to be here a short time. Don't bother her."

"Yanni doesn't bother women. Yanni makes women happy."

"Oh, shut up," said Stavro and stubbed out his cigarette.

"So, how much do you like it here?"

"What?"

"You said last week that you would stay longer if you liked it here. Remember, in the plaza, when Stavro introduced you to Yanni and me. So, do you like it here?"

"A little."

"Just a little?"

"Just a little."

"Okay," said Abraham and lay on his back and tossed the blanket over his legs. "You know, you should like it a lot more than that."

"I should? Why is that?"

"I don't know. Maybe because of me."

"Do you want me to like it here more because of you?"

"I think so."

"You think so?"

"I think so."

Sophia laughed. "I see where this is going. Well, if you really want to know, I like it a lot more than I expected to before I got here. And that's because I met you."

He turned and smiled at her. "You really mean that?"

"Of course. Why else would I say so?"

"I don't know. Sometimes I just don't know what to think with you. You come from another place and you've seen a lot and traveled a lot, and probably met a lot of people. I just don't know what to think."

"That doesn't change the way I think about you, though."

"You're not bored here in the village?"

"Bored?"

"Yeah. Is it fun here for you?"

"Well, I came here for other things than fun. I needed to come for reasons of my own, so fun or not, I'm here."

"Because of your father?"

"Because of my father."

"You know, Sophia, it's admirable that you did this, coming here. It really is. I mean, I don't know the whole story — if you want to tell me you can, when you're ready — but you told me a little and I admire you for it. I like you more because of it."

"Thank you, Abraham."

"You're welcome."

"Maybe I'll tell you one day. The whole story."

"Whenever you'd like."

He took her face in his hands and kissed her hard, as if he had been with her all his life and then hadn't seen her in years. He continued to kiss her on her mouth and cheeks and neck and head. He let go of her face and looked at her.

He kissed her again.

Until he met Sophia, Abraham's experiences with girls had been extremely limited. He had never been intimate with a girl from his village, but had met a couple of girls while he was working in Gjirokastra a few summers back. He realized that what he had experienced with the two girls seemed much more mechanical than the intimacy he felt with Sophia. When he met one of these girls late in the evening after his shift, he envisioned the act of sex, not the exploration of it. From the start, the act was mechanical and, limited. He was concerned with his own pleasure and satisfaction, not the girl's, though not disregarding or degrading her, either.

But Sophia took him on a journey he had never experienced before. She relaxed him and exposed him to exploring and being adventurous, not focusing on the ultimate climax, but on the path that would eventually lead there. She slowed down the movements, made sex more spontaneous, rather than knowing what to expect and how long it would take to get there. Abraham had never known it could be this way; it could be enjoyed slowly and adventurously, and it could be surprising. A whole new avenue opened for him, one he felt to be natural. He wasn't frustrated or anxious with Sophia. He felt calm and good and loved.

Making love with her, he began to understand what a woman's body needs and desires. He became more aware of her breathing, of her movements, of her soft moans. This awakened in him something he had never thought he possessed. He felt chemistry with her, a jolt in his spirit and emotions. It was unusual for him to feel this way, but this true meaning of making love captivated him. The crudeness he had experienced before, the rushed movements that accompanied the intimacy he had in the past, the selfishness that overwhelmed him before, all evaporated into the air. He felt connected not only with Sophia but newly connected with himself as well. She opened his boundaries, and the truth in him was released when he was with her. His insecurities, his passions, his desires — all were right in front of his face. It was as if Abraham and Sophia were signaling to one another the characteristics that ultimately defined them, defining themselves in ways they were in control of — massaging the truth, and molding it to fit their needs.

What word might Sophia use to describe her father? Would she choose one that defined him as an individual, or one that explained him in relation to others? Would she define him when he was healthy or recall the last days before his death? She remembered once asking her father what he wanted for his birthday. He quickly replied that he needed nothing but her love. His response to her question added to the complexity of her father's thoughts, though it was a simple exchange of words.

After he had arrived in Greece with his brothers, they ended up finding a place to sleep in an abandoned apartment in Ioannia. Right at the edge of the town, away from the university, was a neglected neighborhood that had become a haven for those who were not a part of the university or the familial people. Sophia's father and uncles crammed themselves into a one-bedroom apartment. The day after they arrived in Greece, they began to search for menial jobs in the city.

Her father found a job at an upscale restaurant in the center of town, a few miles from the apartment. Taking advantage of the situation, the owner forced him to work long hours seven days a week for minimal pay. Her father took the job gladly because this was what he had left his country for; he took advantage of this opportunity that was in front of him.

Sophia's uncles found work around the city center as well—busboys, cooks, delivery boys. Anything was an opportunity to them, a gift from the outside world that they could never receive from their country. The roles were reversed: owners of restaurants and cafes believed they had found young boys from an impoverished country to take advantage of, but Sophia's father and uncles had a different agenda in their thoughts.

They had expanded their minds with the notion that their situation was temporary. They realized that there was more to life than this. Having witnessed the vast change in their environments, the sudden switch in opportunity between Albania and Greece, there had to be better opportunities.

They set their eyes on America.

Sophia walked to Old Man Arseni's house to see if he would talk with her. After finishing her tea, a mountain tea that she'd been told could do wonders for any sickness, she mentioned to Penelope that she was going to visit him.

"Arseni? You want to visit him?"

"Yeah. Since he was my father's friend, I think it would be appropriate to meet him and talk with him. Interesting, too."

"Okay, go ahead. But I just want to let you know that he's very uncomfortable around people, especially those he doesn't know. A few neighbors stop by his house to see how he's getting along, but no one really visits him for conversation."

"I'll be fine."

"I know you will," Penelope said, putting her arm around Sophia's shoulders. "But I don't know about him."

Sophia stood on Old Man Arseni's front porch a moment, deciding whether to knock on the door. He had already been out on his porch this morning—a coffee cup was on the table and the coffee grounds on the bottom of the cup were still wet. The curtains concealed the inside of his house, and it seemed empty, even abandoned. She felt nervous, like she didn't belong there, as if she were doing something that made her suspect, a criminal. She considered that she was invading the man's privacy, his self-imposed seclusion, just for her curiosity's sake. And he didn't know her. Who was this girl on his front porch knocking on his door for the second time? Didn't she know that he wanted to be left alone by the rest of the world? Maybe the kids in the village knew something that everyone else didn't. Maybe he really was crazy. A weird recluse. Who knew what he might do to her on his front porch?

As Sophia was thinking these things, the front door opened and Old Man Arseni was standing right in front of her.

How short he is, she thought. Her eyes were riveted on the deep creases in his forehead and around his eyes. His pants draped loosely over his legs; a tan rope tied around his waist served as a belt. His slippers were extremely worn, and a flannel shirt exposed his upper chest—browned and leathery from the sun. A gold chain hung around his neck; a cross lay buried in his gray furry chest hair.

"Good morning. You're Arseni, right?"

He looked at her for a moment and responded that he was.

"Hello, Arseni," Sophia said, extending her hand. "I'm Sophia."

"Yes, I know who you are," Arseni said, taking her right hand with his left.

"I'm Nonta's daughter, your old friend Nonta."

"Yes, I know."

She stared at him silently, waiting to see if he would tell her how he knew. He said nothing, and then invited her to sit with him on his porch and have a coffee. Confusion overlay the awkwardness of introducing herself, as she continued wondering how he could know who she was. She thought it impolite to ask, but the thought stayed in her mind throughout their conversation. It wasn't until much later, near the end of her stay in the village, after having been to his house for coffee a dozen times, that she asked him how he knew her.

They sat and talked, Sophia's nervousness fading quickly. His cordiality warmed her. He spoke as if he had known her all his life, made her feel comfortable and welcome. At times she felt like she conversing with her father once again.

Her father used to talk about Arseni, and had said that thinking of him was one of his few good childhood memories. Arseni was the friend he always spent time with, who opened up his mind and shared secrets with. The only times they weren't together were when Arseni, who was a shepherd, would leave for several days to roam the valley with his flock. Arseni had always asked Sophia's father to come along to keep him company. Though he knew his friend had to farm, Arseni just wanted him around. Sophia's father never went; he always replied that he had his responsibilities, that they would get together when Arseni returned, and resume where they had left off.

After talking for a while and drinking two coffees, Sophia told Old Man Arseni why she had really come to visit. "I wanted to ask some questions about my father, Arseni."

"I, too," he said, sipping his coffee. He looked at her longer this time. His eyes were glazed, and the corners of them slightly yellow. He placed his cane against the wall, shifting in his chair. He offered to make her another coffee. She politely accepted, though she had already drunk too much. He came back from the kitchen and handed her a cup. He asked her where her father was, what had become of him, and why he had never come back.

NINE

Sophia walked to the nurses' desk at the end of the brightly-lit hallway with its clean white walls. She noticed they were going about their business in a different way today, acting as though they weren't working in the Intensive Care Unit. Perhaps this was how people had to make themselves work and act and feel to survive watching people deteriorate every day, being unable to help them, just taking care of them for the moment.

Sophia passed the desk. Two nurses who knew her by now nodded hello when she glanced at them. They had seen her here so often, and asked her so many times how she was doing. Lately they'd stopped asking; they understood how she was feeling during these moments. Now they let her go into her own world as she passed them, walking to room 408, the last at the end of the hall.

She crept quietly into the room and peered just beyond the bathroom wall that obstructed her view of her father. When she first walked into the room each day, all she could see was his feet beneath the layers of blankets. And every time, she thought how small his legs looked, as if kidney failure somehow shrank the legs. She felt his legs through the blankets to make sure that they were still there. Sometimes, when she wasn't thinking clearly, Sophia wondered whether they were his, if the doctor had replaced his legs, too, just for the sake of replacing them, since they had been trying to find a solution for everything else that was wrong.

When she spoke with his doctor on the phone earlier, he told her he had drugged her father a little more than usual today because he had been trying to pull the IVs from his arms. Her father, the doctor told her, felt he didn't belong there — he was fine and he wanted to go home. When Sophia heard this, a sharp pain shot through her forehead and spread over the top of her head, like water dripping through her hair and soaking her scalp. She cried quietly as she finished her conversation with the doctor. She drove to the hospital right after class, to see how her father was feeling.

Though he looked at her right away when she walked into his room, he appeared much too drugged to be even a little coherent. Tears welled in Sophia's eyes as she stood by his bedside and kissed him on the forehead as she had always done. She looked at him for a moment as his head swayed slowly from left to right, left to right, always making eye contact with her as his head moved to the right. The expression on his face looked like he was trying to absorb her —wide-eyed, as though seeing her for the first time in his life. He recognized his daughter, yet at the same time he didn't. The drugs had overtaken his comprehension of what was happening around him, and Sophia had to force herself to believe that he knew she was there. She sat on the edge of the bed, holding his hand and rubbing his forearm. He looked at her, then looked away, breathing laboriously, and again he swayed his head and looked at her. He coughed and cleared his throat; pain went through her heart. His breathing had become heavy, wet.

Often when Sophia visited him she would stay for hours, bringing a book to read at his bedside. Just being there next to him was all she needed to calm her. She came to the hospital every morning and night, before and after class. Sometimes she would write a paper while he slept, placing her notebook on the edge of the bed next to his feet. She wrote late into the night, endlessly, until the entire floor was asleep. When all the visitors had gone and the hospital was quiet, the only sound she heard was her father's breathing. Deep breaths, in and out, in and out, struggling to get air down into his lungs. This rhythmic melody would soothe her, letting her know that he was still there with her.

The smell of medicine surrounded her. "How are you doing, Pop? Feeling any better today?" she asked him holding his hand. He answered with a grunt and continued to move his head back and forth. He tried to say something, but she couldn't understand him. He slowly lifted his arms in the air, frustrated that he couldn't talk. Finally, he blurted out, "Wa-ta," and licked his lips. "Oh, you want water. Hold on, Pop, I'll get you some."

Sophia went into hallway and walked to the nurses' desk to ask if her father could have some water. One of the nurses said she would be there in a minute. Sophia walked back to the room and sat next to him again. "They're coming with water. They'll be here in a minute." She sat facing him, holding his hand again, the sound of the TV behind her. A nurse came into the room with a cup of water and a small wooden stick with a green sponge at the end of it.

"He can't drink a lot of water because of the tube down his throat, but we can wet his mouth with this. The IV is hydrating him, but his mouth is probably dry from being open all day."

The nurse walked around to the other side of the bed and placed the wet sponge in his mouth, wetting his lips and tongue. He clamped his mouth around the wooden stick, desperate to get as much water as he could. The nurse did this a couple of times before setting the cup on the tray table next to him. She told Sophia that he could have two to three sponges of water at a time, every hour or so. Sophia thanked her as she walked out of the room.

Her father lay, looking at her, but still swaying his head. She told him about her day at class and about the big term paper due next month that she hadn't even began to do research for. She told him how the weather was and what she planned for dinner that evening—pasta with tuna. She told him she had started playing squash at the health club with a few people she had met there.

She told him that he had to get better so they could go to Albania and visit his village and their relatives as they had planned. They had decided to go when she graduated from college, before she would start graduate study. She squeezed his hand and repeated that he had to get better. She started crying as she said it to him again and again. He continued to look at her wide-eyed, and started to mumble. She leaned over him to hear. "Wa-ta, wa-ta," he whispered into her ear. Sophia reached over her him for the cup of water from the tray table. She placed the sponge into his mouth once, twice, three times, then a fourth.

"I love you, Pop. You've got to get better. You have to so we can go to Albania. Come on, Pop, get better." She put the sponge in his mouth yet again.

He closed his eyes and fell asleep.

I was nervous. I didn't say much since I walked into the home, the house where I was born. No one noticed my uneasiness, but I knew I seemed anxious and insecure about what might come, what I might see, what I might find out from my mother.

Everyone was happy I was there, that I had come back after all these years. They pulled out photos I had sent of myself with my own family, the family I created in the States — the natural extension of my family here. They even had photos I had forgotten sending. I was in a world of my own; I wasn't there with them as I stood in the room getting to know the family I left so long ago. Athina went into the kitchen to fix coffee, and Stavro and Vangelli went out the back door to bring more chairs so everyone could sit around the table in the living room. Lord, they've grown since the last photos they sent me. Athina is turning into a young lady, no longer the little girl I had pictured in my mind.

I looked around the room, observing, penetrating — the cracks on the walls, the couch, the photographs, the painting on the wall — my mind scrolling backward.

A person's perception of the past is molded by how he first reacted to an experience and what has happened to him since. Memory changes the way things had actually occurred. A person might lock up all his thoughts in the back of his head and try to ignore them. Then, at a later time, he might try to sift through his mind and see what he forced himself to forget for so long, the stories that want to be dusted off and read once again.

What I was thinking was incomprehensibly foreign to all of them, something none of them could ever decipher. What I had in my memory was intangible, like a spirit in my head, unable to get out, continually whirling and bumped against the walls of my skull. Releasing these memories from the back of my mind didn't hurt, but they knew by the look on my face that I felt it.

My memory, my story, it appeared, was about to be dusted off.

"Papou! Come. Follow me. I'll take you to her room."

I followed Kosta as he made his way past everyone and to the back of the house. I put my hands in my pockets and lowered my head, walking into my mother's bedroom.

"Yiayia, Nonta is here. He just arrived a moment ago."

My mother turned onto her left side and looked up at Kosta. She was dressed in black, and a knitted blanket lay over her legs, just below her knees. I looked around the corner into the bedroom and saw her on the bed, Kosta standing in front of her, blocking my full view of her. My heart thumped as I walked closer to the doorway, the voices in the living room fading into a deep tunnel. I paused for a moment in the hallway, listening to Kosta talk to my mother. Her voice seemed old and tired and warm — she sounded like history.

Kosta walked out of the room and met me in the hallway. "Your mother wants to see you. She's waiting for you. Go in and talk with her."

To wait for someone is to hope that that person will arrive. My mother harbored this hope in her chest for fifty years. Waiting for her sons, hoping that at least one of them, maybe all of them, would come back to the village. When a person hopes that long, the whole body becomes numb and restless. It wears away the other senses. She didn't mind, though. I came back. I finally came back.

"Mama?" I slowly walked into her room and shut the door gently behind me. The word "Mama." I haven't spoken it in fifty years. An understanding and a relation. I suddenly felt a huge release inside me — calmness, comfort.

"Pop? Dad? Wake up. The nurse brought your food. Let me raise your bed a little so you can sit up and eat dinner," Sophia said, gently touching her father's shoulder.

Sophia went to the hospital before class the next morning. She walked out of the elevator and through the glass doors to the well-lit hallway and the clean white walls. She passed the nurses' station, but none of the nurses said hello to her this time. They looked at her as she walked past. Sophia put her head down and walked faster toward her father's room, finding his doctor in the doorway. She peered into the room and saw her father on the bed. The doctor looked at her.

"Sophia, I'm glad you're here. We were going to call you at home, but I guess you beat us to it."

"How's everything? Is my father okay?"

"As well as he can be. This morning, I and the other two doctors who are treating your father decided it would be best that he gets discharged today, that he be in his own bed."

It took her a moment to process what the doctor was telling her. Discharged? In his own bed? Her eyebrow twitched when she figured it out. "He's as well as he can be? You think this is best right now?" She paused for a moment and her throat tightened. "Are you sure there's nothing else you can do for him here?" she forced herself to say.

"There's nothing more we can do for him," he said. "His body is rejecting the kidney and—I'm sorry, but there's nothing we can do," he repeated, forcing Sophia to grasp what he was saying. "He should be at home now, in familiar surroundings." The doctor put his hand on her shoulder and told her one last time that he was sorry. He said they were going to get a wheelchair and bring her father downstairs to the pickup area. She could drive her car around the front and they would help him into her car.

"Are you going to be all right?" he asked.

"Yeah, I'll be fine. I'll call my brother. We'll bring my father home."

"Good. If you need anything else, Sophia, you know how to reach me."

"Thank you, doctor."

Sophia walked to her father's side. He was asleep. She started to pack up his things—his clothes, cards and magazines, his toiletries. She then stopped and stood motionless beside his bed, collecting her thoughts, the recent moment of what the doctor had said to her. She looked at him and he at her; then he slowly put his head down. Nothing else to say. She lifted her father's hand and held it in both of hers. The doctor left the room as Sophia laid her head on her father's legs and cried.

He lay on his bed and felt his daughter's head on his knees—her sobbing, the quaking of her shoulders as she leaned over the bed and cried. He didn't open his eyes, because he didn't want to witness what his daughter was experiencing, the emotions that shook her body. He would rather die in this bed he was lying in.

"Do you ever think about leaving, Arseni?"

"Sometimes I do, but I have plans now, I'm to be married very soon."

"Would you leave if you didn't have a future wife?"

"Perhaps."

This was the conversation he had with Arseni shortly before the escape. He wondered how his friend's life would have turned out had Arseni followed him over the mountain trails into Greece. Maybe his life would have been less burdensome, more uplifting. How wonderful he felt for the short time he was married to his wife, and how awful the perennial sadness he had experienced thereafter. Which was better, to have a brief episode of total bliss followed by utter despair or a life filled with continuous mediocrity? Maybe Arseni's children could have lived and grown in this country.

The sadness he felt for his friend, the pain of so many memories, all wheeled through his mind. This was the conversation he was having with himself. He knew it would be time to go very soon. He lay on his bed and felt his daughter's head on his knees.

At first their plan to go to Albania was gone; there was no reason to go to the Balkans now. She didn't know her father's family, and what matter if she never met them at all? But her mind changed and the decision was made while, several weeks after her father's death, she was sifting through his bureau and came across photos their family in Albania had sent him over the years. Their faces told her stories through the photos in her hands. She wanted to know these stories. She needed to see where her father came from, and visit what had molded and defined him. There might be a sense of closure, perhaps, in meeting these relatives she had never met before, these first cousins and aunts, and uncles who lived in the Balkans.

She had met Kosta before, in Athens, a couple of years earlier. He was working for a small shipping company, picking up goods and heading back to Albania. He was in Athens for a few days, visiting friends who had left Albania earlier in search of work. Sophia was on holiday in Greece, staying in Athens for a while and then taking a ferry to the Cyclades. Kosta had told her that she should visit the village while she was in this part of the world, and that he could drive her there in his truck whenever she wanted. She declined the invitation, but promised him that she would one day go to Albania — with her father. She told Kosta she had promised her father that she would go to the Old Country with him when he was ready to go back.

She heard stories about Albania from the few who had ever heard of it, though most people couldn't even find it on a map if they were asked. The most bizarre, which she heard during her sophomore year in college, was told by Michael, a classmate who wrote for the travel guide the college published. His assignment was to travel throughout Albania for five weeks, researching which cities, towns, and villages a traveler should visit, what historical sites to see, the places that would really exemplify the country's culture, and where to eat and sleep. What particularly interested him, he told Sophia, were the blood feuds in the northern part of the country, which had arisen again since the communist regime's collapse. There was a code of honor to be embraced by all Albanians, based upon the Kanun written by the legendary Prince Lek Dukajin. The prince, who lived during the sixteenth century, had written what the Ghegs of northern Albania considered the country's first constitution. He devised this code to establish a way of life, and Albanians abided it for centuries, until Hoxha and communism put an end to the ancient doctrine.

Michael told her that the country's forty-five years of communism had been only a momentary hiatus, and these old blood feuds, vicious grudges, again fueled anger in men as if they had begun just days ago. The men were expected to uphold their family honor by revenge of blood. Sophia asked him if he had seen any of these feuds while in northern Albania.

"Actually, I saw one while I was living with a family in a town called Shkoder, which is in the highlands. Hospitality is so important in their culture that this family insisted I stay with them even though I was a stranger. Based upon the Kanun, a person is supposed to honor his guest and treat him as family. Anyway, this family I was staying with had three sons and a daughter. The sons were in their late teens, early twenties, and the girl must have been thirteen or fourteen. Their feud with another family had been going on for three generations, going on four..."

She listened closely as Michael told her about the family's revenge. The story seemed more the stuff of legend than of reality, the people he described more like characters in a play, a tragedy. The remoteness of mountain life and the Kanun law he talked about evoked images in her mind of a medieval period—a culture that had evolved very slowly.

TEN

Preferring to let her mind wander through the village, Sophia avoided conversations about her father, except those she wanted to have with Old Man Arseni. She felt it was the right time in her life to explore her father's past with his boyhood friend.

The people her father had grown up with still lived in Chatista. For various reasons, fear being the most common, they had never left the village. Albania had been too unstable for anyone to leave freely, to pick up and leave the country, neither knowing what would become of those they left behind, nor knowing what might happen when they reached their destination. Her father had left with intentions, hopes, and regrets. He wanted to feel life in a different way, to see it from a different angle, perhaps. Sophia remembered asking him once what his childhood in Albania had been like. "Miserable," he said simply, and left it at that. She knew not to ask more, at least not at the time. He had seen too much, felt too much, and experienced too little to go on living that way. He knew there was a world outside his, because people from that other world walked through it during times of war. He felt like he was only going through the motions of life.

Eventually, her father told Sophia about his childhood in the village, and how he used to spend entire summers as "a nanny for the rich." As a young teenager, he left the village and went to the town of Gjirokastra. There he found a job pushing a baby stroller for a wealthy woman as she sat in the plazas, gossiping and drinking coffee with her friends. He would stay at this woman's home with her family, getting barely enough food to stave off hunger, and very little money to bring back home to the village. He told Sophia he could never imagine having someone else push his baby around like he did during these summers.

He had to do chores around their home, too, making the beds each morning, tending the garden, picking up after the family, and washing the dishes after they ate dinner. They owned him for the summer, yet they resented him because he was dirty. "A dirty little village boy," they would whisper if he was in the next room, but he always heard them. He resented them, too — resented that they treated him badly, thought of him as dirty, insulted him because he was from the mountains. He resented that they wouldn't let him eat with the family. He resented that they had money and he had none.

He never went back to the village while he was in the town, and his stay in Gjirokastra would last until the day before school started, when he would hitchhike home. The family he served during that summer never offered to drive him there; they were "too busy," they would tell him, yet said he could come back next year if he wanted his job again. But when he went back to his village, he missed life in the town sometimes — the quaint, winding streets, the clothes people wore, the "stone city" that was Gjirokastra, though at the time he didn't know what that meant.

Sophia's father left Albania because there was nothing there for him. He confessed to her that he had never had "a plan" in his life after leaving, because he hadn't known what to expect. He would take what in the world offered him, whatever was in its outstretched hand. He had his mind on America, although he didn't act on going there until he had been living in Greece for several years. There simply came a time when he wanted more from the world, and thought America would be able to give it to him. By working in restaurants, he saved enough money for a one-way ticket on a ship departing Athens for New York City, where he arrived in 1955. He had a few contacts in the States, friends in Detroit, one of whom was to meet him on Ellis Island fifteen days after the ship left the dock in Piraeus.

Fear and excitement consumed him as the ship docked. The hustle of the largest city he'd ever seen mesmerized him—all the buildings and cars and Americans. His friend met him at the harbor and they drove to Detroit.

Sophia's father told her of an experience that he had shortly after arriving in America. His friend got him a job at a tailor shop in Detroit, where he spent long hours stitching men's suits. Sometimes he would work sixteen hours a day, trying to earn as much money as much as he could. He was able to work quickly, he said, because of the language barrier; he had no one to talk to. But he learned English by listening to the other men who worked at the tailor shop, picking up words and phrases here and there.

After working a couple of years he'd been able to buy a car, a luxury he had been saving for since coming to America. He found an old and beaten Oldsmobile owned by a Polish man he knew from the neighborhood. He remembered putting the key into the ignition and cruising aimlessly around the city, just enjoying the feeling that he was free.

As he wound through the streets of Detroit, a police officer pulled him over for rolling through a stop sign. The officer asked to see his license and thereafter tried asking him a few questions, but her father couldn't understand him. After a few moments, the officer became frustrated and gave up, saying, "Immigrant, you go!" waving his hand in the air.

She remembered her father hesitating sometimes when she would ask about his life in Albania, being part of a minority in a country that is itself a minority in Europe. He shied away from her questions, giving her one-word replies, hardly ever elaborating upon what he had experienced, witnessed, and felt. She looked around the village that she had known for so short a time. Here were the people who persevered in the mountains. It was they who would overcome the hardships they had known, the brutality they had seen in wartime, the forced adaptation to another culture. How could these people continue this kind of life when they now knew that a different life awaited them just beyond these borders?

Those who left after World War Two had predicted it clearly. They had known that the changes in the country would not make things better, that there was no hope for them. And those who stayed behind would come to hate themselves and each other for allowing themselves to become what they hated most. They tried to strengthen each other's spirits, but held one another in contempt at the same time, clawing into the ground as the culture that held them captive tried to pull them down into its abyss. It angered them that no one — not even they themselves — tried to do anything to better their condition. They just accommodated it, stood around and waited, enduring the monotony of this life and waiting for the sun to rise and the moon to rise later. After some time, they knew there had to be something else, a hint of goodness and contentment just beyond their reach, but how were they going to attain it?

The lesson the people learned was enough: things were not just handed out in life; there was always a price to pay, even when the government told them there wasn't. Things are not clear and simple, black and white; there is a hidden agenda in everything people do. They would teach this to their children, to their children's children, and it would be passed on to future generations, regardless of where they were living.

Several years after he had left, Sophia's father heard what happened to his mother from a friend in the States who had escaped about eight years after he had. They were sitting in a coffee shop after work when the subject of the village came up. He hadn't seen his mother since kissing her goodbye and escaping through the mountains with his brothers. His friend was hesitant to tell him what had happened, but Sophia's father insisted that he had to know, saying that he needed closure. As his friend's story unfolded, Sophia's father rested his head in his hands, cupping the sides of his face. His friend tried to calm him by telling him the soldiers hadn't gotten the best of her, that she survived the concentration camp and was able to live out her life back at home in the village. He sat for a moment staring into his friend's face, but looking through him. His vision became unfocused and he looked down at the ground.

He began to cry uncontrollably.

Sophia thought about going back to Old Man Arseni's house to ask more questions about her father, to retrieve the answers about the life he had left here. What had her father known that most other people hadn't? Old Man Arseni was the only one who could give her an accurate picture of him and his thoughts. The answers she got from Kosta and Penelope had been passed on through her family, stories told again and again and again. Images can become distorted through a family's eyes, and the folklore that permeated these mountains could only leave her with more unanswered questions. She didn't know Old Man Arseni, but he had been close to her father, and this made it comfortable to approach him and easy to believe his word. She had to speak with Old Man Arseni to get a complete portrait of their world right after the Second World War, regardless of whether people said he was crazy.

Her father told her once that the Albanians say they were descended from the ancient Illyrian tribe, their blood pure and untainted by foreign blood. If her father were still alive, would he be friends with Arseni, would they have kept in touch somehow? Would her father have helped Old Man Arseni come to America? Would he consider Arseni crazy, as the rest of the villagers did?

One afternoon when the village was napping, Sophia walked over to Old Man Arseni's house. She would take a chance on finding him awake because he seemed to do things his way, on his time. She thought her chances were pretty good. She found him eating lunch on his porch. She approached, not thinking, or perhaps not caring, that he might not want to be bothered. Old Man Arseni was like a history book; he was the person filled with the stories and facts and answers to her questions.

"Hello, Arseni. How are you today?" She asked, stopping abruptly at the edge of the porch.

"Hello. I'm well. Come, come have a seat. Are you passing by or did you come to see me?"

"I came to see you."

He smiled at her.

Sophia sat down and they started talking. This time, though, it was different. He let her into his world. She was a link to his past, and he found solace and a rare level of trust when he spoke with her. He felt relaxed and comfortable talking about the things that were familiar to him and linked parts of his memory that he hadn't touched in a while. He now seemed almost eager to open his thoughts, his memories, and the feelings he had locked up so long. Her questions made him feel like he was opening books about his childhood, as if she had been brought to him at this moment in his life to get him to speak of the things he hadn't talked about with anyone for years. She was here on his porch for a reason. Perhaps it was a reason he didn't fully understand, but Arseni knew it wasn't a matter of chance that this girl from America—the daughter of his old friend who had fled as a teenager because he had known somehow—had come to the village and found him and asked to talk with him. This could not have been chance; such things didn't happen that way.

His mind dwelt on these thoughts, but he had spoken to no one about them because the villagers left him alone. Some thought that he had lost his mind years ago and it was impossible to have a coherent conversation with him; others believed an evil spirit had gotten into him and feared contact with such a man.

Sophia asked him what her father had been like when he was

young. She asked if there was an arranged marriage for him, if this was why he left Chatista.

"Oh no, your father wasn't arranged before he left Albania. Your father didn't have a father to arrange a marriage for him. Your father didn't know your grandfather. He left the village to find work in Constantinople when your father was only two. He found work binding leather, from what I can remember, and I think he's buried there, near Hagia Sophia."

"He never came back?"

"No, no one has seen him since he left. It was very difficult to travel back in those days. Roads were no good."

"Did he send money home or just leave?" Sophia asked, a question laden with implications.

"He sent some money. Not a lot. It was difficult times back then in the 1930s. Finding jobs was tough, and the foreigners always got the low-paying jobs."

"It's like that everywhere, Arseni."

"Yes, the immigrant doesn't have enough difficulties when he comes to a new land. He is forced to work for low wages, too."

"Just the way things are, I guess. There's always someone who will try to take advantage of someone else's situation. How was my grandmother with all of this?"

"She was all right. It was hard on her, raising her kids by herself, but she managed." He paused. "We didn't have it easy then, and it's still not easy now."

She nodded. "My father told me when she died about fifteen years ago—my uncle Kosta sent us a letter. Was she very sick before she died?"

"Her body just gave out. She was tired and weak during her last days."

"What type of woman was she? You must have known her well if you were close with my father."

"She was a very kind woman. Her roles were two: the mother and the father. She was always good to her kids. Your father was the closest with her, more so than your uncles. He took care of her more than they — not that they didn't, but your father was more attentive to her. You could tell that he was your grandmother's favorite."

"Favorite?"

"Yes, her favorite."

"So why did he leave?"

"Well, there's a little history behind his reason. After the war, and the Italian occupation, and then the German occupation, life had become really hard in Albania. The people were exhausted and frustrated and angry. But they had hope. This was when a young man named Enver Hoxha became the communist party leader. He was an educated man, educated in Western Europe, and he had plans and solutions that sounded appealing to the people right after a war. And the people embraced his ideas, his vision. Albanian, Greek, Jewish, Catholic, Muslim, Orthodox, or Roma, it didn't matter — they had hope. The communists took over, changed the way life had become, and gave structure to the nation, made it more integrated. But this comes with a price. People's identity was being taken away methodically, a premeditated act that lay sleeping until it was wakened at the right time, like a lion abruptly awoken from a nap. They knew the right time to take our identities away from us. And your father, your father knew something or saw something that most people didn't, and he left after the communists took over the government." Old Man Arseni was silent for a moment. "Yes, there was something your father knew."

She hadn't expected this answer. She had anticipated something a little simpler. "You say this now, Arseni, but did you know it then? Did you know that something revolutionary was happening in this country and you wanted to be a part of it? Maybe people did know what my father knew, but he saw it from a different perspective and acted on that."

"I think people knew, but at the time they weren't aware of knowing. Subconsciously, people knew something extraordinary was happening, something that was going to change their lives. People were tired of the fiefdoms and clans and Turkish landowners who ruled the country; they had been suppressed by the Turks for centuries. The people saw the opportunity for a change in government, so they embraced the communists, especially here in southern Albania, where the Mohammedans owned all the land, all that you see here," he said, pointing out into the valley. "And they would farm it for them. The country lost control of its land and people under King Zog."

"The what? Who?"

"The Mohammedans. King Zog. The Turks who owned the land here were called Mohammedans. King Zog was president of Albania and then changed his title to king. He went into exile during the Second World War. But people started to realize that the new communist president was just another dictator. He took the power of the people and molded it for his own self-interest. No one could say anything or they'd be jailed or executed, so people watched what was happening from their homes and said nothing.

"But people loved communism at first because the concept of this type of government was appealing compared to what we had experienced. The whole idea of a communal effort to run this country intrigued people. All power wasn't given to one individual; it was supposed to be collective. They were all involved. All the people could put their imprints on the country.

"When Hoxha first came to power, he told the people they should unite and become one under the Albanian flag, the double-headed eagle. Albanians had been segregated, with their own chieftains and regions, their own little worlds, but he changed all that. He told them to think bigger, to think beyond the village, the valley, the mountain, the town, the city. He wanted people to be visionary, to see the idea of Albania in its entirety, and the nation embraced this. People felt they were a part of a larger picture, a greater vision, and it felt good. He made efficient changes, and they saw their world transforming right in front of them. And they were a part of this transformation, making it happen as a people and a nation and a culture. And the people embraced all of this.

"And at the same time that the country was busy building and organizing and uniting itself, the president was collecting his power. Every year he controlled a bit more, slowly and strategically moving toward the role of dictator that he had always wanted. By the time people started to figure it out, the government was untouchable. The president became Albania; he defined the country, ruling as he saw fit. He even abolished religion in 1967, saying that Albanianism was now the official religion. And there his soldiers were, destroying beautiful churches and mosques on his orders. It was such a shame. He ruled with a tight grip for several decades until he died in 1985. But when he was alive the nation was his, the people were his.

"Although Albania had been isolated for so long, the momentum of the world swept over the land. Communism had collapsed everywhere in Eastern Europe, and here was Albania, completely apart from the rest, marching to its own drum. Or so it thought. The weight of the fall of communism took Albania down, too. The country wasn't untouchable. The curtains were just closed for a while. The people realized this later when they opened again, and saw how far behind they were compared to the rest of Europe. The people believed they were so intelligent and powerful and self-sufficient. They believed they could've stopped any foreign army at the border. They believed they needed no one who was outside the realm. How foolish they were."

"Were you living here at that time, Arseni? Here in the village?"

"No, back then I was living in Gjirokastra—the president's hometown."

"Did you know all these things then? Did you embrace communism like the rest of the country did?"

"I did not."

"Why?"

"I just didn't."

"But why? You're telling me all this like you weren't a part of it, like you were just observing from a distance. You weren't impressed with all that the president was saying?"

"They murdered my wife." He stared at her.

Sophia sat looking down, eyes fixed on the floor.

She didn't know what to say. How could she possibly have lived her life so unthinkingly when people in the world were living like this, suffering like this? And here she was, an American, who comes here and hears this. How different her life would have been if her father never left, if she had been born and raised in this village. *What would have happened to me? I'd have spent my entire life here. Tired, hopeless.*

"Sophia, what are you thinking about? You have a strange look on your face," Arseni said.

Sophia shook herself out of her thoughts. "Oh, I was just thinking about how tough people are here. How strong a person has to be to survive in this country."

"There aren't any strong people, just tolerant," he said, "and patient," he quickly added, a forced grin wrapped around his face. "People here have learned how to expect failure in their government. Expectations have run low; we have lost hope. And I say *we* now, not they. In the last century, we have been a crossroads for other countries, a steppingstone to the other side of the sea. But the communists changed that. We were completely isolated, as if we existed on some remote island, far away from the other countries on this same continent. And now, the aftereffects of communism and its demise persist here. People are hungry and greedy and naïve. They don't know what it's like outside of Albania. They think they're brave, and leave the country to find work and a better life, but become timid when they have to deal with the simple things that everyone else deals with every day. And the young men, who have turned to crime, are impressed by the Mafia and their business in the Balkans. You see it all the time in Tirana, even Shkoder and Gjirokastra. The Mafia plucks the bored and the restless and the impressionable from the streets and tells them to join, promising money and power and women. But they don't realize that they're just the peons of the business. They do the dirty work, the work they're told to do, work the Mafia leaders would never degrade themselves doing. Our young boys, they don't know any better. They feel power when they have a gun in their hands and are able to act tough.

"This is what's happening to the culture here. The government offers no alternative for people. What do you expect them to do, stand on the street corners and watch the day go by? The government offers nothing. These young men have forgotten their morals, forgotten how to treat women properly — they are willing to force women into prostitution."

"Prostitution is a problem here?"

"It has become a big problem in the past few years. And it's not going to get any better. It won't go away."

"How are they forcing women into prostitution?"

"Many ways. They lure women into working somewhere in Europe, thinking that they have found work in housecleaning or in a restaurant. But they're sold as sex slaves, forced into prostitution to pay off the debt they owe from their sale. And once they're about to pay it off, the man who bought them sells them again to someone else and their debt starts over again. The girls can't leave. They're threatened that they'll be killed if they try to escape. Some do, but others are too scared to run away and go home again. They're worried that their families will disown them or will be killed by those in the sex ring. And most of the time, the family does disown them."

"They do this *here?*" Sophia asked, embarrassed at being so shocked.

"Yes, they do. Sex slaves exist all over Europe, mostly in the Balkans — Kosovo, really. And these girls are young, some as young as twelve and thirteen. They're enticed to work abroad and send money home, hungry to get out of their situation back at home, the poverty, and they become a part of this."

"What do the police do about it?"

"Nothing. Most turn their heads; many are part of the whole sex-slave ring. Get a bribe here and there and just look the other way." Old Man Arseni looked at her. "It's not easy being a woman in this country, Sophia. Women have a very difficult and off-center life here."

"What do you mean, 'off center,' Arseni?"

"Because they don't have peace within, their souls are unbalanced. Therefore, they are discontented. They might seem to be happy women, and they are to some extent, but to experience complete happiness, to feel fulfilled and at peace and comfortable in your own skin, your lifestyle must be centered."

Off-center, Sophia repeated to herself. She had never thought to look at her life in this way. And what was she? Was she off-center? She didn't know. "I like that, off-center. This phrase could reveal a lot about a person."

"Yes it could," Arseni said, puffing on his pipe.

The most painful part of living in a poor country is the breaking up of families to pursue economic promise. The men move to cities in neighboring countries to find jobs, hoping to make money and return home after some time to reunite with their families. And the tension that this creates is overlooked and pushed aside. It is forgotten that the pain lingers even after the father returns home, but he must do this to provide for his family—he is the man of the house, after all. He is the power for the family's survival.

The men leave for a time, kissing their wives goodbye and telling them they'll see each other sometime soon. But the "sometime" is what penetrates the mind, the soul. That word is what a wife remembers as she watches her husband leave her. And so she must tend to the family, await his return, and become the pillar of the home, the guiding force, the voice for all. And, hopefully, the husband will find work in the city.

She knows the cities are filled with men like her husband, just as desperate and determined as he is—an immigrant, searching for something he has not found in his own country.

Sometimes, when the husband returns from his life in the city, he is burdened by family life, unaccustomed now to a confining space among his crying children. But he does his duty as the man of the house, fulfilling his role as patriarch, providing for the family. And after a few months in his own home, his mind dwells on thoughts of freedom: he looks forward to leaving for the city again, so he can be with other men and sit in the cafes and play backgammon. And bring his culture and traditions to this country.

When he leaves again, his absence from home tends to be just a bit longer. He enjoys the city life, new friends, and the liberty of being alone and doing what he pleases. He finds new solace in this lifestyle and begins to relish it. Sometimes the husband never returns to the village, and deserts his family. Now his eldest son is the man of the house, or perhaps he follows in his father's footsteps, curious about what his father has found in the city.

The mother continues her life in the village. Her honor is bruised, but her pride is intact. She provides for her family as well as she can, continues to farm their bit of land, teaches her children to fend for themselves, perhaps arranges a marriage for a daughter to help ease the burden she now shoulders. For her, life will move along as it always has — without her husband, but he will always be in her memory.

She will keep her shoulders straight when she passes the other women in the village as she walks to her garden plot. She will stare straight ahead as they stare at her with those eyes. She will answer their questions quickly and clearly: "Yes, I received a telegram from my husband. He is doing well in Skopje and misses his family very much. He says he's making a lot of money for us. We can't wait to see him again." She will farm the land as she is supposed to, as is her responsibility. She will store the crops in the shed that her husband built two years ago, in preparation for the winter storms to come. She will come home and prepare meals for their children. She will do the household chores and bathe herself and her children in the evening.

She will go to bed alone at night and cry into her pillow.

Not long ago the government invented a clever economic fiasco in which everyone who had invested in the Federal Bank lost everything. It promised the people a large percentage on investments deposited into the bank, and many people invested their money — their life savings — out of greed, gullibility, or hope. This lasted a couple of years, and everyone was happy, believing they were on their way to becoming wealthy. This is how democracy and capitalism works, the government had told them: their money would build roads and highways and schools and communities, an investment in their own country. All of this would happen before their very eyes, during their lifetimes, and their children would benefit the most. The people were happy. They had hope.

After a year had passed, someone would ask why no roads were being built, why nothing new at all was being built. The government would say that construction had begun at the other end of the country and would work its way to wherever the question had been asked. But most people never questioned anything — they were receiving forty-percent interest on their money.

When it became clear that all the invested money deposited was gone in an instant, cleared from the computer screens, a massive revolt exploded like an erupting volcano. The world became chaotic and hostile. Men broke into the country's military warehouses and took the weapons. Civilians were now armed with Kalashnikovs, roaming the streets, angry and wired and hopeless. Unrest spread everywhere and those who governed had to leave to save their lives. Humiliated, many civilians left as well, to extricate themselves from the chaos and to find work in other countries.

In search of a job, Abraham left for Ioannia. "Don't worry, Father. I'll take care of things," he said one day, taking it upon himself to provide for the family. It sickened him that this had happened to his family; that they had been foolish enough to believe that so much interest could be given. "What did we know? We didn't know that this was unbelievable and impossible," Abraham would explain to people in Ioannia when they asked him about it, laughing underneath their breath. He tried to hold onto his pride, though, even as he felt ashamed and out of touch with the world. He promised himself that he would save up enough money to build a nice house in Chatista for his parents, something they had planned to do with the interest they were receiving from their bank account.

In downtown Ioannia, Abraham found work at a popular restaurant where the college students spent their afternoons drinking frappes and smoking and gossiping between classes. Most of them were near his age, but to him they seemed so much older and worldlier. Their clothes and shoes and cell phones and hair and cars amazed him—he began to realize how far behind the rest of the world Albania was. When the people he worked with found out he was from Albania, they avoided him like a fatal disease, annoyed by him, and made it difficult for him to work there.

Ultimately, he was pushed out; forced to go home, back to the village.

Supreme egotism dwells in a dictator, and compassion falls before him. He speaks not from the spirit, but from precise calculation: *What do I want the people to believe of me? What do they want to hear that will satisfy their little dreams?* He cultivates the ability to appease the people and simultaneously discourage them from free thought. The fate of an entire culture, an entire heritage, rests on one man's words. A dictator's government builds its strength upon bringing order out of confusion—*his* order out of *their* confusion. In this continuous contradiction, an overall pattern and certain constants are revealed, exposing a government's underlying structure. Not knowing that there is something different outside this realm, the people learn to accept it — fear, fate, comfort, conformity, acceptance.

When people cease to look at themselves collectively and begin to think for themselves, regimes fade into history, becoming memories of cyclic tyrannies. Paradoxically, to break free of these regimes, people need to come together.

The people's strength derives in part from their own desperation, their irrepressible hope that one day they might be able to believe in their government, believe that its promises will be fulfilled. As they wait and wait for those promises to become real, the people become old, and the hope is passed onto their children, and their children's children. And maybe one day in the future, they will be able to trust their government, believe it, feel loyal to it, and, ultimately, embrace it.

But the influence of the old regime lingers. It was a part of their daily lives. Their religious beliefs and cultural practices suffered from its authoritarian rule, even deep in the countryside. The old regime told them that they were being cared for, and that this was what they wanted. They seemed content because they didn't know any other way of living.

It's not what you've been through, but what you've been exposed to.

The government thought everyone was happy and patriotic because it couldn't hear the resentment — the fear was too overwhelming. The regime cracked, but those who had dictated were still around afterward — nothing but the name of the political party had changed. They were still in office, controlling as they always had. Just under a different name.

When everything was at stake, when people were on the verge of losing hope, life seemed to conquer the catastrophe somehow. It was like this for years: there was no obstacle that couldn't be overcome, no disaster that couldn't be survived. And the people believed it because they had hope, believed that this was how things were and there was no alternative. And they prayed in the confines of their bedrooms, and practiced their cultural traditions within the shelter of their homes, and this was all right. Why would they think otherwise?

Pity the men who believe their politics to be truer than the ideals of their culture.

"We've been isolated for so long that we've become our own people here, evolved on our own. I can tell you that we are neither Albanians nor Greeks. We are, in essence, the true Illyrians. "I've lived here my whole life, left the village only a couple of times — during the 1980s and then just recently after they opened Albania's doors to the rest of the world. I went to Italy, lived in Venice for a while. I couldn't believe how prosperous the Italians were compared to us. We're so backward in so many ways. We're not an ignorant people, just lagging behind. Most of the time the world has forgotten us — a careless oversight. But at the same time, it's nice not to be bothered. We live our own lives here; for the first time in a long while, we can do what we want to for the most part. At least until the world goes to war again — and this area is prone to war, it's war every day. There's always fighting in this land, and if men aren't fighting, they're planning to fight. People who live here never forget. They remember what happened to their ancestors centuries ago, so warfare will always be here. When there's another war, a larger war, these hills will become a gateway to other regions of the world. This valley will become a walkway for the world's soldiers. And then, when the war is over, we will be left to live our lives again.

"But what defines this village, Sophia, is not the country. The inner patterns of the people are what make this village, what define our village, our world. No historian, no professor at a great university, can come here and analyze us and define us. We're a complex people, yet we live a simple kind of life. That's something you need to understand. There's a difference between a simple life and a primitive life. There are many people who are very complex, but enjoy simplicity. We have no choice in this matter; this is our God-given fate. There are other people in the world who enjoy this lifestyle, too.

"It's true that a society affects its people, but here it's the people's traditions and beliefs. Nowhere else in the world will you find people like those who live in this region. We are different. We don't have material possessions, don't have jobs in the cities like other people do, but we possess dignity. We are proud of where we come from, and we can endure all sorts of hardships — we have proved this in the past.

"Your father and his brothers did a very unusual thing, Sophia. When most men thought communism was going to save them from the wealthy Turkish landowners, they thought otherwise." *How did Nonta know?* Arseni seemed to ask himself. "What was it they knew that none of us knew? The Turks owned all this land," he said, waving his hand in front of him, "as far as your eyes can see. Men who lived in the village couldn't hold even a small plot of earth. When communism swept Albania at the end of World War Two, we thought we'd keep our land to feed our families, that it would be ours to pass on to our children. We didn't know what the government was capable of. In time, the communists took everything for themselves. It took most of us by surprise — how could something so communal give us nothing? It ate the hearts of grown men, and brought them to tears. Never have I seen such devastation happen so quickly. We ended up farming the same piece of land, but it wasn't our own.

"But whatever happened to us didn't kill us. We persevered, and we're still the same people with the same traditions and beliefs, passed down from one generation to the next. This is how we define ourselves, by the inner pattern of the villager. We can be exposed to any army or any nation, and we still maintain our traditions and our culture. And we won't become tainted by the outside world."

Old Man Arseni looked out into the darkness and kept his eyes on something he saw in the grass. He didn't move for a long time, frozen by what was lurking in the dark. Sophia stared at him, saying nothing, waiting until he came back to her. She thought for a moment, realizing that the people here had no idea what was going on outside their land. Some people thought that it was Albania, this tiny country hidden between Yugoslavia and Italy, defeating every enemy who came to its realm. They had no clue as to who really controlled the wars here.

Arseni scratched under his chin and refocused his eyes on his surroundings, on Sophia.

"Yes, we won't become tainted by the outside world—ever," he said to the darkness.

Eleven

Abraham always kept a close eye on his younger sister Teresa. It was just the two of them in the family, ever since their older brother had died in a farming accident several years before. The government had brought a tractor to the village to help them farm more efficiently, and Niko was out in the fields one day, harvesting the hay with a couple of other men. He got too close to the tractor as it went past him and his arm got caught in the blade. He bled to death before the doctor arrived from Gjirokastra. Ever since, Abraham felt a sense of heightened responsibility. He lost the security of being the younger brother, the one who always had the family's lesser expectations. Now, here he was faced not only with being the eldest brother, but the only brother, the only son. He needed to take over as the other man in the house, right behind his father.

Teresa looked up to the only brother she had left. She tried to act just like Abraham, following him around the village throughout the day, helping him with household chores and with farming in the valley, and coming home from a whole day outside smelling like a boy. But when he was going to meet with his friends in the evenings, he would tell her she had to stay behind, and promise her that she could spend the day with him tomorrow. As they sat in the plaza, she'd sneak up on them and try to listen to what they were talking about, but she wasn't as clever as she thought—her giggles echoed through the valley.

Teresa didn't have the domestic qualities of a girl who was raised in the village, the qualities that are expected from women and taken for granted by society. Their mother tried tirelessly to teach her a woman's work around the house, a woman's duty as a wife and mother. But Teresa quickly got bored helping her mother; she would seize any moment to sneak away and find Abraham in the fields or in the plaza. Her mother never gave up on molding her daughter into an optimal woman, until one day when she asked Teresa to wash the clothes in the large metal container in the backyard. Halfway through the washing, Teresa left the clothes in the water and left to find her brother. Wondering how she was coming along with the washing, her mother went out to the backyard and found a kitten tangled in the clothes, floating lifeless in the water. When Teresa returned home a couple of hours later, her mother showed her what had happened. Guilty and grief stricken, Teresa confessed to her mother that she hated women's chores, that she wanted to be out in the fields with Abraham and her father—she liked man's work better. Her mother never again asked her to do any domestic chores.

Abraham enjoyed his sister's company in the fields, but one day asked her why she didn't like to do things around the house like their mother.

"I don't know, Abraham. It's really boring for me. I like being out here on the farm. I like the animals and the fields and the outside. The sun on my face—"

"But don't you want to be a good wife when you get older, and cook and wash clothes and do the housecleaning?"

"Yeah, I do, but I'm sort of young to worry about those things. I'm just thirteen. I have a lot more years before I have to think about a husband."

"That's true. Pa won't marry you for another few years. But you have to think ahead, plan your future so you'll be ready."

"You know better than anyone, Abraham, that there's nothing to plan for in Chatista. Everything you can expect out of life comes true here. What am I going to plan? I just have to change my ways when I get married, that's all. I'll be living here the rest of my life. When the time comes, I'll do the cleaning and washing and cooking for my husband's family. And maybe sometimes I'll come out to the valley and farm because that's what I love to do. It'll work out for me here; I'm not going to have any surprises. It's going to be easy."

Abraham looked at Teresa for a moment and realized how free and sensible and brave she was, and how true.

The fact that Sophia and Abraham came from entirely different worlds didn't affect their attraction to each other. To him, she was a new adventure from the outside world. He could learn things from her that he'd never known existed; she could explain the world that he had missed his entire life—that the whole country had missed. Sophia was attracted to Abraham's kindness and curiosity, his desire to find something new, to move away from the mountains and get more out of life than he'd been exposed to. She knew he was a bit naive, perhaps, but who could blame him for that? In his naiveté was the potential for rediscovering himself, and he was intuitive at the same time. It seemed to her that his Albania was a faraway island lost at sea, and only gypsies had ever touched upon it. And she was attracted to his voice, the voice that put her in a trance whenever she was alone with him. She didn't think he knew how powerful the sound of his voice was.

But when they met in the middle of the night, it was as if they weren't from different worlds. There was no separation between her world and his. They became one, connecting as if they had known each other from another lifetime, and their need of one another, and their bodies' need, overwhelmed them. The softest touch of his hands on her face and breasts and stomach comforted her. He treasured the way she held onto him when they made love, her hands clasping at the small of his back.

Abraham would withhold himself, trying to make it last a bit longer for Sophia. When he got close, he would stop awhile and pleasure her with his mouth; then, when he regained control, make love to her again. The rundown schoolhouse, the wind outside, the mountain air, the moonlight through the window, their movements silhouetted on the walls by the candles on the floor — all of these intertwined to make these moments surreal for her. When he finished, Abraham would lie on her chest, Sophia running her fingers through his hair, scratching his moist back, following the path of his arched spine. He had never thought such love could be part of his life.

Abraham felt important when Sophia asked about his life. She was interested in the things he had experienced; it wasn't always about her, about her worldliness and all she had seen. He sometimes caught himself rambling about a comical memory from his childhood, and when he became aware of what he was doing, he'd quickly change the subject, embarrassed. But she enjoyed these stories, thought they were funny and warm. How sweet it is to live in a village, she would say to herself, but she would never say these words to him — they were thoughts she wanted to selfishly keep inside.

He showed her old photographs of himself because she asked to see them. He brought several of his family and late brother to the schoolhouse one night. Sophia had asked him, because she wanted to connect the fragments of his life that she only imagined, wanted to see the creation of his world before she had met him. Too many gaps filled her head, and she wanted these photos to create bridges that might give her an accurate image of Abraham.

Several years after she had left Albania, Sophia still remembered one photo he had shown her. Abraham must have been eight or nine, riding a pony in the valley. He told her his father had taught him how to ride that day, and took a photograph because he thought his son a natural rider and was so proud of him. The expression on

Abraham's face was one of fearless determination, like he had just mastered an art. Sophia knew by looking at his face that, even when he was a boy, he'd been eager to do things and not sit idly, waiting for life to come to him. He wanted to capture the world, however large it seemed to him.

The person Sophia had become with Abraham was different from who she was with William. She felt freer and more deeply in love, bound by nothing, and able to express herself in ways that were not possible with William. Now she understood what people meant when they said they felt like their true selves around the one they loved. She understood what it was to love someone so much that it hurt, a constant burning in the chest, a surrender of the soul.

Sophia was always uncertain whether William's words were sincere, and unsure of when and how it would all end. She later felt that William was in control of their relationship, that it wasn't theirs, but his. She always questioned why he was with her, whether because she pursued him or because he really wanted her. The thought that there was someone else continually gnawed at her toward the end of the relationship, when she was preparing herself to end it abruptly. This was how things worked best for her; she was the type who needed to see closure right away — clear and concise, with no element of hope or doubt or question. Residual elements bothered her even more. Yet there were doubts now as she put that part of her life in perspective, thinking more clearly now because she had stepped outside of the relationship; a stranger to the person she was before.

She remembered a day when William asked her to meet him in his office after class. As Sophia approached his door, William's wife opened it and smiled at her. She was dressed for the evening — cocktails and dinner, perhaps. Looking in, Sophia saw William in a dinner jacket. "Oh, come in," he said. "Honey, this is Sophia, one of my students." His wife turned to her and smiled again. "Did you need anything, Sophia?" William asked professorially. Feeling foolish and humiliated, Sophia made up a story about class. William answered her as a professor would. Looking at the scenario, the professor, his wife, the student, Sophia said to herself, *this is where he belongs, this is what it has to be, and what it always was.*

She thanked him, told his wife it was nice meeting her, said good-bye, and walked out of his office, downstairs, out to the courtyard and down the sidewalk to her home.

After class the next day, William apologized, telling her sweetly that he would make it up to her somehow. He'd forgotten that his wife had made plans for them the evening before and he had had to run back to the office to pick up a few things. Sophia smiled and said nothing, not knowing what more to expect. Was he experimenting with her, perhaps doing research for a better, more adventurous relationship with his wife? Yes, maybe she was his experiment — he was a professor, after all. She was only for the moment, yet the idea of not being able to be with William completely was appealing to her. He was forbidden; she was not supposed to close his office door and hold him. If he were not her professor, maybe just another student, would she be attracted to him? His playful glances at her during his lectures, would he do that if it were forbidden?

But Sophia felt something much more powerful when she was with Abraham. The way he stroked her hair with the lightest touch of his fingertips. The way he looked at her, searching her, for her. He would be spellbound by her eyes, her shoulders, her neck, and run his hands over the soft skin on her arms and chest. She would close her eyes and let him touch her any way he wanted, let his hands wander all over her body. This was what she wanted him to do.

Sophia felt comfortable with him because he was pure and genuine — nothing had corrupted his innocent, romantic view of life. He thought no obstacle too great before facing it; only when he did, would he understand the consequences. But he always kept his idealism, as if his memory filtered out what could tarnish his spirit, and kept what was good. He seemed to never lose a beat in his thoughts — a rhythm flowing continuously from his heart.

Old Man Arseni came out of his house and stood on the porch. He looked out across the village, stretched his vision toward the sky. The sun was low against the mountains, illuminating the dew on the grass. The old man sat down in his usual chair and allowed his mind to wander again to the images that so often occupied him.

The sunlight struck his eyes, and he squinted and turned away, trying to readjust his vision as he awoke. He felt a fly on his left leg, but didn't bother to swat it away. He watched it sitting on his skin, hide in his hair. Perhaps it believed his leg to be the perfect refuge — hidden from the rest of the world by these thin black strands surrounding it. Old Man Arseni watched the fly a moment longer, and then it flew away. "Where are you off to, dear fly?" he said, trying to follow its path with his eyes until it was beyond his vision.

He looked out into the valley toward the farms, the gardens, the village stretching to his left. Beyond the mountains ahead of him was Greece. He watched another fly land on the table and walk across the cloth, nearing the arm Old Man Arseni rested on it. Was it the same fly? Did it come back to visit him? It moved quickly and then abruptly stopped, seeming to stare at his arm. Old Man Arseni kept his arm still. The fly did not move. It sat as if it had fallen asleep. He slowly shook his arm. The fly did not move. He shook it again. Still, the fly sat there. He slowly moved his arm closer and closer to the fly. As his arm was about to touch it, the fly sprang into the air and flew away.

"Hello, Arseni. How are you?" he heard from his left. It was Sophia, come to visit him.

She paused a moment before sitting in the chair across the table from him. His mind had been elsewhere, a place out of reach by other people. He motioned for her to sit down. "Here's our girl! How are you today?"

"I'm doing well. And you?"

Twelve

When the shepherd found the young girl in the mountains he quickly closed her eyes. Nervously, he asked himself how long her eyes had been open; worried that he was too late to prevent an evil spirit from entering her body, another death in the young girl's family.

While tending his sheep he came across her near the divide, where the river lay, spotting her when he lit his pipe and looked ahead to the horizon. He first noticed her arm, which lay in the trail, the rest of her hidden in the grass. Moving slowly, he approached, and gasped when he saw the knife stuck directly in the center of her chest. Blood stained her blue shirt, her eyes slightly open. The girl looked peaceful. She had rid herself of the burden.

He lifted her in his arms and carried her to the village. He knew whose daughter she was, and walked straight to the house to return what the family had lost. Her mother and father were in the garden as the shepherd approached. When she saw her daughter in the man's arms, the girl's mother fell to her knees. Screaming and crying, she threw her hands to her head, pleading with God. Neighbors ran to the house to see what the commotion was. Some took pity, some were shocked and confused, and others saw their darkest thoughts confirmed. The shepherd said a few words to the young girl's father and walked away, dipping himself into the fields again.

Later that day, the girl's family placed her body in the coffin that had been quickly built for her, and the procession of condolences in their front yard began. Her friends wept and screamed like her mother and aunt had; her father and brothers stood stiffly next to the girl, their hands clasped in front of them while the villagers knelt beside her coffin and said a prayer. Some believed that Lania, the dragon woman who kidnaps children in the mountains, had had something to do with the young girl's death. Perhaps she had had an argument with the goddess Hera, and was revenging herself upon the village. The choir stood behind the girl's family, several village women chanting lamentations for the dead. One stood slightly forward of the rest, singing and wailing. After the ceremony, the villagers went to the girl's home and washed their hands. The family stayed in their front yard until the girl's body had become a silhouette beneath the moonlight.

Years afterward, on the anniversary of the young girl's death, the women still went to the cemetery and wept and wailed in front of her grave.

A formal funeral awaited her. The family was overwhelmed with grief. *Why did my baby girl do this? Why did she kill herself in the mountains?*

The whole village had helped the family with anything they needed, and they all came to the funeral. *Who is going to build the coffin? Who is going to make the dress she will wear in it? Who is going to find the priest?* The girl's family let others handle all these duties. Their responsibility was just to let grief overtake them.

Everything was prepared for the girl's funeral, which was held at the church the following morning. The day before, the shepherd who had found her had offered the girl's father to travel to the next village and ask the priest to come and say a prayer and give her to God. The priest arrived early that morning, holding his Bible close to his chest. A group of young men built the coffin and carved a cross on the lid and sanded it smooth. The woman who lived next door offered to sew a dress of the best fabric for her. The girl's mother lay in bed until the funeral began.

Sunlight penetrated the valley and seemed to singe the tips of the trees. The day was bright and hot for this time of year, the sun beating down like an act of condemnation. The village gathered for the funeral. Everyone dressed in their best clothes: little boys wore their button-down shirts and the shoes their mothers had dusted off; little girls wore the dresses their grandmothers had made them for such occasions as this. Everyone met at the iron gates in front of the church and waited for the family to come out of their home. The priest was with the girl's family, said a prayer in their house, and then led the procession, the men of the family carrying her coffin as they made their way from the house, down the path toward the church, and beyond the iron gates. The priest chanted a prayer from the Bible as he asked God to have mercy on her soul. The girl's mother walked wearily behind her daughter, grasping her husband's arm.

Thoughts suffused the village. And the young boy who had told her he loved her and wanted to marry her stood with the rest, his hands in his pockets and his head lowered. He stood with his family as the priest lead the procession into the church, brushing his arm against the boy's. He looked away as the priest passed, allowing the sun's rays to penetrate his eyes, blinding him for the moment.

Sophia stood next to Athina and Stavro as the procession moved toward the church. Sophia watched the priest as he led the way, his face buried in the Bible, chanting a prayer suggesting that God have mercy on the girl's soul. His words filled the air with assertive precision. He didn't miss a step — controlling the vulnerability and uncertainties that gripped this village.

Sophia looked at Athina, who had a perplexed look on her face, yet a sort of discernment. As the procession walked toward them, Athina made the sign of the cross, holding her three fingers tightly together, and touching her forehead, stomach, right shoulder, and left shoulder. Sophia wondered whether Athina knew something everyone else didn't. She gently touched Athina's arm and held it until Athina looked at her.

"What's going on? Are you okay?"

"Yes, I'm fine."

"The look on your face makes me think otherwise."

"You can tell?"

"I can. You look like your mind's somewhere else."

"Well, something is bothering me."

"You want to talk about it?" "Later?"

"Yes," Athina said, "when all of this is over."

Everyone followed the priest and the coffin and the family into the church, and stood looking at the altar as the priest turned to the villagers, continuing to chant the prayer. Women fanned themselves and men pulled handkerchiefs out of their pockets and dabbed their foreheads. Little boys stood obediently at their mother's sides. The air in the room was still. Everyone stood quietly, feeling the sweat drip down their backs.

Near the far end of the little cemetery, near the old tree, there used to be an empty patch of grass. Now, freshly overturned dirt was raised slightly above the ground, and colorful flowers encircled the mound. At its head rested a tiny piece of concrete with newly carved letters: ELEKA STAYA, 1981–1999, GOD HAVE MERCY ON HER SOUL. The grave lay next to those of a mother and her two children. Sophia looked at the children's dates of birth and death — twins, three years old.

Athina and Sophia were in the corner of the cemetery, sitting on a large rock shaded under a myrtle tree. They sat quietly next to Eleka's grave, their minds elsewhere. Athina picked restlessly at a branch, breaking off twigs and then breaking the twigs with her thumbs.

"So what's going on, Athina? Do you want to talk now?"

Athina looked up from the grave and toward the village. Tears welled in her eyes, and she sighed softly, "Ah, what's happening to us?"

"Athina, are you going to tell me what's going on?" Sophia said softly.

"Sophia, if I tell you, you cannot tell anyone."

"Of course I won't."

"No, look at me. You cannot tell a soul. Do you promise me?"

"Yes, Athina. I promise."

Old Man Arseni walked out of his home and put a small icon and a lighted candle floating in olive oil on the porch table. He crossed himself three times and stood there for a moment, looking left toward the church. He looked at the icon and made the cross one last time before he walked into his house and shut the door, loosening the tie he wore.

The young girl slightly swollen with child could not bear to face her family so she went to the mountains. Late that evening, her father went to search for her and bring her home, but could not find her. He came back hopeful, knowing he would wake up the next morning and continue the search for his little girl.

No one knew why she had killed herself except for a couple of her friends and, of course, the boy who had made her stomach grow. The young girl couldn't take it anymore; she knew that people would notice her swollen belly and begin to whisper and point. *What will I say to my family? Who will be responsible for doing this to me?*

And the young boy sensed what was going on inside her. He felt it when he was making love to her that night by the pond under the big tree. The sensation was so strong that he just stayed there and did not move, but let everything release from inside him. He knew it happened that night, and didn't tell her. But he told her he loved her, and held her closely as he lay on top of her, burying his head in the grass, feeling her body breathe underneath him. And he lay there assuring her that he loved her and would always be there for her, and he rubbed her hair and kissed her forehead, all the time thinking about what he had just done in her, telling himself, convincing himself, that everything was going to be all right. And she lay beneath him, telling him how much she loved him, too. Feeling happy and safe, she told him she wanted to spend the rest of her life with him. Stroking his hair, she whispered how much she loved him and would be a good wife to him always.

She began to get sick in the morning, running to the outhouse as she did her chores. Her mother thought nothing of it at first. *A flu perhaps. Maybe I've been working my daughter too hard.* But she began to notice this daily ritual. And the young girl told her mother it was nothing, that she was coming down with something. But she became more tired as the days moved on. By late morning she would lie down on her bed and close her eyes, praying that this was not happening to her, begging God to leave her alone just this once, and promising she would never do that again. *I will never meet him under the tree again. I promise, I promise.* And she would raise herself from her bed and notice that her belly was swelling, gradually growing. *Am I eating more? I'm normally not this plump under my belly button.* And she would try to remember the last time she had her period. *It can't be. Should I tell him about this? What would he say to me then? He's told me he loves me and wants to marry me.*

She was perplexed. People would begin to ask questions, ask her mother, her father, her brothers. *Do you know what's happening with your daughter? Do you know what she has done to you?* And they would be angry and ashamed and angry again. They wouldn't be able to contain it for very long. Her mother and father would look at their daughter's stomach more closely, pulling up her shirt and seeing that her stomach wasn't flat anymore. And they would beat her within an inch of her life, or maybe hide her, or send her away somewhere, anywhere, to rid themselves of the shame she had brought on them. Maybe they would even try to get rid of it behind the chicken coop, sheltered by trees. Lay her down on the grass in the middle of the night and reach into her with a farming tool for the thing that grew inside her. And they would rid her of it, this shameful thing that would disgrace the family. And then, in their eyes, all would be okay — simply because it was out of her body.

One Saturday afternoon she went for a walk with Athina. The girl knew she could tell him today because he went fishing at the pond every Saturday and she would find him there. She would try to get him alone and tell him that she loved him, and always wanted to be with him, and ask him what *they* should do. He loved her, he had told her that. She asked Athina to distract his friends so they wouldn't hear what she was about to say.

They found them at the far side of the pond, shirtless, their pants rolled up to their knees, feet at the edge of the water. The girl suddenly became nervous and her heart began to race. *Maybe I shouldn't say anything. I'm not exactly sure I'm pregnant.* Athina and the girl approached them, and he smiled at her with his big goofy grin. He was happy to see her.

They talked for a while, the boys fishing with the tiny worms they found in the grass after the morning rain. Athina talked with his friends, asking them about their plans for the coming summer.

"Are you going to Gjirokastra to work at the café you worked at last summer?"

"I think so, they paid me about fifty lek a day and I saved a lot of money. I'm hoping they'll pay me a little more this year."

"I'm going to stay here this summer and tend to the farm. It's supposed to be a good season this year; we'll raise a lot of crops," another said.

And the third said, "I don't know what I'm going to do just yet. I'll just see where my life takes me."

"You'll never get anywhere that way. Do you expect to make a living thinking like that?"

"I don't care. I like it here. This is where I want to live for the rest of my life."

"But you've never been anywhere else your whole life!" the others laughed at him, at his naiveté.

"Maybe this is what I want to do. I don't need anything else. I'm a simple man!" They cried out with laughter at their friend's wisdom. The boys chased him around, trying to push him into the water. The girl knew his friends were distracted enough that she could talk to him. It was her chance to tell him what was happening inside of her, maybe.

"I have something I need to talk with you about. It's important," she said trying to smile at him.

He felt a sudden panic at the pit of his stomach. *What does she want to talk to me about? I didn't do anything that night.*

"Remember that night under the tree? Remember how you held onto me and wouldn't let go? Remember how you told me you loved me?"

"Yes."

"I'm late," she said abruptly.

He knew what she meant and he felt his heart sink. *This can't be happening. Why is she doing this?*

"What do you mean, you're late?" he asked.

She looked at him, shocked. "I'm trying to tell you that I'm *late*."

He stared at her, then quickly looked away. He didn't want to hear this. He didn't want it. This wasn't happening to him.

"Well, what do you want from me?"

Why is he doing this? Why is he saying this to me?

"You told me you loved me and wanted to be with me. You told me this the last time we were with each other under the tree. Don't you remember that? Look at me! Why won't you look at me?"

He began to get flustered. "What do you want me to tell you? What do you want to hear? That everything will be all right? That I'm going to marry you and take care of you, have kids with you?"

"I want you to tell me you love me and that you still want to marry me. I want you to be there for me. That's what I want from you. And as for kids, we might have one right now." She looked down at the ground, confused and scared. "Oh, I don't know——"

"Listen, don't do this to me. I don't need this, any of this! I don't want it! You can't just tell me you're late and then everything will be okay. Do you expect us to have a house here and raise a family?"

"That's one thing we could do. We could also maybe live at your parents' house. Or maybe we can run——"

"I don't want that."

"I thought you loved me," the girl pleaded with him, tears filling her eyes. She tried to touch his arm but he jerked it away.

"If you think I'm going to leave Chatista and run away with you, you're sadly wrong. Where are we going to go? We've never been out of this place. Do you think that would be easy for us?" He looked beyond her and watched his friends running around at the edge of the pond. "I don't know what else to tell you."

"Tell me you love me."

"I don't know what else to tell you," he repeated.

"Just tell me you love me," she cried.

He took a step closer and faced her. "Nothing that you want from me will happen. I told you, I don't want any of this."

"Do you think I want it? Do you think I want this happening to me?"

He was already walking away from her. He threw his hand in the air when she said this.

The other two guys pushed the "simple man" into the pond and dove in right after him, trying to dunk his head. Athina laughed as she watched them. She hadn't noticed her friend walking away until she saw him walk past her and pick up his fishing pole. "Hey, stop it, you guys. You're scaring the fish away," he said, absently. Athina turned around and ran to catch up with her friend, and said nothing when she saw her crying. She tried to put her arm around her shoulder, but the girl squirmed away.

"Do you want to talk about it?"

"There's nothing to talk about."

The girl went home and lay on her bed, thinking about what had happened. Shocked and angry, upset and confused, she lay there until darkness shrouded the village, wondering what she should do, what she could do.

Perplexed by the limitations that faced her, condemned by her actions, she walked out of her bedroom and out of the house, straight into the mountains that nestled the village in seclusion.

Sophia, Athina, and Stavro sat at the edge of the pond. Stavro faced the moon, his face bathed by its light. The crickets around them made the noises they do to find mates for the evening. Sophia thought that she would hear Stavro out — her cousin who never said much — this was a time for confession. He lit an after-dinner cigarette, which was his routine, and lay back on his elbows, looking out at the water. Sophia wanted to know what he had thought about the girl committing suicide over his friend. He sat quietly for a moment when she asked him, unsure of how to express himself. Stavro had known both of them his entire life and had worked with him last summer in Gjirokastra.

"How could he have married her? Even if he had wanted to, he wasn't ready for the responsibility. It's just too bad that she had to resort to this — ending her life in such a way."

"What did you expect her to do, Stavro?"

"I don't know. I really don't know."

When Stavro talked to anyone, he always looked the other way — a shyness that hinted he had more to say, but he never said anything more. He would just look, and observe, and his body language would speak for him. He often came across as aloof and uncaring, but those who knew him believed otherwise.

"Is that all you can say? This guy was your friend, I understand that, but do you think this was right? At least tell me that."

"I don't think it was right," he said through a puff of smoke.

"Well, what do you think? You're not saying anything."

"What do you want me to say? There's nothing more to say — it's done."

"Don't talk like that about her, Stavro," Athina said. "You, of all people, know better than to talk like that."

"I'm sorry, but there's nothing else anyone can do at this point."

Sophia realized that she might never really get to know Stavro. He was too isolated in his own world and in his own thoughts to attach himself to others. He simply believed in the things he believed in, and was never, ever, influenced. She was amazed by his composure in a situation such as this, and she didn't like it. He was too practical, too calm.

Athina had once mentioned to her that Stavro had fallen in love with a girl from the village a few years back. They had seen each other occasionally in secret, behind a tree after dark, in the abandoned schoolhouse in the middle of the night, in the mountains during an afternoon. Stavro never talked about his relationship with this girl, but Athina knew of it somehow. When the girl told him one day that it had just been arranged for her to marry a man from the next village, he was devastated. All he could do was contain his emotions as he watched the girl and her family prepare for her wedding day. But they continued meeting each other until her wedding, Stavro whispering what he felt when he lay next to her.

On the wedding day, everyone went in procession, accompanying the bride to the neighboring village for the ceremony. The entire village was abandoned; everyone went to the celebration except Stavro, who stayed behind and planted corn for the coming season. He hadn't seen the girl since the previous night.

Sophia thought of the time when she and her father had traveled to Greece, making their way to the northern part of the country. "Just past these mountains is Albania," he told her, "my old village where I grew up." She remembered the sun setting below the mountains that divided Albania from Greece—a political division, not a cultural one. She wondered which nationality the wolves thought themselves when they roamed these mountains.

Vangelli walked into his bedroom and looked at his cousin's backpack leaning against the wall. Hesitatingly, he moved closer, as if it were something to be scared of, or a gem that mesmerized him as he approached, its power illuminating the room. He closed the door.

Vangelli tried to adapt to this new addition to his small family, a relative who had come into his life and was foreign to him. He wanted to see what she possessed, what she had brought to his world. Because he was so young, Vangelli's life was simple; nothing could have been defined as complex as he lived his days in the village. And as he watched his cousin move into his home, life was gradually becoming more complicated because she helped define it now.

Vangelli touched Sophia's backpack and tried lifting it, but it was too heavy. He thought of opening it to see what was inside, but then decided not to, fearing that she might come home and find him going through her things. On the nightstand at the side of her bed—his bed—was a notebook. Flipping through the pages, he found words he could not read, a language that was foreign to him, one that moved the world. He turned again to her backpack and unzipped the largest pouch. Clothes neatly folded, a book, and photographs were what he found. He went through the photographs—one of his family, one of her father. When he put them back into her pack, he felt a small box between her shirts. Vangelli pulled out the box but didn't dare to open it; this was an object that piqued his curiosity. He shook it and turned it over and looked at it closely, curious about his cousin from America.

Vangelli placed the box back into her backpack and zipped it shut. He walked into the living room, seeing his sister, Stavro, and Sophia walking up the path.

Thirteen

Talking with Old Man Arseni, Sophia realized that his intellectual capacity was enormous, and beyond the comprehension of anyone in the village. Before she introduced herself to him, she had heard that he had lost his mind and that it was better to leave the poor man alone rather than disturb him with her mere presence. An isolated man, his mind had evolved untouched by other people — or, rather, it had evolved and expanded by emotion and memory. But he was off-center — a phrase he used to define other people when he spoke with her. The balance in his life was slightly off; the only element keeping him together was his memory, his thoughts about life.

Sophia asked Old Man Arseni one day why he, too, hadn't left the village when he was young.

"Well, there were a couple of reasons. I had my parents here; my mother was sick and I didn't want to leave her. Also, I was planning my wedding. It was already arranged for me to marry a girl from the next village."

"And you married her?"

"Yes, I did. I was lucky, too. I was betrothed to a girl whom I fell in love with right away."

"There wasn't an awkward period between you?"

"Of course there was a little, but we were both very happy with the arrangement. If I could have chosen my bride, I would have picked her."

Sophia smiled, pleased to hear of a moment in Old Man Arseni's life when he was happy. She had begun to feel sorry for him, wondering how he managed, living alone in the mountains. Though his neighbors stopped by from time to time to see how he was doing, they left him alone for the most part.

"So what was your secret to a happy marriage?"

"My secret? The secret to my marriage was an enormous amount of understanding. I knew my wife better than I knew myself, and she knew me just as well. We had a deep respect for each other, which allowed each of us to be our own person, our own being."

"You're talking as if you don't come from a village. I don't know many men in Chatista who talk the way you do."

"Not many couples whose marriages are arranged by their parents find love. Like I said, Sophia, I happened to be very lucky. For a short time, though," he quickly added.

At night the pain would swell in Old Man Arseni's mind — this was when his thoughts were the most active. After his nightly cup of coffee on the front porch, he would fall asleep in bed and then waken to the sounds of his wife's voice. He could feel it echoing through his body, touching every limb, stroking his hair, soothing him while he slept. But when he awoke, fear overwhelmed him.

He took up the shepherd's trade, as his father had done, and his father's father. He enjoyed taking walks through the countryside, leaving the village for a time and roaming the world as he saw it. He would go for weeks, returning when the leaves on the trees had begun to change their colors. He would come back with stories to tell his wife and children, and they would look at him with admiration, she wondering about the people he had met, the villages he had seen, the stars he had fallen asleep under. She thought he was so intelligent, so knowledgeable of the outside world. As he told his story, his children's already wide eyes would widen, waiting for the next sentence to come out of his mouth.

He told his wife once that being a shepherd in a shepherding family must have been his calling, and that he found his place in life because he had found her. She smiled at him when he said this, and this was when he knew he was truly in love with her. They married just when the Italians came to Albania "to help the government of Albania to modernize itself." Arseni remembered how beautiful she had looked, holding onto her father's arm as she walked through the valley with the wedding entourage. She seemed like an angel to him. The men in her family fired their rifles into the air, and the guests from her village walked slowly behind her in procession. He waited for her anxiously, honored to be her husband, proud to have such a beautiful wife.

The emotional celebration after the ceremony was joyous and filled with love. Arseni's cousins roasted lambs in the pit set up in his parents' backyard, and his mother and aunts prepared salads, breads, and fruits. The guests ate heartily, sang smoothly, and danced wildly. Arseni danced with his wife that whole evening, singing softly into her ear.

During the early hours of the morning, while the guests were still reveling, Arseni stole his wife away so they could be alone. He led her to their new bedroom, an addition he had built onto his parents' house. Her relatives had already brought her belongings there — a tradition still kept in the village. He fixed up their bedroom and made it cozy for her, decorating the walls with paintings, laying a new blanket over the bed, and placing a vase full of flowers on the center of a trunk that sat at the bedside. She looked around the room and smiled with satisfaction, feeling warmth in her new home.

Arseni stared at his wife while her eyes searched their bedroom. Then he took her into his arms and held her close. They made love a few moments later as the revelers danced their hearts out into the night.

Old Man Arseni thought back to when he had fallen in love with his wife. Her beauty was what did it for him, the long black hair that lay smooth against the sides of her face, her large brown eyes that were furred with long eyelashes. How much he loved her, and she loved him. There were moments with her that he thought would last forever, that he would be with her forever. He didn't see his life any other way, though before meeting her, he had never believed he would be so in love with a woman.

The first time they met, his parents invited her family and her to their home. It was time he settled down and started a family, his father told him one afternoon in the plaza, just the two of them talking while the village was asleep. "Arseni, you're getting older now, you've become a man. I think it is time for us to look for a wife for you."

Arseni looked at his father questioningly. "Do you already have someone in mind, Pa? Someone you'd like me to meet?"

"Well, your mother and I have been thinking of a young woman in the next village. Your mother knows her mother, and I've met her father a few times throughout the years while herding sheep. They're a good family, a decent one, and I'm sure you'll like her. Meet her, at least, and give it a chance. You'll have to get used to meeting girls now."

"Yes, Pa," Arseni agreed, but he wasn't expecting to marry this soon. He supposed that it was about time, but he never brought up the subject—he waited for his parents to tell him that he had reached the next stage in life. But his father had brought it up so quickly and unexpectedly that the time he was given to adjust, to change his way of thinking, was not enough. He knew this, but he agreed to meet the girl, this girl from the neighboring village, to please his parents. She was the first girl, anyway. Was he going to marry her the day he met her? No, he would not. He would smile, and talk with her parents, and talk with her just a little. It wouldn't be appropriate to have a deep conversation with a prospective bride, even if she could possibly be his. But he would smile at her subtly, glance at her, and perhaps make full eye contact. He wanted to play with the idea that he was available, that he was potentially reachable, attainable. He would play this game without her knowing. He would portray himself as a mysterious figure; heighten her curiosity with his silence and looks and smiles and politeness. She would wonder about his thoughts while their parents were engaged in conversation. And she would think he was so desirable.

But things didn't turn out that way. Arseni waited nonchalantly in the living room for this girl and her family to arrive, sitting on the couch, fixing his collar. But when she walked into the room, he was completely taken by her beauty. He became speechless, not because he wanted to convey a mysterious image of himself, but because he was mesmerized. He stood up and greeted her parents, but immediately said the wrong things to her and then became self-conscious, his blunders coming one after another, piling up right in front of her. She smiled at him, at his embarrassment, his shyness. Throughout the evening, he was polite and talkative with her parents, was able to converse with them, but when he spoke with her, his thoughts were muddled.

All of his strategy, his plans to intrigue her, entice her, had diminished, as if God had played a trick on him and handed him a beautiful girl who could possibly be his wife. And the art of planning gave way to a genuine attraction to her.

As they were leaving, concluding the first meeting with the potential young husband and wife, her father put his hand on Arseni's shoulder and shook his hand. The parents kissed one another on either cheek, and Arseni looked down and said goodbye to her, but he could not look up and meet her eyes. She accepted this, resolved to think he wasn't interested in her. She left with her parents believing that this was the last time she would see Arseni.

His father shut the door behind their guests and turned to his son. "Well, Arseni? What do you think of this young woman?"

"Don't ask him just yet," his mother quickly said. "Let him think for a moment. She's the first girl he has met. If he's not interested in her, he'll meet others."

"I think I like this one," he said to both of them.

A few days later, Arseni's father walked to the neighboring village and sought to speak with the girl's father. He left right after breakfast and told his wife he wouldn't be back until the afternoon. Arseni felt excited to see his father walking toward the next village. He wanted to see the girl again, perhaps accompany his father, but tradition would not allow it. It was the fathers' duty to discuss their children's prospective union; it was inappropriate for the families to meet again until the men had finalized the marriage. He knocked on their front door and the girl answered. The first expression on her face was shock; then, perceiving what was happening, she grinned. She hadn't expected to hear from Arseni's family, certainly not this soon. Arseni's father looked at her, smiled faintly, and said, "Good morning, Maria. Is your father at home?"

She stood at the doorway for a moment, her mind racing with what she had hoped for. She stood in front of him, overwhelmed by what she was thinking.

"Well?"

"Oh, I'm sorry, sir. Yes, he's home." Maria found her manners. "Please, come in. Would you like something to drink? Some water, perhaps?" She left him in the living room, poured a glass of water in the kitchen, brought it to him, excused herself again, and ran to the next room.

"Papa, Papa! Arseni's father is here. He wants to speak with you."

Her father looked up from his work and smiled at his daughter. He walked across the room, gently patted her head, and left her there alone. Closing the door behind him, she jumped onto the bed, fell back, and lay there laughing to herself, overwhelmed with joy.

"Welcome, my friend. It is a pleasure to see you today," she heard him say to Arseni's father.

Arseni kissed his wife on the forehead and left for Tirana on the bus that stopped in the village once a week. He told her he would soon return with the soap, lantern, and candles she needed. "I'll be back in a week or so, my love. Tell the children I love them." She blew a kiss as he turned to look at her once more. He waved goodbye as the bus rattled off toward the capital.

Two days later, Arseni's wife put their twins to bed for the night, laying them close to each other on a cot in the corner of the bedroom. Three-year-olds, a boy and a girl, they were small enough to sleep comfortably together, and they wanted it that way. As she did every night when she tucked them into bed, Maria told them a story. Sometimes, Arseni would stand in the doorway and listen to her storytelling. *Her stories are so vivid,* he thought as he watched her. The twins listened and squirmed that evening as she told them the story of the three *Fatias* who had come down from the mountains and gathered at a bonfire in the middle of the night after their birth, determining which characteristics her children would have. The first Fatia spun the thread of life; the second took the thread from the first and measured its length; the third Fatia took the thread and cut it, at which moment her children's fate was determined.

"What is our fate, Mama?" her son asked.

"The thread was cut to a certain length that was very special for both of you," she said, and they smiled at her. "Both of you are courageous little ones."

When she finished the story, she told them they had to go to sleep now because tomorrow they were to help her plant tomato seeds in the garden. She kissed them, tucked the blankets closer under their chins, wished them good night, and carried the lantern out with her.

The whole village helped put out the fire. Men ran to the pond with large buckets, and women filled cooking pots with water from the well, but the house was entirely aflame before the smoke that filled the night air awakened anyone. Some of the men tried to reach Arseni's wife and children, but the blaze was too strong. It was three hours before the fire was reduced to a smolder.

The village did not want Arseni to find what lay there afterward. There was nothing more than a pile of smoking ashes. They looked for anything they could salvage—a toy, jewelry, or maybe a photograph.

Three days later, Arseni came back to Chatista on the same bus that had taken him. The funeral was held the next day at the church at the bottom of the village. They say that Arseni was never the same since he laid the flowers on his family's graves and walked away.

Fourteen

Awkwardness enveloped them when they were around people. Sophia felt clumsy behaving as though there was nothing between them. It felt artificial, and she thought it must be evident that she was disguising her feelings. She couldn't be herself in front of others when Abraham was around, because of what they had—a secret only the two of them knew. When they were with other people, Sophia barely talked to him, and when he spoke to her as if just talking with a good friend's cousin, she would respond tersely, making no eye contact. *If I look at him, people will notice my lingering gaze. The sound of his voice taking me in.* Noticing this, Abraham thought it was charming that she was so open and comfortable when they were alone—sharing her secrets, her desires, her ideals, but could pretend indifference when they were in company.

They lay on the blanket, looking at the sky through the mountain air. Sophia felt relaxed and safe next to Abraham, her head resting on his arm as he playfully pulled her hair. *I don't want this feeling to end.* She didn't have another thought in the world. Escaping from everything, she had reached that peaceful plateau where she wasn't concerned about next year or even tomorrow. She wasn't off-center, relishing the warmth his body gave off, the slight movement of his chest, the touch of his fingers against her scalp, softly pulling her hair and then releasing. The sounds of the mountains surrounding her. Wishing it would never end, she closed her eyes, leaned against his shoulder, and thought about the things young women think about.

"You don't want to talk to me when we're around other people, do you?" he asked her. "Why? It's as if you loathe me."

"That's not true. I talk with you."

"You answer when I ask you questions, but that's it. You're distant."

"Abraham, I just don't want people to know about us. If I start talking to you like we really know each other, don't you think people are going to catch on?"

"I don't think that's it, Sophia. I think it's because you're so in love with me you can't stand it," he joked.

"Yeah, that's exactly it," she said.

"Sophia," he said her name again. "Do you have someone back home in America?"

She opened her eyes. She didn't turn to him, but looked up into the night. "Why would you ask me that?"

"I just want to know. Do you have someone back home?"

"No, I don't."

"Could you ever live in another country? I mean, not to visit, but actually live there?"

Sophia turned to him and put her hand on his face. She stroked his cheek and looked into his eyes. They were the kind of blue that gave off tranquillity, yet made a person feel completely vulnerable, surrendering to the blue. He stared at her without blinking, trying to read what she was feeling.

"I think so. Yeah, I think I could live somewhere else besides America."

Abraham smiled and looked at the sky, thinking he'd grasped what Sophia was feeling. *This is how people are supposed to feel when they are in love. To sneak out in the middle of the night and meet one another in the schoolhouse, or perhaps follow each other through the valley until they reach the deserted monastery between the mountains. Climb onto the roof to make love beneath a dark blanket of sky, lie on her back when she had finished, looking upside down at the cross in front of the church.*

If someone just happened to cross their path and saw them, there would be whispering and pointing and smirking when they got back to the village; the *kotsoboli*—gossips—would relish the story. But Sophia found a rhythm to her movements that allowed her to leave unnoticed during the night. It became second nature for her to act dead tired after dinner and go to bed, everyone thinking she was soon fast asleep. She would listen for footsteps on the kitchen floor, ragged slippers sliding across the concrete, Vangelli's endless jokes, listening until the noises faded to soft whispers and then ceased. Athina would come into the bedroom and fall asleep in the bed next to hers, but Sophia didn't worry—Athina could sleep through an earthquake. Once she heard Athina's light snoring, Sophia knew she was clear to sneak out and meet Abraham.

"You're getting pretty good at this," Abraham would say when they met.

"I've become a chameleon, blending into the night," she would say, throwing her arms around his neck.

Innocently, Athina asked Sophia if she was interested in any of the guys in the village, saying that she was asking because the guys were wondering what Sophia thought of them. Sophia took this as simple curiosity about someone new, a girl who hadn't grown up with them in the mountains, and a foreigner—an American foreigner. To them, America seemed untouchable, a very far-off land where everyone was so modern and united, and whose decisions could make sweeping changes throughout the world. With an American girl here in Chatista, they felt that they too had a connection with this powerful country. The idea of her intrigued them; they viewed Sophia as a personification of America.

Sophia answered Athina's question vaguely, as if she took no notice of any of them. She wasn't here to find romance, she said, but to see her father's village—Athina's village. Athina told her that a couple of the guys thought she was pretty. Sophia didn't know how to respond to this. She told Athina that nothing could ever happen between anyone who lived here and herself.

Sophia believed she was careful enough about meeting Abraham in the night, and that her image of a girl traveling to Albania to see her father's homeland was intact — but truth is a matter of perception, not scientific fact.

"The idea of equality in a body politic is very noble, and the certainty of being provided for is a generous notion. Communism was based on these ideals, but it strayed from functioning within their scope. When something becomes too theoretical, all common sense is thrown out the window. Regardless of its stated intentions, communism does not provide for equality and does not give society a sense of being provided for, and it never has. Communism gathers its strength from the act of providing just enough to exist, while making people believe that they are living in a utopia, industrial or agrarian, and by making them afraid. It does not allow personal ambition, individualism, intuition, or creativity in the people, but forces them to obey for the sake of obeying.

"We are not machines. We observe what is around us, and we don't just do things mechanically — our senses allow us much more understanding than that. Also, every human possesses two traits that oppose how communism wants to define us: greed and envy. We cannot simply turn away when we see others with things we will never have under communism. Given the chance to have these things, we always want more. What we currently have will never be enough. This is why communist nations falter.

"When a country collapses from within while embracing these ideals, or believing that it does, each individual can make choices, but what is forgotten is that while these choices exist, guidance does not. People who have been suppressed for so long — generations at a time — are ill-informed about the fundamentals of democracy and free enterprise. Only those who have been in power have access to the country's assets, its factories, farmland, and bank accounts. Still, a person looks at his neighbor and wants to have what he has, and this is where greed plays an essential role. When he acquires as much as his neighbor, it's not enough. Human consciousness was not meant to remain on a plateau.

"So, the rhetoric that began with the Bolshevik Revolution moved westward toward the Balkans and promised the people that things could be better under communism than within the existing Ottoman Empire. *What have these Turks done for you? What have they provided for your people?* After the Second World War, this ideal came to Albania, after the Italians and Germans marched in, carrying different flags through the land. The communists took over, idolizing Stalinism, and believing that it was the Albanians' turn to be 'provided for.' Somehow, the communists persuaded the Albanians to stop believing in their Muslim neighbors and King Zog, and believe in something more secular, more 'equal.' And the man who came to power was our leader, our provider, for quite some time — or so we thought.

"There are young men in the village who have big dreams, and these are not as farfetched as some perceive. Show them an opportunity, and they will becomes less remote, perhaps less mechanical, and something grand may arise. Would you like more coffee, Sophia? There's a little more on the stove," Old Man Arseni said.

"No, thank you, Arseni. I'm sorry to cut our conversation short, but I told Athina I'd meet her this evening. Can we continue another day?"

"That's fine. I apologize for keeping you."

"You don't keep me, Arseni. I'm always happy to speak with you," she said, smiling.

Abraham watched Sophia as she sat in the plaza talking with the village girls, intrigued by how gracefully she handled herself with them. He imagined their conversations — the backaches while washing clothes, the cold mornings when they would walk to the barn to feed the animals, the prospective arranged marriage that was to come, laughing at the prospective husband's oddities. Sophia was more the listener, the observer. He knew that she was absorbing the conversation because she done this with him. He recognized the tenderness about her right away, her compassion for those who lived here. Her presence made them feel good: now they too had a connection with America, the world outside.

He loved the intimate moments he shared with her. Her ease with him made him feel he was doing something right. He would hold her in his arms after they made love, her hair tickling his face as he snuggled behind her, their breathing in unison. He felt content when he lay beside her; there was nothing more he wanted. In his world, there was uncertainty of where or how to direct his life, but he had stability when he was with Sophia. He had always felt that his whole world was whirling quickly around him, but with her, the spinning suddenly ceased, and he felt tranquil and lucid. He would lie next to her, feeling her sleep, forcing himself to stay awake, marveling at how this could possibly happen to him. Had someone told him a year ago that he would soon fall in love with an American girl, he would have laughed and said that person was crazy.

Remembering when he asked her if she could live in another country and she told him she could, a smile swept across his face, his heart beat rapidly. He was one step closer to her, to having her, breathing her, to their becoming one entity.

"I truly do love you, Sophia. Really, I do. I've never met anyone like you before. I never even thought I'd ever meet anyone like you."

Abraham said this to Sophia in the schoolhouse one evening. The words came out of his mouth from nowhere, just slipped into the conversation as they talked about his life in Albania. These random thoughts frequently raced through his mind and occasionally would be expressed.

He was naïve like this — unleashing his thoughts and allowing himself to be completely open to those around him. Sophia quickly realized he was sheltered in this sense.

Initially, Abraham didn't notice that he would speak random thoughts until Sophia pointed it out to him. He was never conscious of it. Her noticing this about him gradually made Abraham self-conscious of it and gradually become more aware of what he would say. He lost this element of naïveté merely in reaction to Sophia's awareness of it.

Abraham was becoming transformed not by Sophia's intentions or his own, but by their interaction. He was changing as a man, becoming more aware of the thoughts in his head, the words coming out of his mouth. Becoming wiser — allowing the energy of a conversation, the energy that exists between two people, to take the lead.

This is what Abraham loved about Sophia, that her small observations about him would catapult his feelings toward her to a higher level, that she was so in tune with who he was. It made him feel important and wanted that someone, this Sophia, could be so observant to even these minute details of him. This is how it was supposed to be. This is why he was so in love with her.

"A person like me?" she responded.

"The way you make me feel. The way you touch me. I've never met anyone like you."

"I love you too, Abraham. With all of my heart. I am very happy at this moment."

She took his hands into hers and kissed them. She continued to do so.

"All of my strength is from you. You are the one who makes me feel alive, makes me want to continue. Now there's a goal. There is a reason for why I live."

These were the words that came from Abraham when he was alone in his bedroom after they parted that evening. It was a few days before he planned to tell his father about Sophia, before he planned to tell Sophia about their future together. She had come into his life for a reason, and these were the answers that danced in his head.

He wondered why his friend Stavro had never mentioned having an American cousin named Sophia. That she was someone with whom he could easily fall in love. Stavro never spoke of family other than those in the village. Why didn't he say anything?

Abraham was happy with the words he had put together in his head. The way he was going to say them to her. The way he was going to look at her.

The way she was going to look at him.

He wanted so much to have an unconcealed relationship with Sophia. It hurt to have to hide what he felt, that he couldn't tell everyone this was the girl he had fallen in love with, and hold her hand when he sat in the plaza talking with his friends. He wanted to tell the world that she was the girl he saw himself with for the rest of his life, the one he would greet when he came home from the fields, the one who would care for his children. Would anyone understand what they felt for each other? Here, love didn't happen with an initial attraction between two people, then move on to dating and finally a serious relationship that meant bringing someone home to meet the family. Love was more a gradual development after years of having been married by an arrangement. Traditional constraints didn't allow for love that was adventurous and spontaneous, flirting in the plaza with a pretty girl. People were bound by the restrictions their culture placed on them. Love was a level of comfort, a convenience; perhaps two people might eventually fall in love after years of happiness and heartache and unexpected babies and routine. The highest priority was functionality.

Abraham tried to think of a way to break this mold as he sat and watched Sophia talk with the girls.

Sophia left William in his office, his belt unbuckled. She had said what she wanted to say to him, her speech well prepared for this last time that she would enter his office and lock the door. He rested his hand on the bookshelf as she spoke her final words to him, looking attentively at her face, watching her eyes become animated, then sad, then animated again. He focused his eyes upon her, but his vision became distorted, blurred, even though his face was inches from hers. He watched her lips form the words as he stared at her, her teeth, her tongue rapidly moving behind her lips. He was sucked into the vacuum of her words, but he heard nothing. The movement of her face and the expression in her eyes were telling him what he needed to know, yet didn't want to hear. He was alone in his thoughts while Sophia talked to him.

She told him she couldn't be the person between the life that he shared with her and the life he presented to the world. Though she had often told him that she didn't mind how the relationship was, and how they had initially created it, now the thought of being the other woman made her sick to her stomach. Now, after her father had passed away, she was rearranging her life and this was something she needed to be rid of. That she was invisible in his world, the world that everyone knew, and by which he was defined, diminished their relationship in her eyes. That no one knew of the relationship was precisely the problem. If he were having dinner with friends at a restaurant, she could walk past him and no one would know who she was. He would look at her briefly and turn away as if he didn't know her, as if she'd never been inside his office with him. She was happy when they were together, but when she was away from him her mind obsessed with how he was spending his time with his wife: a Saturday afternoon walk, a Sunday night dinner, lying together on the couch, watching a movie moments after he had left her.

When Sophia had said all she needed to say, she asked William what he was thinking — a question one usually asks someone they have just begun dating. It took him a moment to refocus his eyes and get his mind back on his surroundings, the situation he was in.

He told her he wanted her to be happy, and if this was it, then she should do it. He didn't even know what "it" was, but he thought it the safest answer. He had been concentrating on her beauty, her moving lips and radiant eyes, rather than her words.

She knew this was the only answer she could possibly get out of him. Reaching over and kissing him on the cheek — an act that would confuse him even more — she told him to take care of himself. As she began to open the door, he quickly closed it and pressed her against it. He told her not to leave, that he wanted to continue seeing her. She asked him how she could continue seeing him if he had a wife. He didn't answer.

Dusk had begun darkening the air, which had become crisp since she had entered his office. Sophia walked down the outer steps of the building and through the courtyard grass, thinking about how things would have been different had she never met him, never taken his class. She wouldn't have the heartache she felt now, and knew she didn't want this any longer. She felt like her life was at a standstill when she was with him, not moving either forward or backward — a sort of limbo.

Sophia looked back at the building and noticed his office light still on. She contemplated going back and telling him to forget what she had said a moment ago, that she was out of her mind and just needed some air, a short walk. She felt confused, and feared she might regret what she had said and done. *Don't leave, Sophia. You know I love seeing you, and things would be different, well, if the situation was just different.* These thoughts spinning in her head, she forced herself to turn her back to the building and his office. A couple leaned against the library doors as she made her way off campus and across the street to her apartment.

After Sophia closed the door, William sat down on a chair, listening to the sound of her footsteps on their way down the stairs, hoping they would get louder rather than softer. Then he heard the door that led outside creep open and then slam itself shut. He felt trapped in his office. He walked backwards to the couch they'd been lying on only moments ago, and let his body sink into it. His left eyelid twitched as he stared at the coffee table, knowing this time had really been the last. He remembered the book he had forgotten to give her, the one she had previously mentioned wanting. It was a travel guide to Amsterdam.

Sophia walked into her apartment and threw her bag onto the chair under the mirror in the front hall. She stared at herself for a moment, looking at her arms and legs, torso and face. She turned to the side to look at her profile, noticing that her right side was shaped slightly different than her left. She thought that her right was her better side.

She decided to take the trip to Albania that she and her father had planned before his death. She wouldn't procrastinate any longer; she needed to get momentum back into her life, the natural forward motion that had eluded her for a time. Instantly, she felt relieved by her decision, because it honored her father and the promise she had made to him and to herself. After what she had experienced with William, she saw things from a new perspective. No longer would she let others control her life, her destiny. She was ashamed to have allowed such a relationship for so long. She wanted to make the decisions, direct her life as she thought best. She felt she had focused on trivial things, and allowed her relationship with William to divert her pursuit of what she had set out to do before meeting him. Their relationship had become trivial now — there was nothing more she could done and nothing more she could offer, and nothing he could offer her. Everyone, at some point in life, gets sidetracked, but the ride was over.

And who would be the next student to seduce him, if that was what he was about? She was the one who had asked him for help after class, the one who stood close to him as he answered her question, the one who slid onto his office couch. And he was the one who lost concentration and began to mumble before he climbed on top of her. Who was to be the next to hear his words in her ear as he practiced his charm?

Sophia walked into the bathroom, undressed, and started the shower. Stepping into the tub, she felt the hot water pour over the top of her head, stream through her hair, and drip down her body. She stood, motionless.

BOOK III

FIFTEEN

The war in Kosovo was escalating, and refugees poured into Albania faster than the world had expected. The government made a plea for help from the international community — the same world powers that had been there earlier in the century, after the Great War, when they drew the borders and didn't seriously consider the problems that would inevitably arise. They hadn't looked closely at the region's ethnic diversity or how the people and the land had been divided.

They carried what they could on broken-down, mule-drawn wagons. The men led the caravans carrying their belongings and the women held their children's hands, reassuring them that everything would be all right, but couldn't explain when or how. They took with them mattresses and blankets and cooking pots and clothes. A photograph of the family, perhaps, before all this began. The peasants met in the towns and were to travel with the rest of the Albanians who had been told to get out of the country. The line of departing cars was long and slow — it looked like a trail of ants moving through the mountains on its way to the neighboring countries.

Some men were not with their families. The guerrilla movement that was formed, made up of political hard-liners and armed peasant farmers, appealed to these men. They joined the militants in the fight for their land, the land that was theirs because they were the descendants of the Illyrians and Dardanians, the original inhabitants of Kosovo. The men who were too old to fight left with their families and waited for those who were not.

The people left their country tired and fearful — what was to become of their homes, the only possession that symbolized family and identity and their lives? A heavy weight of dread rested on their eyelids. What would they come back to if they had the chance to return? Would everything be destroyed? Could they live as they had before? Could they ever possibly go back?

Macedonia and Bosnia and Montenegro opened their gates and took in the ethnic Albanian refugees, requesting help around the globe. Camps sprouted from the landscape just over the Kosovo border to accommodate the people, giving them a small sense of community while NATO did its work. But Albania was the country that took in the most.

The central train station in Tirana was cramped with even more Kosovar deportees. The world news said that soldiers filled boxcars with people and shipped them out of the country, no longer wanting them on Yugoslav soil. They were pushed and pulled in every direction, forced onto the trains; families were broken apart in the confusion, children yanked into boxcars with people they didn't know. Frantic mothers tried to find their children, get hold of their hands, but were dragged away and forced onto the trains with nothing. Men were pushed like mules as they tried to fight the soldiers, trying to regain some sense of control over what was happening to them, to their people.

Packed in cramped spaces, they stood side by side in the boxcars, gasping for air. The stench choked them as the trains moved slowly across the landscape. They pleaded to the air to be free, but their cries were muffled by the noise of the train, the noise of people, the noise of children crying, their minds trying to grasp what was happening to them.

Images arise in a person's mind when he looks down from a mountain upon a village recently razed. The village looks small, like a picture a young child painted for school one day. He knows what he sees, and his perception shows promise, but his artistic talent is not yet fully developed, so the picture looks disordered and out of proportion—just like a razed village.

Serbian soldiers infiltrated the Albanian villages in Kosovo; they slipped in, establishing a presence, demanding. Fear filled the air, suffocating the people. Every village had its own story to tell, its own secrets to protect. Seemingly random, the soldiers' acts were calculated, dictated over the long wire of military bureaucracy. A man was shot in the back of the head as he walked down the road toward his home, a young girl picked from her bicycle and raped throughout an afternoon in an abandoned home, the family's belongings still inside, left behind when they were ordered to leave. These were the images that would remain in the Albanians' minds, and it was these images that compelled a people to act out vengeance. They believed that this was the way the world worked because this is all they had been exposed to—everyone lived in terror and violence, and only sometimes joy.

A person will accept something if he sees it as justifiable, will allow things to happen if she becomes too weak to fight any longer. In this part of the world, both happened. Some people accepted an attack, but would retaliate. Others would surrender themselves when the enemy came to their village, but not submit spiritually; their souls endured elsewhere, away and protected.

Some wanted the truth to be told and others wanted it buried deep in the earth, but truth had become a matter of perception in this part of the world. It was not black and white—a tapestry of colors portrayed the Balkans: the mass graves unearthed in isolated regions; the disappearance of men and boys during an afternoon; the women who were too ashamed to go home again and protect their children. These truths were sometimes told, jeopardizing the safety of individuals and their families, a whole village, perhaps, and fueling the men to justify future acts of revenge.

The world cried out when photos of ethnic Albanians being transported out of Kosovo were plastered all over the Earth. Some were dramatic enough and sufficiently comparable to recall visions of the Holocaust—another people's story. This wasn't the Holocaust, but it was the beginning of a mass exodus of a people, a lasting error by a world leader who, after the Great War, drew the Balkan borders as he saw fit, unaware that a generous number of Albanians lived outside Albania's borders. No one could have known then what would happen decades later, when the tensions among the people would ignite. The world saw it as spontaneous combustion, not realizing that these problems had always existed—it just took several decades to part the curtain and expose the stage.

For several centuries, the Balkans seemed integrated, the people living together in rhythmic harmony. The Ottoman Empire stretched to the west, claiming its stake in Europe. The people adjusted their lives for comfort, putting aside their ancestors' religion and adopting Islam. The sultan took their boys hostage, educating and training them at court in Constantinople. Brought back to the Balkans and now Mohammedans, the young men would relish their newfound power and fame, some forgetting their roots entirely. Perhaps things would have been different had all the kidnapped boys grown up to be like Albania's national hero, Gjergj Kastrioti Skenderbeg: *I have not brought you liberty. I found it here, among you.*

Albania was then part of the grand empire within the sultan's vast reach. Albanians defined themselves as subjects of his empire, an imperial temptation that, in the end, devastated them all the more. With impressive ideologies and the art of rhetoric, authoritarian political culture infested even these isolated regions of the globe, proliferating the myth that this part of the world was one and whole. A man came and promised them that he would lead—an old story that persists here still.

Decisions made in Constantinople found their way to this region and defined those who lived in it. A deed to the land was their profession, eternal admiration for the empire their spirit. This was life for hundreds of years, until the Great War came and collapsed the Ottoman Empire from within.

The traditions and cultures that made up the empire were suddenly liberated, and people didn't know how to breathe — the sultan had always dictated how to think and how to behave, how to admire and how to condemn. Now, life had changed, but the freedom was ephemeral: men from other parts of the world wanted to lead and dictate how the globe would turn.

What became a war between secular enlightenment and communism, and religion and democracy, would be resolved easily. These conflicting ideals were too extreme to coexist; one would have to collapse. The disillusionment of capitalism and free enterprise, forcing people to live in a competitive society, gave way to security, conformity, and secularism — in short, communism. It swept over the Balkans methodically, moving strategically over the land, the people unaware that they were being suffocated.

Soon enough, its reach slowly shortened, and the grip of its extended hand loosened. What was once a pillar of life, a great ideal of culture, a systematic method of government, began to eat away at itself. Internal corruption took its toll, everything shattered, and when the dust settled, the people were liberated again. This time, things were different. The chiefdoms that had previously existed began to sprout from the rubble, and the war was no longer between capitalistic democracy and authoritarian communism, but between Christianity and Islam. Both sides used the principles of fundamentalism, gaining force by authentic persuasion, manipulation, and hypocrisy.

Depending upon how deeply a person probes into history, each side was correct when they cried out their claim. It went on and on, the bloodshed persisting because people were afraid to step a little further back into time and perhaps prove themselves wrong. So they stopped only as far back as they wanted, and continued the fight.

The struggle between Muslims and Christians, essentially a conflict between Albanians and Serbians, left the Greek Orthodox people living in southern Albania forgotten. Separated from everyone, they sat in the mountains and dreamed, and remembered while trying not to—mementos of the war years were all over the landscape, making it impossible to forget. Occasionally, the region's borders shifted, always defined by someone else.

Kosovo balanced itself precariously on a cliff, the province's back toward its edge: the mass graves found in Pec; the mysterious abductions of local officials; the soldiers' carnal pleasures with young women; the old women crying themselves to sleep at night; the children screaming; the men murdering one another.

Scars are reminders that our past is real.

The men became soldiers, guns their passion. They vowed their loyalty to the government, and placed their trust in its soul. The soldiers reflected the government's mind; their obedience would never allow them to think any other way. Orders were seen not as incomprehensible, but reasonable, and a soldier's order to murder was part of his daily life. They believed they were doing God's work by massacre. *They are infidels and do not believe in Jesus Christ.* After the soldiers ransacked the homes, the women came and cleaned up, and it looked like no one had ever been there. No one could tell the difference.

The people had become bitter and angry. Their leader instilled distrust toward those who lived in these particular villages in Kosovo, fueling nationalistic hatred. They lost everything—their property, learning, and way of life. All they had ever asked for was equal status in official and legal matters.

Life became a succession of impersonal manipulation, by means of charismatic domination; the agony of civil war; war followed by war, followed by catastrophe, followed by shame and dishonor.

And always there were the ancient resentments, acts of vengeance, conflicting political and social interests, uncertainties, and random violence. The absurdity of violence always seems to take hold in regions whose inhabitants are the most religious zealots.

Sixteen

When Sophia was younger, on her father's return from work, she would run up to him and jump into his arms and kiss him. She would call him during the day sometimes, and ask him when he was coming home because she missed him. This made him work harder, a validation of his efforts, a reason for his sweat. Her mother, Sophia thought, resented the relationship she had with her father.

Much younger than her brother, Sophia was the baby of the family. "A mistake," her mother had told her. "We didn't plan you — you just happened. We were content with one child, and since our first was a boy, well, that was even better — you know, to carry on the family name."

Her mother would remind her of this explanation when Sophia and her father would come home from spending the day together, or at dinner when she noticed how well they got along, just the two of them laughing at their inside jokes. Her mother slipped these words into her conversations with Sophia, like sneaking an extra layer of custard into a birthday cake: no one notices it except the person taking the bite, but it's there.

Her mother's anger arose from the fact that she wasn't close to either of her children. She had her own agenda; she seemed to speak with her children only when she was bored, when her mind was free for the moment to think of them. Her mother tried to establish a closer relationship with her son, trying to make Sophia jealous with an image of how great life could be were she close to her mother. All of a sudden, her mother wanted to spend more time with Sophia's brother, be a part of his life, ask him questions that would make him open up, allow him to confess himself to his mother. And he appeased his mother, not taking sides, but reciprocating the attention she was giving him at the time, regardless of how transient it was, how quickly he knew it could vanish. He had become the observer in the family, and noticed how close Sophia was to their father, and how distant his mother had become as they had gotten older. It didn't bother him, though — he had his own life to think about, his own interests, and his own plans to make.

If Sophia needed help with homework, she had only to ask her father and he would be there to help her. If she wanted someone to play ball with, he would unhesitatingly drop what he was doing and follow her outside. Even if he were about to fall asleep on the couch from his long day at work, he would smile and lift himself up and let her lead him to the backyard.

Her mother criticized Sophia for little things that meant nothing to anyone else, but were extremely important in the World of Mother. And they became more important when she would notice Sophia and her father spending more time together, as if the issues that were bothering her needed to be addressed immediately. The way Sophia dressed, the way she held herself, the way she talked, her manners — nothing was never good enough, even when Sophia wasn't trying to be good enough. Her mother yelled at her for nothing and blamed her for everything she did not do. It became routine, something expected, like the morning's mail.

Once, Sophia's mother slapped her face for answering the phone. Sophia was in the kitchen with her, standing next to the phone when it rang. Her mother was washing the dishes, so Sophia answered it. Right after she said hello, her mother's wet hand flew swiftly across her cheek. She felt the stinging right away and automatically handed over the phone to her. Dumbfounded, Sophia just looked at her as she pleasantly began chatting with her friend, as if nothing had happened. When she finished her conversation and hung up the phone, she said nothing to Sophia. She went about her business in the kitchen, like a good housewife.

Mother had been expecting a call from a friend, so there was no reason Sophia should answer the phone. This was the explanation her mother gave her years later, when Sophia was already out of the house and the two were having one of their arguments—old resentments surfacing easily between them.

Her father never witnessed the worst of his wife's behavior—she saved that for when she and Sophia were alone, before he came home for work. These were the same moments when her mother demeaned Sophia's relationship with her father, telling her that her father was bored or felt obligated to spend time with her because she seemed lonely and awkward. Sophia knew she was an eccentric, but she thought her father didn't mind. She had always been a little aloof, the last to be chosen on a team in gym class even though she was athletic. When Sophia was fourteen and waif-like, her mother told her that she would probably have big hips when she got older, would become an obese woman.

When Sophia was in the fifth grade, she was given the leading role in a school play and had to sing a song. It was the finale of the play, and she practiced her singing in her bedroom for weeks, trying to memorize the words and reach the high notes. A couple of days before the opening, when she thought she had the song down pat, Sophia wanted her parents to be her first audience. During dinner that evening, she asked if she could show them how hard she had been practicing. She stood up in the middle of the kitchen and began her song, both her parents watching, pleased. Halfway through the song, her mother said to her father, "Oh, I forgot to tell you, I made an appointment to get the brakes fixed on the car. I'll need to take it tomorrow." Sophia looked at her mother, then ran out of the kitchen and into her bedroom.

A few minutes later, her father softly knocked on her bedroom door and asked to come in. He found her lying on her bed, crying. He sat next to her and gently stroked her hair, and asked her if she would sing her song for him, from the beginning. He asked again, saying he really wanted to hear it. Sophia sat up, cleared her throat, and began to sing for her father. She sang every note perfectly and remembered every word. When she finished, he told her that her song was beautiful. He kissed her forehead and asked her if she would sing for him at the show that weekend.

Later that week, a friend at work asked him what was that beautiful song he kept humming to himself.

"In a week I will be leaving to find work outside the country."

"You're leaving next week?"

"I think it's best that I leave next week, yes."

"Where do you plan to go to find work?"

"Perhaps Constantinople."

"Constantinople?" his wife cried. "Why Constantinople? Why so far away from us? We have young children and another on the way. Do you have to leave now, and so far?"

"I think this is best. But don't worry, love, I will send money and be back before you even miss me," he said, taking his wife in his arms.

She smiled at him because she didn't know what else to do. She let him hold her, feeling the strength of his arms wrapped around her body.

A storm rolled over the village, blanketing it with darkness. She looked out the window and saw a lightning flash illuminate the valley below their home, the swaying of the crops, the sound of the thunder that was making its way to the valley. The storm was moving toward them — their home, their village. This made her even sadder, sapping the strength that was left in her.

He kissed his wife on the forehead and told her he had to make sure the animals would be safe during the storm that was quickly approaching.

"Don't worry," he told her again. "I'll be back and everything will be all right, I promise," he said as he slipped out the front door, kissed his palm and waved it toward her.

Abraham watched Sophia as she undressed, taking in the successive images of her: fully clothed, then gradually removing a piece of clothing, then another, and then one more, tossing them onto the floor, until she was completely nude before him. He stared at the angles of her face, her shoulders, her stomach, and her slender legs, taking her in with his eyes as she lay on the floor waiting for him. And she looked at him, her eyes saying that all was okay.

He lay next to her on the floor, his clothes still on, and ran his hand through her hair, tracing the angles of her face. She watched his eyes as he did this, the small freckles on his nose and cheeks, letting his hand move down her neck to her breasts, touching them with the tips of his fingers, then caressing them with his entire hand. He led himself down her stomach with just his thumb, lightly touching her skin, making a trail until he reached between her legs. She closed her eyes, softly breathing through her lips.

After making love, late in the night, Sophia looked at Abraham and wondered how he would get along if he were to move to the States — not necessarily with her, but just move to America. How would he adjust to a way of life he had never experienced? He might get sidetracked and lose his focus, a focus that made him want to change his life. Maybe he would be content with the things her country offered, things that Americans take for granted for the most part: hospitals, schools, libraries, movie theaters, cafes on every corner, cars, clothing stores, bars, and, of course, the generous safe loans American banks gave people these days. She could help him with what he wanted, what he needed, but she knew she wasn't ready to accommodate him the way someone would in a relationship that required delicacy because of a precarious situation.

She continued to look at him carefully, at his hair, his eyes, his freckles, his jeans and ragged shirt and dirty shoes that lay next to him on the floor. He was from a different world than hers. There were things he didn't know even existed, and if he moved to the States, she would have to explain everything to him, as if he were seeing the world as it was for the first time. It would be like teaching a child how to ride a bike: she would hold on to the seat and guide him, and when he seemed confident and secure and bold enough, she would let him go.

"What are you thinking about?" Abraham asked.

"Would you ever come to America?"

"That is what you're thinking right now?"

"Yes. My mind works in strange ways."

"Of course I would, but how would I get there?'

"Can't you get a visa in Tirana?"

"It's much more complicated than that, Sophia."

He's right. It's definitely much more complicated than that. A person from this part of the world can't just easily pick up and leave and travel halfway across the globe without any complications. She realized at that moment how she, too, presupposed the things most Americans took for granted. The accessibility one experienced in her country was so vast and profound that it became easy, often effort-less. Things in countries like Albania weren't so accessible—there were always a lot of obstacles, complications, and bureaucracies. Sophia's even asking him the question was like a tease, an impos-sibility that she dangled in front of him, just out of his grasp. She felt badly about it, that she could hurt him even slightly in this way, expose the hope in his heart by suggesting it to him.

Sophia knew that Abraham had thought about coming to America—who from this country hadn't? But for him it was an implausible thing; he had never believed he would really be able to go anywhere, especially to America. He had known no one in the States before he met her; for him, the thought of going there was a daunting, intangible dream. His country has been so locked, so hidden from the world for so long, no one coming in and no one going out, that it was part of the country's culture to think this way. In America a person was tied by nothing; here, he was held down by everything.

She thought about his life in the village; such days, defined by monotony, creeping up and then quickly moving on, would have worn her out. It was a life of just getting by, asking nothing more than that you would eat that day and maybe sell some crop in the nearest town. It was a simple life, yet it exhausted people to live this way. Abraham had lived here his entire life, untouched by what existed outside Albania's borders. His imagination had always wandered beyond the village, but he never left until he went to find work in Greece. The idle lifestyle that infected Chatista was wearing thin; he knew he needed more to complete him.

Patriarchal order was manifest in the society he had been born into, and it extended to the family unit. Highest respect was paid to the eldest male of the household, the father, perhaps the grandfather. Children never questioned what they were told; they simply nodded and did as suggested. If in old age the patriarch became senile, he continued to be the force in the family—this was his right as a man, and the family respected his wishes regardless of how outlandish or even dangerous they might be.

Abraham was one of these children. There was no room for rebellion—the villagers would hear of it and question the family's integrity. There would come a time when he would be the family patriarch, and his mind would get the chance to grow senile, yet still make decisions for the family and be respected. This was a great paradox in Albania's rural culture—the mind deteriorates while gaining power.

Children were considered respectable if they obeyed the rules presented to them—never questioning their parents or contradicting other adults. They were extensions of the perception of the family, the seed that was to pass on the family name. Manners were taught in the home, and were taught so well that they seemed inherent traits.

Abraham told Sophia of a time when he was a young boy, and his father was roasting a lamb in an open pit in their backyard. Abraham accidentally tripped into the fire and burned his left hand badly. His grandfather suggested that rubbing butter on the hand would cure the burn and prevent it from scarring. Abraham's father did this for several days, noticing that his son's little hand was getting worse. Never questioning the grandfather's advice, Abraham's father continued to rub butter on his son's inflamed hand. His mother silently stood aside and allowed this to continue. She never suggested that maybe they should go to Gjirokastra and see a doctor. All this time, Abraham simply told his father that he was all right, though when he was alone, he would let himself cry his pain out. He still had the scar on his left hand — a reminder.

When he was younger, Abraham used to run down to the pond early in the morning and jump in, scaring away all the fish the men were trying to catch. He would float on his back like a fallen leaf, aimlessly moving wherever the wind would take him, keeping just his face above the water, his ears dipping in and out of it with the ripples. He knew the fishermen were talking to each other and telling him to stop jumping in the water when they were trying to fish, but he didn't hear them — his ears were submerged and he heard only the rapid beating of his heart. To be able to hear the insides of his own body thrilled him.

Abraham enjoyed his privacy, walking for hours through the mountains, surrounding himself in his thoughts. Those who knew him were aware of this and let him seclude himself. He knew the mountains better than most people in the village, leading the way when they roamed the hills and crossed through neighboring villages. Sometimes he would lead them in the dark — he knew when to follow a certain path that would eventually bring them home.

But the awkwardness of village life followed Abraham when he went to Tirana one summer to work. People knew he wasn't from the city just by looking at him. His clothing was disheveled, his hair matted, and his shoes were worn and had a permanent layer of dust. As soon as he spoke, they noticed his accent—a mountain inflection that drew out the words and made his every sentence sound like a question.

He looked lost as he walked around Tirana's town center. He walked the streets looking at everything around him. The buildings, roads, street lamps looked very foreign to him, luxuries he never had seen before. Faded communist logos stained the walls of buildings. A statue of the former dictator still stood in the center of the square in front of the old communist headquarters. People wore nicer clothes and looked well groomed compared to him, and he noticed that they didn't have dirt under their fingernails—something Abraham wasn't accustomed to.

The morning after his arrival, he started a job, found with the help of his friend, Thanasi, as a busboy at the bar in Hotel Dajti in Skenderbeg Square. The bar was very popular among the wealthy politicians and their visiting friends.

He was working one Saturday evening, and it seemed that the whole capital was out for the night and somehow ended up there. Abraham was hustling through his work, making sure that he kept up with cleaning the tables and brought the dishes back to the dishwasher fast enough so they wouldn't run out. He overheard a conversation at a table next to the one he was wiping clean. A woman mentioned to her friends that she had just purchased a new watch. He had never heard of anything that cost so much. She spoke as if it were no big deal, something expected in her world. It humiliated him to know that people bought such expensive watches, when he relied on the sun.

Abraham stayed in Tirana the whole summer, the larger world opening his small one. A man whom he had befriended had a beat-up old truck and taught him how to drive. They navigated the outskirts of the city, weaving through the streets like drunkards. While driving around, Abraham felt a rush of emotions he had never felt before. He thought about what his life would have been like, how different it would have been, had he grown up in the city.

He wouldn't be a peasant.

He remembered going back to Chatista at the end of the summer, feeling better acquainted with the world, knowledge one obtains only in a city. His friends questioned him about the capital — the restaurants, the cafes, the cars, and the girls. He told them that everything was so much different than in the village, and that they had to go and see for themselves. They looked at him differently for a while; he was something larger than they were — a phenomenon, perhaps. The novelty of their friend's living in the big city wore off after a few weeks, and they began to treat him like one of them again. Abraham never forgot that feeling, though, and thereafter acquired a permanent restlessness in the village.

Abraham's idealistic view of life didn't fit the practicality of a village. When in Tirana, he began to read books by Marx that expressed communism in theory, not the way it is truly practiced in communist countries. What Abraham didn't realize was that these theories breathed life into abstract models that didn't pertain to the human condition. Still, he always felt that the government's duty was to lead the way for its people. He became disillusioned with how communism had evolved in his country: in the end, it had become something entirely different. He didn't need to know what was happening in the capital, because he knew what was happening in the countryside. Abraham questioned why things were so, while other men, in utter hopelessness, would accept what was given to them. His unbridled mind would dwell on what could be different for people like himself, and it pained him to realize that this was how things would always be because they had been like this for centuries. Although he was one of them, he didn't feel one with them. He wanted something more and it was aching inside him. Perhaps he was out of his element and just needed to get out.

His desire to satisfy his curiosity about the world was what attracted Sophia to Abraham. Mischievous in his own charming way, his non-threatening manner yet defined him as adventurous. Sophia thought that if things were different, if he were from anywhere but here, a relationship between them could have a chance. But no change was likely; she knew she had to make the best of what was given to her — to them.

Lately, the world's perception of Albania was slowly being transformed. The country had awoken from a deep sleep in 1990, when the government faltered under its own corruption and distorted definition of communism. For years, Albania had been seen as a microcosm of the Soviet Union, loosely modeling itself on Soviet ideals, yet, looking for ways to apply its own ideology to its own people. After President Hoxha's death, the people knew that sweeping changes were inevitable. Those in political office knew that after the dictator died, there would be a power struggle, and that the winners would reap the fruits of the people's oppression more easily. Politicians began salivating when they dreamed of the unlimited possibilities for themselves, their families, and their cronies: a yacht docked on the Dalmatian coast; a villa in Italy; a garden estate in Cyprus.

For the peasants, the people who had perennially defined Albania, things wouldn't change. There would just be another politician controlling the country in very similar ways, and they had only to adjust their daily lives to survive under the new regime. A small modification here and there could make survival just a bit easier.

Once the borders opened, people started leaving quickly; they'd been starving for so long that they just walked out, heading for other parts of Europe. It was especially the younger generation who were moving away, finding work, and sending money home to their families. And when the security blanket of socialism disappeared, the change was a rude awakening for the people who stayed behind. The paycheck once had been given, the clothes received from the government, the food rationed to the public — they now had to work for all these things. The economy became stagnant, and massive inflation followed.

Abraham was decidedly an individual, yet a product of his environment. He had the energy to pursue what he wanted, but the opportunities were not there. He was hobbled by the society that had groomed him. Everything that he owned he carried within him; no material possessions, no education, no foothold. He knew it, knew that what defined him was his heart and his soul, not what he owned, where he went to school, the clothes he wore, or the job he held, as people were defined in America. Sophia had not met many people like Abraham—he was a rarity, and it saddened her that she was from so shallow a world.

The security Abraham had known throughout his childhood, the security one feels when living deep in the mountains in isolation, was a farce. His country had afforded him no security; rather, it was mere isolation laid upon him by the president's paranoia, compounded by the topography and location of the village. Albania gave him nothing more than what he already had—safety in the mountains. His own man now, Abraham began to understand this truth when he asked his father about the life he had led when he was younger, and realized that nothing had changed. Abraham was leading the same life, only in a different era. The leaders of the country during the last century had seized power, becoming the stronger ones by stripping the manhood of others. Many invested their souls and minds and lives in such men, believing that a dynamic leader would confer worth upon them as well, but they failed to realize that this undermined their manhood, their being.

In essence, they became nothing—living for and through someone else.

Sophia looked at Abraham and smiled, not knowing what else to say about the matter. The more she thought about it, the more complicated it got. He was a product of his environment.

"I love you, Abraham," she said, touching his face.

"And I love you," he replied.

The next day, Abraham saw her swimming in the pond with Athina. He walked down to the plaza to smoke a cigarette and sit with Stavro and Yanni who had just come in from the fields. Not wanting to take part in their conversation, he sat a little away from them and nodded when they spoke to him. His thoughts had been spinning since he had awakened, and he was trying to make sense of his feelings and decide what he would tell his father.

He thought of different ways he could be with Sophia. It frustrated him that there were so many traditions in his culture; that he couldn't just sweep the girl he loved off of her feet and run away. The straight path of tradition presented so many obstacles. *Maybe I should suggest that we go and live together somewhere in Europe, or even America.* But after this, he had no other ideas, no agenda. Abraham's life was an open book with a blank page looking back at him. Where would he go? How would he make a living and support her? The idea of discussing it with her never occurred to him. Abraham believed it was entirely his responsibility to make this decision — he was a man, after all. He was a man.

He decided to speak with his father that night about his feelings for Sophia and her feelings for him. He wanted to look his father in the eye and tell him that he had fallen in love with the American girl and wanted to marry her, wanted to start a life with her, somewhere. He would explain their secret; that they had been seeing each since she first arrived, and their relationship had evolved into something serious. Abraham wanted to tell his father all this, receive complete support from his father, and prove that he knew what he was talking about and must act on his feelings because Sophia was planning go back to the States soon. He needed to make decisions about what he was to do with his future wife. How were they going to arrange everything? How would she bring her belongings here if they did, in fact, plan to stay and live the peasant life?

Abraham would make sure that his mother and sister weren't

there — it was going to be just his father and him — two men talking about something of importance. He looked toward the pond and saw Sophia staring at him. She smiled. This was all he needed to make it feel right. He flicked his cigarette away, asked his friends what they were talking about, and joined in the conversation.

"Yanni, why do you look so angry? What's bothering you?"

"There's a lot of stuff going on. My head is going crazy."

"Well, there's nothing you can do about it now," Stavro told him.

"I just want to get out of here, go somewhere, anywhere. Do you ever feel that way?"

"All the time."

"Is there somewhere you want to go?"

"Where are you thinking?"

"I don't know, Stavro. North, maybe."

"Where north?" he asked pulling out his cigarettes.

"Toward Kosovo, maybe."

"I'm not going there. Why would you want to go there?"

"To get away from here."

"Bad decision. Don't do something so foolish over this. Things will get better for you. Just hang in there and keep your head low. No one knows about this. No one will know."

Abraham moved closer to them. "What are you guys talking about?" he said, gesturing to Stavro for another cigarette.

"Do you want to go to Kosovo, Abraham?" Yanni asked him.

"What would I want to do in Kosovo? Especially with all that's going on over there now."

"Yeah, you idiot. Why would you want to go to Kosovo?" Stavro asked, playing dumb.

"To get away from here — all of this. To do something," Yanni said.

Abraham stared at him.

"I'm not going anywhere," said Stavro through a puff of smoke. "I'm staying here. If I'm going somewhere, it'll be Greece — south, not north."

"How long have you been thinking about this?" Abraham asked.

"I don't know, few weeks. Come on, Abraham. You're always the one who wants to take off. Let's go," said Yanni.

"I have other things going on."

"You have nothing going on."

"We'll see," Abraham said, leaving it at that.

"What have you got going on?" Yanni asked.

"Don't worry about it. You'll find out soon enough."

"What have you got going on?" Stavro echoed. "Nothing's ever going on here."

"Just leave it. I got something going on, but just leave it alone."

This stopped Yanni's pestering. Stavro wanted to know; knew not to ask, but was intrigued. "You guys want to get a drink at the café?" he asked, breaking the silence.

"Yeah, let's go," said Abraham.

They started walking toward the cafe. Yanni grabbed Abraham's arm. "Just let me know if you change your mind," he said.

Abraham nodded, appeasing his friend for the moment.

Abraham walked home the long way — up the side of the mountain near Old Man Arseni's house. He approached the village from behind, and looked down at the tiny houses before making his way home. The sun's glare shimmered in his eyes as he walked down the path.

His father was sitting alone at the kitchen table, sharpening his pocketknife on a stone. He told Abraham that his mother and sister were at his aunt's having coffee. Abraham sat down across from his father. His father did not look up.

"Can I speak with you for a minute, Pa?"

His father scraped his knife a couple of times before answering. "Something on your mind, son?"

"Yeah, well, there have been a lot of things on my mind lately."

His father put down the stone and knife and looked at Abraham, studying his face, noticing a deep crease in his son's forehead. "What's bothering you, son?"

Abraham pulled out his cigarettes and lit one. He inhaled, and then blew a cloud of smoke between them. "Pa, I'm in love with a girl here in the village."

His father leaned back in his chair and smiled. He folded his arms across his chest in thought for a moment. "Is this girl in love with you?"

"Yes, but there's a problem."

"Are you in love with Stavro's cousin?" his father had answered his son's concern with just one question.

Abraham turned red. "How'd you know she's the one?"

"I see it in your face when you're around her, and I see the way you look at her when you're down in the plaza with Stavro and Yanni. You think I don't notice, Abraham, when my son is in love?" He paused, then asked, "Have you been spending time with her?"

"We've kept things very quiet."

"Yes, I know. I expected this of you, a gentleman."

There was quiet between them. Abraham finished his cigarette, letting his father absorb what he had said. And his father allowed his son a moment to collect his thoughts and decide what he wanted to say. He wanted to see which path Abraham would choose.

"I want to ask her to be my wife."

Abraham's father leaned closer and rested his elbows on the table. He sat quietly, looking at Abraham. Then, tilting his head sideways, he said, "You cannot ask her to marry you, Abraham." He wished this wasn't the path his son felt he had to choose. "You just cannot do this."

"You wouldn't approve of this marriage?"

"It's not a matter of approval, Abraham. The two of you come from very different worlds. What you expect from a wife is not the same as what she expects from a husband."

"But Pa, we get along fine. I've never felt this way before. I want her as my wife. Arrange it for me, Pa. Talk to her family and arrange it."

Abraham's father rubbed his face and pushed back his hair. He let out a deep sigh and said, "Abraham, they don't have arranged marriages in America. Anyway, whom would I arrange it with?"

Saying nothing, Abraham stared blankly, so his father continued, "This is what I mean by saying the two of you are too different. You don't even know the culture she lives in. You don't know how things are there."

"I understand, Pa."

"You feel you know this girl, but did you ever stop to think that she might not want to get married?"

Abraham looked up. "I know she loves me."

"Ah, my son, life in a village is different. Things aren't quite as simple in other places. Just because two people have feelings for each other, or the parents arrange a marriage for them, doesn't mean they just get married and have a bunch of kids —"

"Okay, Pa, I understand," said Abraham.

"Do you expect her to stay here and raise your children?"

"I could move to America!"

Abraham's father laughed. "Don't you think this whole country would move to America if they could? There is so much paperwork you must fill out, requests, loopholes, and waiting games — a giant bureaucracy. You don't even have a passport, Abraham. Do you think they let just anyone leave the country? Especially people like you."

"What do you mean, people like me?"

"If they let all the young men leave, do you know what would happen to this country's economy? Worse than what it is now. You can't just pick up your things and —"

"Okay, Pa, I said I got it!"

They didn't look at each other for a long time. Abraham lit

another cigarette. The room darkened as the sun dipped behind the mountains. His father reached to light the lantern on the table. "Abraham, I know you love this girl. I know she's different and perhaps exciting, something you've never experienced before. But we are too different here. She would never be able to handle the life here, a peasant's life. She couldn't survive, she's seen too much, done too much. And if you were living in America—let's just say that could happen—you probably couldn't keep up with her. You don't know how she is in America; you don't know the people she spends her time with. I know you're having fun now, but you don't know each other that well, and this is probably what's making you so interested in her. I'm sorry if what I'm saying hurts you, Abraham, but what brings two people together is exactly what can break them apart. Remember what I'm telling you now."

He watched his son begin to cry at hearing what he needed to hear. Abraham sucked deeply on his cigarette as he tried to reconcile his feelings for Sophia and his father's words.

"But Pa, I love her," he said, as tears rolled down his cheeks.

"I know you do, my son, I know you do."

Abraham sighed. "Ah, it just hurts, Pa."

"I know it does, Abraham," his father said, rising from his chair to touch his son's face.

SEVENTEEN

It was cold that day, but Abraham and Sophia still planned to meet in the night. They had by now created a secret language that allowed them to communicate privately with one another in the presence of others. It was an initial look, then a rub of the face with two fingers if they were to meet at two in the morning, and finally a simple nod of agreement — a way they had found to talk to each other about things that were theirs alone.

They were sitting by the pond. The wind chilled them, brushing the leaves of the trees, shifting the silence that surrounded them. Abraham looked out into the village, the dark sky hovering over the cottages making them appear vulnerable. They sat closely beside one another, leaning back on their hands. Abraham took Sophia's hand and gently held it. She turned toward him and started to kiss his neck, behind his ear. She snuggled close, feeling his warmth, his smell.

"The fighting is getting worse in Kosovo."

"Yes, that's what they're saying," Sophia said absently, and started to kiss him again.

"They've terrorized villages. Women and children are being assaulted. Families are leaving their homes and coming here," said Abraham. "It's unbelievable. Refugees in their own land."

Sophia stopped and looked at him. "Is something on your mind, Abraham?"

He was looking at the stars, thinking about what he was going to say to her tonight. "Do you see that eagle in the sky, Sophia, up there in the stars?"

She looked up and saw it in the moonlight. "Yes, I do." She paused, remembering, then asked, "Did I ever tell you the story of how my father was attacked by an eagle when he was five years old?"

"No, what happened?"

"He was playing outside with his friend Arseni. Do you know Arseni, the man who lives right over there?" she said, pointing at his house.

"Yes, I know him. Arseni is a very nice man."

"I've met him a few times. I went to his house to talk to him."

"What did you want to talk with him about?"

"A lot of things. I wanted to talk with him to piece together my father's life. That's the reason I'm here. And, of course, to spend time with you, now — the time we have."

He looked at her. Sophia went back to her story. "An eagle came down from the sky and tried to take him away. My father held on to a tree branch and fought with the eagle, struggling to free himself. The eagle held on to his thumb and tried to lift him. It gave up after a while."

"That means your father was the chosen one."

"What do you mean?"

"In Greek mythology, there's a story that if an eagle chooses a child to capture and feed its young, this is a special child. The eagle searches for this child, and lifts him up to the clouds. Your father was a chosen child, a special child."

"I've never heard this story before."

"The story says that this child has special powers. He can do magical things. It's sort of strange that this happened to your father here, and then he escaped from Albania and made his life in America, and now..." he became quiet, "...now I'm here with you."

Sophia looked at him. He looked into the darkness of the valley.

"Abraham, what's on your mind?"

He paused for a while, staring straight ahead. "I'm going to Kosovo to fight."

She raised herself and looked at him. "What do you mean, you're going to Kosovo?"

"I mean exactly what I said. I'm getting out of here. I'm leaving with Yanni and we're going to drive to Kosovo. We're going to fight for our people, our land."

"What do you mean, your people? You're not even Albanian."

"The Greeks think I am."

"Who? What Greeks think you're Albanian?" Sophia said tongue-tied.

"Sophia, listen to me," he said, jumping to his feet. "I have always seen myself as Greek, Greek in culture and heritage. I'm Orthodox. When I went to Ioannia to work and make money for my family, the people treated me like an Albanian. They treated me horribly, like I was not even human. They said I was the same as all the others who come to Greece, a conniving Albanian. They treated me this way because I come from the other side of the border. And the Albanians who live in this country don't even see us as Albanians; they see us as Greeks. I'm completely lost in it all. No one can name us — *I* can't even name myself. Those people in Ioannia taunted me until I couldn't take it any longer; that's when I came back to Chatista. How could I come back to my village without any money for my family when we needed it most? I'm supposed to take care of my family and I couldn't even do that — "

"What does all this have to do with you going to fight in the war in Kosovo, Abraham?"

"This is an ethnic war, Sophia, a cultural war, and it has nothing to do with anything else. This war goes back centuries; the problems here didn't start recently. If you think that, I'll tell you right now that you're wrong. We don't forget our history here like you Americans do. If I'm shunned by what I thought was my own race, the culture that

I thought I was a part of, then I'm going to fight for the Albanians who live in Kosovo. Then I'm Albanian, aren't I? Why should I care if I'm Orthodox or if I speak Greek if they don't?"

"What do you mean, like us Americans? We don't remember our history now?"

"Sophia, I asked you how people think in the States, and you told me how Americans forget the past, they just move along without remembering what happened only thirty years ago. Remember when you told me about this civil rights movement in the 1960s with the blacks and this man named…what's his name?"

"Martin Luther King."

"Yeah, Martin Luther King. This happened just thirty years ago, and now look—how do people in the States go about their lives like that, the white people? Have they forgotten what they did to a culture all those years, treating them like that? Wounds are deep, Sophia, and it's the same thing here. If you can't even see this, after your country did the same thing to another people, and just recently too—"

She interrupted him, knowing he had a point but not wanting the conversation to go in this direction. "Are you going to tell me exactly what you're thinking about? What does all this matter to you? This war going on in Kosovo is between the Slavs and the Albanians, not the Greeks," she yelled, pointing at him. "Why would you put yourself in this situation? Did Yanni tell you to do this? Did he persuade you to go with him?"

"Serbs are like Greeks, aren't they?"

"They're both Orthodox, if that's what you mean. Abraham, you're not answering my question. Did Yanni put you up to this?"

"You're not listening to me, Sophia. People in Greece think I'm an Albanian, so I'm going to fight for the cause of a Greater Albania."

"But you're not even Albanian. How many times do I have to tell you? Answer me! Did Yanni put you up to this?"

Abraham looked at her for a long time, peering into her intense eyes.

"Did you ever think about me, how I would feel?" she asked.

"I'll never forget you, Sophia. I'll find you again someday." He stepped toward her and kissed her, put on his shoes, and walked toward his home.

"Abraham, I look at you with eyes more full of love than understanding," she said to herself.

"What do you love most about me?"

"Your smile. I love the way your mouth shapes when you smile. It's more like a grin."

"That's what you love most?"

"That's what makes me happy, allows me to be free."

She moved closer to him on the schoolhouse floor, wrapped her leg over his.

"My smile. And would you like to know what I love most about you?"

"No, I wouldn't."

Sophia strongly resented his reply. To control the emotion, she took a moment to allow herself to calm down. Feeling her heart slow, she asked, "And why not?"

"Because I hope you love all of me the most. That's what I would want to hear."

Sophia went back to Kosta's house and lay in the dark and quiet bedroom, that conversation in her mind. She wanted to rid herself of this disintegration—of the relationship and of herself. Her mind dwelt on all that was between them, recalling Abraham holding her, making love to her, the arch of his spine, the sweat on his chest. She tried to shake off these thoughts, but it was useless. She had lost her connection to the self-control she had believed was hers. Sophia ached all over, her hands clenching on her stomach, her legs stiff. "He is leaving," she whispered into the darkness, and a sharp pain shot through the top of her head, like the time when her father's doctor had phoned her from the hospital.

He told me he was leaving. He is leaving me. He has left me.

"Could you live in another country?" Abraham had asked her once. She remembered his question and her answer: "Yes, I could."

And now he had left her.

Sophia squinted at the ceiling, seeing nothing. She lit the lantern that sat beside her bed. Athina's back was toward her. Sophia looked around the room. The shadows of the furniture surrounded her, towering over her, their images looking as if they had somehow gained life. She stood on the bed, raising the lantern closer to the ceiling, trying to see the cracks in the paint. She stood, swaying the lantern side to side, trying to discern the image that rested on the ceiling.

The cracks had spread, touching the corners of the room, surrounding her with all that defined this world. Moving toward the walls, the cracks forced other elements, foreign ones, to become entangled in the ceiling's mess. Sophia switched the lantern to her other hand. She stared at her image on the wall, the lantern's movement rocking the shadow that was supposed to stay still. Her arm extended, her legs apart, balancing herself on the bed. Her silhouette was large, shadowing the wall almost entirely. She lowered the lantern and stood facing the wall, both arms extended, looking at herself, at the image against the wall, the cracked paint on the ceiling.

After a while, Sophia blew out the light and remained standing on the bed in the gloom, the cracked paint above her. She lowered her arms to her sides, the extinguished lantern in her hand.

"Leave it, Mama. I got it, I said. Just leave it."

Abraham was in the kitchen with his mother. He grabbed the water container from her hands, lifting it above his head and onto the shelf. "You're going to break your back if you try lifting something this heavy."

Her son was acting different this morning, edgy and short.

She didn't know what was wrong with him. "Do you want me to boil you some eggs, Abraham?"

"No, Mama. Just leave me alone."

She looked at him. "Did I do something to you?"

"No, Mama. Just leave me alone," he said again.

She got out of his way as he went to the refrigerator. He took out a couple of eggs and placed them on the counter. He found a pot in the cabinet, poured water into it, and lit the stove, then leaned against the counter, waiting for the water to boil.

His mother was looking at him.

"What?" he said to her. "What?"

"What's the matter, Abraham?" she asked softly.

"Nothing, Mama. I'm just having a bad morning." He looked around. "Is there any coffee?"

"I could make some for you."

"Why isn't there any made? There's always coffee ready in the morning," he said, knowing she was the one who made the coffee.

"I haven't made it yet, but if you'd like I'll make some right now," she said, taking the coffeepot from the cabinet and pouring water into it.

He slid the eggs into the boiling water, sat in a chair at the table, and then leaned over, rubbing the right side of his head. His mother came over and softly stroked the back of his hair. He sighed, and the tears that had been waiting began to fall. His mother's hand on his head told him it was all right, that the tears were supposed to come out now—it was safe.

He wrapped his arms around his mother's waist and held on to her as he cried. She continued to stroke her son's hair, her fingertips feeling its silkiness, the shape of his head, the warmth of his neck, the sound of her son crying into her apron. She cradled his head in her arm, letting him rest his head on her hip, feeling his warm breath through her clothing. She continued to stroke Abraham's hair until he had let out everything he needed to.

"I have to go to the fields, need to start early today," he said after awhile, getting up and wiping his face.

"What about your eggs? Don't you want to eat something, Abraham?" she asked, trying to avoid talking about whatever was making him feel this way.

"No, Mama, you can have them—you can have anything you want," he said to his mother, because he could not. "I'll see you in a little while," he said, and walked out of the kitchen.

He met Yanni in the fields. Yanni's father and a few other men were way ahead of them.

"Where have you been? We've been out here at least an hour," said Yanni.

"Bad morning. Don't want to talk about it, either."

"Okay," Yanni shrugged.

Abraham stretched his arms over his head and sighed loudly. "Ah, another day in the fields."

"Another day," Yanni said.

"Well," Abraham said, "I guess we should get to work."

"Let's go, my friend."

They walked toward the group of men in the valley, trying to catch up. Abraham lit a cigarette and offered one to Yanni.

"Hey, I might take you up on that offer. You remember, about going north, maybe Kosovo? Were you serious?"

"Yeah, I was serious."

"Well, I might take you up on it."

"Just let me know, my friend," Yanni said, flicking a bug off his sleeve.

Eighteen

Everyone is born with a trait that stands out from all the other traits he possesses. A person can be identified by this particular characteristic, and the world can judge that person based upon this trait, thinking its judgment complete and accurate.

Sophia did not have this outstanding trait. There was no one element that could define her, yet most people didn't know this. When people met her for the first time, they automatically identified the trait that was most apparent at that time, her mood in the moment. But judging Sophia by her moments would yield a false characterization — a limited view of her.

The characteristic in Sophia that perhaps identified her best was her understanding that people behaved the way that they did because they were reacting to something else. Everything in the world was linked together in some way, she thought; no phenomenon that just floated in the air. People were born like smooth clay, and what they were exposed to in life molded them. And over time, they tended to react rather than act — emotions seeming to find their way.

She often wondered if this understanding was something to be thankful for. If she didn't have it, would she be better off? Would she just accept what people did, and feel no compassion, remorse, or resentment? Maybe it would be better not knowing that there was such a link in every encounter. Perhaps she would have handled

Abraham's going off to war a little better. She wouldn't have known the real reason behind his decision, and wouldn't have felt so helpless. Because she did know what he was thinking, she felt she could have helped him see things another way, make him understand, perhaps, that this was not his war.

Sophia knew that Abraham was going to Kosovo because he was reacting to everything he had encountered in his life — the economic debacle in his country, his working in Greece, his restless frustration with village life. He took these things personally, as if someone had done these things to him intentionally, or if God put him on this earth to punish him. But Abraham reacted differently than anyone she had ever met. His reactions were more sweeping — revolutionary, perhaps. He held things inside for so long and then suddenly exploded, changing the direction of his life with one bold decision. She wondered sometimes if he ever thought things through completely before acting upon them.

Abraham was beyond all the men in the village. Charisma exuded from him. His movements were graceful for a mountain man's, how he walked, how he held a glass, how he sat down or shifted his legs while sitting, the way he used his hands when he spoke — it all seemed like an art. His warmth was effortless, too. It was natural for him to show compassion toward others, a vulnerability to which people were drawn, but which some had taken advantage of. And his eyes commanded attention. They were large and slanted a little in the corners, and, in contrast with his olive skin, a stunning blue that seemed illuminated from within. His eyebrows formed a small ridge above his eyes, shading them, giving them mystery, and making his face appear sympathetic. His lashes, long and dark, seemed to stretch out forever.

Abraham's upbringing was typical of a peasant's. He was born in the village, his mother, aided by her sisters, birthing him on the living room floor. Right after he came into this world, his aunt gently washed him in a bucket of warm water and swathed him in a blanket. He attended school only until he was thirteen, thereafter farming with his father, and knowing at thirteen what was expected of him, of his life—he would farm the same plot of land his father farmed, and, like his father, grow old tending this plot of land. There was nothing more to a peasant's life—his life.

Abraham had been torn between leaving his family and acting on the passions in his heart. He felt responsible for his aging parents and for taking care of his younger sister until she was ready to wed. When Abraham thought about leaving to fight in a war that he was uncertain of, a wave of selfishness swelled in the pit of his stomach. These were the times when he noticed his parents' aging even more—their weathered skin, the deep cracks on their hands, the missing teeth, the gray hair conquering the brown. His father sometimes walked crookedly, his back muscles stiff from physical labor. Late at night his wife would massage his back to loosen them as he lay on the living room floor.

But what settled Abraham's decision was the burning memory of working in Ioannia. Humiliated and disillusioned by the way people had treated him there, he felt that his only outlet, his ticket to the world, was to fight in Kosovo. This, he would say to himself, will be a steppingstone to something great.

And the fact that he could not be with Sophia any longer? This in itself had repercussions that were beyond his comprehension—and hers.

Restless and bored by the slow pace of mountain life, Abraham left the village to work, but always found his way back home—finding a job in the city and then coming back to the village became a monotonous dead end in itself. Nothing in this cyclical, mechanical routine progressed. Torn away from civilization, accustomed to exile and the predictability of village life, the monotony of day-to-day living can deteriorate souls.

It is a misperception that warfare instills a sense of predictability in people—the villager's world becomes even more arbitrary when warfare arises.

When Abraham spoke of this boredom to his friends, they never understood his desire to do something different, to find something that simply made sense. They told him he shouldn't have watched the television when he was working at that bar in Gjirokastra a few summers back — it made him think beyond mountain life and what was expected of him.

Sophia's heart was heavy, and the top of her head, where she had her worst headaches when things were troubling her, throbbed, consumed with how Abraham was going to manage. She knew he had no idea what he was getting himself into, fighting someone else's war, thinking it was or ever could be his.

Sophia remembered traveling in Spain with Vanessa and a few other backpackers they had met in Pamplona on the way to San Fermin. Arriving on the first Sunday of the festival, they walked from bar to bar, drinking sangria until they found themselves in the central square with its large statue, the one people jump off like doves, and the people below catch them. Everyone feels as if they know each other, though no one really does. Each jumper puts his life in the catchers' hands, the entire scenario a matter of trust. But there must be a tiny element of uncertainty as the jumper floating in the air for a moment, relying on these people, then falling into their locked arms.

That was how Sophia felt now.

It was more difficult than ever to get a minute of Abraham's time. The news spread through the village like summer wildfire. While out in the fields, Abraham's father told a friend that his son had told him the night before that he and Yanni were leaving for Kosovo, but he didn't mention to his friend the conversation he and his son had had about the American girl not long ago. The friend told his wife, and it was then that the wildfire took off — several of his wife's friends came over for coffee that afternoon, and Abraham's plans were revealed. By the end of the day, the entire village knew, and probably some from the neighboring village, who occasionally met shepherds from Chatista.

Abraham went about the days not noticing the gossip that coursed over Chatista's valleys and farms, doors and windows. He filtered the world out of his mind, directing all his energy to leaving in a few days. But there was one person he was afraid to speak to, or ever look at. His mother had been very upset since his plan to travel to Kosovo had been broadcast by the *kotsoboli*. He knew he had to discuss it with her, confess his thoughts to the woman who had given him life. He approached his mother in the kitchen.

"Hello, Mama. Can I talk with you for a moment?"

She turned from the counter where she was slicing potatoes, her eyes tired, red, and worn.

"Why? Why, Abraham? Why do you think you need to go and fight in this war? We've had too much heartache here. Don't start this pain for us again," she said to him.

He looked at her, wondering which pain she was speaking of. They had had to bear so much in their lives that he couldn't decipher which she thought of at this moment.

But he told her this was something that he wanted to do, needed to do. The restlessness he had been feeling for so long was taking its toll on him.

"Is this what it's all about?" she asked him, her mind wandering back a few days, when he was in this very room, crying into her hip. "You feel bored living here? Is that it? You can go to Tirana and find work there if you feel bored in the village. You don't need to go to Yugoslavia."

"But Mama, Tirana is having its own problems now. Thousands of people are coming to Albania. You can't find work in the capital now — there isn't any, and even if there was, I don't want the work. What you're telling me, it doesn't make any sense, Mama."

"Then why don't you get married? Your father can arrange a marriage for you with a girl in Chatista, or from another village if you don't like any of the girls here. If you're restless, start a family, raise children, maybe it's time you settled down, but don't tell me this is something you need to do. This is not our war."

"How can I explain it to you," he said, more to himself than to her. "I want something else in my life. I don't want this, any of this," he said, waving his hand across the kitchen.

"Then what is it you want, my son?"

There was no explaining to his mother, and he wasn't being completely honest with her, either. He sat with her and tried to calm her, saying again that he could not go to Tirana to find work, nor did he want to get married and settle down with a girl from the village. He didn't have it in him at this moment to tell his mother that he had found love with a different girl, a girl who would have shocked her. It would only have added to the confusion, and he was emotionally exhausted at this point. He wanted to be rid of everything that he had to deal with right now, walk away from all that he knew.

His mother pleaded again and again, begging him not to go. But Abraham told her this was something he needed to do for himself. He felt numb. The pain inside him had been so great that his body had shut down; he was just going through life's motions.

Abraham hugged his mother as she cried on his shoulder, placing his hand on the babushka that covered her head.

Old Man Arseni sat on his front porch and breathed in the life that was his. A throbbing pain came into his mind, forcing him to flinch and twist. He shifted his legs underneath him, and breathed the air.

He thought of Sophia. Where her life would lead. What course she would finally follow. How fortunate he was to have met his old friend's daughter. How he now held on to this connection to his past, a path to his future.

He rubbed the back of his neck.

"Nonta, do you want to travel to Gjirokastra with me tomorrow? I have to go to the city and find a very special gift for my future wife."

"I will go with you, Arseni, and help you find something for her."

Old Man Arseni smiled.

The wind shifted, blowing hard through the village. His glass of water fell, spilling onto the ground. He moved his feet to avoid stepping on the broken glass, then slowly got up and began to pick up the pieces.

Sophia was walking toward his home.

A few days after telling his father he was leaving, several days after he had told Sophia, Abraham and Yanni set out for the highlands. Abraham had told his father the truth, that he was going to fight for the Kosovar Albanians and that he would return home someday. His father knew that his son wanted to fight in the war out of desperation. There was no solution to the problem Abraham was faced with, the situation he had brought upon himself by meeting with Sophia during so many nights. This desperation that consumed him came not from the atrocities happening to the people in Kosovo, but from the restlessness in his heart.

He wanted what he could not have, someone he could never have. He felt foolishly childish for believing that he could marry Sophia and raise children, perhaps here in the village. It embarrassed him to have thought that she would want to stay here and raise a family. That he had even suggested the idea to his father made him certain that his father thought he didn't know any better. When he thought about this alone at night, smoking a cigarette on the porch, he would bury his face in his hands, ashamed of his thoughts. Looking out into the darkness, this humiliating memory tortured him, creeping up on him repeatedly. When he got to the moment when his father told him his relationship with Sophia was impossible, he shook his head, trying to jar it loose from his mind. The way his father had stared at him when he said those words haunted him. To think that a girl from America would want to live in Albania, that maybe he could move to the States and make a life there. How naïve some people could be.

Abraham knew that he was leaving to fight in a war that wasn't his, but he never told anyone. His heart wasn't in this war, but his time here was done. There was nothing left for him in the village. He had tried to make something of his life, but there was nothing tangible for him to hold on to. Having lost hope, he surrendered himself to fighting in someone else's war, a cause he knew very little about. All because he couldn't have what he wanted, and would fight in a war he did not want. This was his reasoning, his justification.

When Abraham told his father he was going to Kosovo, he didn't need to explain why. His father saw in his eyes that what he was saying and what he was thinking were two different things. He sensed it in the quickness of his son's voice, his eyes staring at the floor, the wavering thoughts he expressed. Abraham never raised his head when he told his father he was leaving. And his father wished Abraham would look up, just for a moment, to see his devastated look as his son spoke those words.

His father sighed and shook his head when Abraham told him, feeling that he had just lost his last son, thinking that perhaps he had failed as a father — failed to give his son more opportunities, more optimism. A greater vision. His son's vision had become limited and resorted to warfare, and he took it as his own fault that a young mind would think in such a way.

Abraham left Sophia with myriad thoughts churning in her head. For the first time in her life she felt hopeless about something she really wanted. There was no clear solution to making it all work, but her emotions insisted that things could, somehow. So the old story goes: a girl will try anything to make the impossible happen — even turning a blind eye to the cruelest obstacles on the horizon.

Sophia said goodbye to Abraham like everyone else did. She waited in the line that grew in the plaza, the men shaking his hand and wishing him well. "Always go down, Abraham, never go up," his neighbor told him, the mantra of mountain life. The women hugged him as if he were their own, perhaps because his mother wasn't there — she couldn't bear to see the actuality, the fact, of his going.

Yanni was already in the truck, compelled by conscience to be there at this moment. He had said his good-byes quickly, avoiding the usual lingering talk. And the question of why.

Right after Athina, it was Sophia's turn. She looked at Abraham quickly and gave him a hug, held him for a moment, but not long enough for anyone to notice anything more between them.

"Be careful," she said to him, not knowing what else to say at this point.

He looked at her, his eyes telling her everything she needed to know. "Thanks, Sophia. You take care of yourself too."

Sophia planned to stay in the village a little longer, spending the days with her family and having long talks with Old Man Arseni. She was going to travel to Greece, ultimately to Athens, and then return to the States. For the time being, she would live the life of a peasant, emotions worn to exhaustion.

From the time Abraham had told her he was leaving for Kosovo to the moment he actually left Chatista, something within Sophia had escaped. She became certain that he was leaving the village, his resolve etched in stone. She knew there was no changing his mind; this was what he wanted to do with his life at this moment. It was strange how similar they were in this way, their lives filled with vividly defined moments that existed detachedly, rather than as a natural progression eventually reaching some distant goal. It became clear to her that people who come from this part of the world had to lead their lives in this episodic way — things just came at them, and they had to address what was in front of them at the time.

Sophia felt a momentary loss, then a sense of failure, and finally a calming resolve. Her body just let go, allowing things to take their natural course, come what may. The relationship had taken its course, regardless of how wrong she felt it had gone in the end. If she could have had it otherwise, things would have been different. But these were moments when her soul gathered its strength and integrity and tried to move on to the next episode in her life.

What else could she have done? Was she supposed to stop Abraham, tell him she loved him and take him away back to the America with her? Was she supposed to grab him by the shoulders, shake him, and insist that he was making a mistake by going to a war that didn't belong to him? She shook her head at these thoughts. She had come to Albania to go back to her father's roots, hadn't she?

After telling Sophia that he was leaving, Abraham had become distant with her. He was already on the mission and couldn't be distracted. He didn't ask her to meet one last time in the schoolhouse — for him their last time had come and gone. He had to focus, travel to the north and join the militants on their way to support their people. As far as she could tell, he was already gone. Still, there were moments when she wanted to grab hold of him and shout that he was out of his mind for wanting to fight someone else's war. She couldn't understand why he was doing this, however noble it was. And she didn't care who would see her plead with him and realize that they had a connection, a history between the two of them.

The night he told Sophia he was leaving, she could see the anger and resentment that flowed in his blood. She listened when he talked about leaving, hearing him speak more and more quickly as he got deeper into his story, recounting history that didn't belong to him. She told him that he needn't see himself the way others insisted on seeing him, but the pain in his heart, the anger and the humiliation, compelled him to.

"How useless it is to hold on to people or life. The unpredictability of it burdens me. I can't escape the feeling of total loss. I can't plan or control my life, have no idea what my future is. I can't even understand the predictability of circumstance that assures someone of a future. Who knows what is to become of me, where I'll be ten years from now, or next year? I can't come to grips with this. I follow a path of impulse, of surrender to all that surrounds me."

When he talked like this when they met by the pond, it scared her. His words reflected how scattered his thoughts were. Sophia tried to get more insight about Abraham from Stavro, another perspective on the man she thought she knew. She tried to be subtle, but curiosity overtook her, and she pried more and more until Stavro asked her, "Why so many questions about Abraham?"

"I don't know. I'm just curious, I guess."

He looked at her a moment. "Something came over him in the past couple of months. He hasn't been himself lately."

"What do you mean?"

"He's not thinking straight. He's been like this ever since you got here," he said, smiling.

"Me? I have nothing to do with Abraham," she said.

"I know. I'm just teasing you. But I notice he acts different when you're around."

Sophia's eyes began tearing. Stavro looked at her again, then approached her and rested his hand on her shoulder. "Why are you crying? What's bothering you?"

She wiped a tear that clung to her eyelashes. "I'm crying about a lot of things. How people deal with life here — does it make any sense to you? I'm crying because I know that this won't be the end of it. You talk about things as if they were expected, Stavro. You really have no opinion about anything, do you? Is this how you live your life?"

He listened, knowing she had been shocked by the story of the pregnant girl who had killed herself because of not knowing what else to do. He knew that she was saddened by the fact that Yanni and Abraham had just left to fight a war in the north, while he remained behind, calm and silent. But Stavro didn't know about Abraham and her. He wondered how her life was in America; everything was probably easy for her. The immediacy of life and death in the village was alien, he knew. What was she to think of the people who live here, who wash the bodies of loved ones, make certain they are dressed properly and placed in the coffin made by relatives, and then bury them with their own hands? What was she to think of young girls who kill themselves because they know of no alternative? What was she to think of the desperation of people who know only one way, desperation that had become an intrinsic trait?

Gently lifting Sophia's head by her chin, Stavro looked at her. He swept his thumb across her cheek, slowly wiping away the tear that was making its way down her face. It was the gentlest touch she had ever felt in her life. Her eyes filled with tears as she let him do this for her, wiping away the pain she had inside. He didn't say a word, just looked at her, holding her chin.

Sophia walked through the village, down to the plaza, and on toward the pond. She was making her way to Old Man Arseni's house, wanting to have another talk with him. She saw him leaning against the railing of his porch, his hands holding the rail. Sophia saw on his face the agony of what he had just experienced. Old Man Arseni leaned over the railing, the pain taking too much from him. Still crying, he straightened, shaking his head to shake off the memories that haunted him.

Sophia watched him a little longer, staying out of his sight. Then she turned around and crept back into the village.

Nineteen

They drove off early in the morning, taking the rocky road that hugged the edge of the mountains. It felt like the journey took forever, but they passed the time with small talk, and stopped to buy figs in the neighboring village, then continuing on. They seemed to be standing still in time, driving through village after village that had evolved pure and pristine, untouched by the outside world, and growing from experiences that were uniquely their own.

"How long to Tirana?" Abraham asked.

"I'd say about four and a half hours," Yanni said.

"And from there, how far to High Albania?"

"Let's see," Yanni said. He puffed on his cigarette. "A couple of hours from Tirana."

They drove in silence, hearing the rattling of the engine and the wind whipping through the windows, which were opened just a crack to let out the cigarette smoke. The weather shifted, and the air became crisp as the previous night's moisture evaporated.

"People never get tired of fighting for their land, especially here. Wouldn't you say?" asked Yanni, breaking the silence.

Abraham was thrown by this question, but he answered. "I don't know if things can ever be resolved here. People don't care how much their country is divided, as long as they feel their autonomy."

The former president's paranoia was evident as they drove to the north. Civil defense bunkers resembling concrete mushrooms dotted the fields, plentiful reminders of the fear that was embedded in this country. *Providing for and protecting from are two different things. But who was out to get you?*

They arrived in Tirana in the early afternoon. Wanting to relax for a little while and get something to eat, Yanni drove the car around Skenderbeg Square and found a place to park near the old City Hall. Abraham awoke as the car stopped. As he climbed out of the car, he saw, painted on the side of the building, "We shall break the blockade of imperialism and revisionism."

"Why didn't you tell me this when it happened, at least before we left?"

"I don't know why, Abraham. I didn't tell anyone," Yanni said, looking at the road ahead.

"Do you think no one will find out?"

"God, I hope not. Abraham, promise me you won't say anything when we go back home. You promise you won't?"

Abraham pulled his cigarettes out of his shirt pocket. He took one and tossed the pack onto the dashboard.

"Were you in love with Eleka, Yanni? Did you tell her you loved her?"

"Yes, I told her."

"Before she told you she was pregnant?"

"Yes."

"And after she told you?"

"No."

"What did you tell her then, Yanni?"

Yanni told Abraham what he had said to the girl.

"Aaaah!" Abraham yelled, leaning his head back, his hands on either side of it. Yanni turned toward him quickly.

"You told her you didn't love her? What the hell is the matter with you, Yanni?"

"I panicked. I didn't know what else to say. I didn't want the baby—I can't have that in my life now."

"Do you think she could've handled it by herself? Obviously not, don't you think?"

Yanni didn't say anything.

"Obviously not, right, Yanni?"

Yanni still didn't say anything.

"Answer me, Yanni!"

"Apparently not," Yanni said.

"Is that all you can say, 'apparently not'? How could you do this to her? We've known Eleka our whole lives. How could you do this?"

"I don't know," Yanni said softly, the words catching in his throat. "Look, I feel bad about it, I really do. I don't know why I'm confessing it to you, especially now."

"Because it's safe, you fool, that's why. We're gone now. You don't have to face it anymore."

"That's not it."

"No? Then what?"

"I don't know," Yanni said, looking out the car window.

"'I don't know.' Good answer, *my friend*."

They drove along the road, headlights leading the way along the winding mountain. They sat, each in his own silence, Abraham smoking his cigarettes while Yanni shifted himself in the driver's seat, leaning toward the door. He looked at Abraham, trying to figure out what to say to him.

"Look, Abraham, I regret what happened. Really, I do. I felt horrible, but you have to understand where I'm coming from. I didn't know what to do. I just panicked. It's not my fault Eleka decided to...do that."

Abraham said nothing for a moment, just stared out into the darkness, smoking. Finally, he turned to Yanni. "Listen to me. I want you to answer me truthfully—no more lies, no more secrets.

Is this why you asked me to go with you to Kosovo? Was Eleka on your mind when you asked me?"

Yanni stared at him, not saying anything, glancing quickly at the road and then back at Abraham.

"Okay, I got it," Abraham said. He sighed, his mind racing.

"We could turn back and go home, you know," Yanni said.

"We're not turning back. Forget it. Forget everything. Let's just get to Kukes and find a place to sleep. In the morning we'll ask around for the KLA camp," said Abraham, shifting in his seat.

"Gjaku I Shpriskur. Gjaku I Shpriskur, Gjaku I Shpriskur," the patriarch of the house chanted. "Our scattered blood. Our scattered blood. Our scattered blood."

They brought the body into the house with no first-floor windows, thus affording them protection from the avenging family. They sat on the floor; the body lay on the bed. The children grabbed at their knees and bawled. The adults sat in disbelief, shame, and outrage, staring at their lifeless loved one. *Why did this happen to Paul? Why did they have to kill him?*

The boy was leaning against the wall, rocking back and forth, his arms locked around his legs. "This will never end, it will never end," he said, dropping his head onto his knees. He rose to his feet and ran out of the house.

Gjaku I Shprisku — a vendetta between two families. The internal struggle remained and the anger never went away. The clans that existed before communism were forced into twentieth-century nationalism, only to revert to clan society again after communism had collapsed.

A sinking feeling in Abraham's chest made his heart feel heavy, hard for him to swallow. He placed his hands behind him against the wall, raised himself, walked out of the room to the kitchen, and out the front door to look for the boy. There was quiet in the village. The reddening sun was low, lying on top of the mountains, and a calm was in the air as if the wind, too, had been satisfied. People were hiding in their homes or paying their last respects. Revenge had been honored. Hold on to the family honor; cleave to your dignity.

Eagles flew overhead, announcing their presence with loud calls. Abraham walked toward the barn. Poking his head inside, he found the boy sitting on an old tractor, swinging his feet back and forth. Abraham sat next to him and didn't say a word. The boy stared at the floor, not acknowledging Abraham's presence. Abraham turned toward the boy and stared out the window, watching the setting sun.

"I can't take this anymore. I never know when someone's going to get killed. I never thought they would shoot Paul. I never would have thought that. Things just happen for no reason here — it's out of control."

"Come on, it will be all right. Things will get better," Abraham said to him.

"How?" the boy asked, crying. "How will they get better?"

"I don't know how they get better, but they just do."

The boy shifted in his seat, staring out the same window as Abraham. He then looked at him.

"What's your name?"

"Abraham."

The boy told Abraham his name.

"Remember what I'm telling you now," Abraham said. "Remember this moment because it will remain with you for the rest of your life. Break this cycle. Don't desire revenge on the family who did this to yours. You don't want anyone to feel the way you do now, right? Remember this hurt you feel at this moment. Don't become what you hate."

The boy turned and looked at Abraham.

"Paul is your brother?" asked Abraham.

"Yes, he's my brother. My only brother."

Abraham's memories of his brother surfaced in his mind. He saw himself, his past, in this boy.

"Will you do this for me?"

The boy nodded.

"Please remember the words I say to you now," Abraham repeated.

"Gjaku I Shpriskur. Gjaku I Shpriskur. Gjaku I Shpriskur."

Mr. Lekaj walked to the olive garden that belonged to the Vulaj household, and sat against one of the trees. He pulled out his pipe and a bag of the tobacco he grew in his own garden. Taking off his sweater, he placed it behind his head.

There are things a person doesn't say in front of certain people, but sometimes, a person forgets and says the wrong things in front of the wrong people. And this can grow into something much larger. An offense against honor is repaid in blood.

Mr. Lekaj leaned back against the olive tree and shook his head as he reflected on what had happened. The story kept replaying in his head, and he realized how foolish it was and how easily it could have been avoided. *But what do I know? I never avenged my own brother's death and now I'm a dishonored outcast.*

There hadn't been any vendettas in their village for some time, but the feud between the Dukajin and the Kastrati families had started up again. *Foolish men,* he thought. *It will continue now, and probably get worse. If I told them to stop, this village would think I was behaving dishonorably, again. They couldn't possibly understand. The people already think I'm a* cakalloz — *a person who acts crazy. But I didn't lose my mind; I just put it on a different level.*

Mr. Lekaj looked out at the dark sky, the shining moon above him. He relaxed and smoked his pipe, thinking about his family. *How I wish I still had my brother close to me. These men, they kill one another for the honor of it.* He saw a light in a second floor window of the house, and silhouettes behind the curtains. A shadow walked back and forth, hands waving in the air, a gun slung over its shoulder. *Spilt blood cries for the family to avenge.*

He let out another puff of smoke and shook his head.

BOOK IV

Did I dream this believe
Or did I believe this dream
Now I can find relief
I grieve

—*Peter Gabriel*

TWENTY

No one knew that Abraham and Sophia had been meeting at night; they had kept it to themselves well enough. Kosta would question sometimes why his American cousin was staying in the village so long. "Most people who visit want to leave after a couple of days. But you, it seems you wouldn't mind living here," he joked with her.

"I wouldn't go that far, Kosta," she said, and then left it at that.

The forbidden act of meeting with Abraham excited Sophia, increasing her expectations of the relationship beyond what actually existed or what she should hope for, but the power of it was beyond her control. Lying in bed at night, sleeping next to Athina, she thought of Abraham. Her desire to see him increased all the more because she couldn't see him on a given evening unless they had planned it. She couldn't roam the village after midnight and tap on his window. If someone were to see her, that would be the end of it; she would have to leave the village. But Sophia was consumed with memories of the previous time they had met, regardless of when that had been. She dreamed of him, and awoke in the morning with Abraham her first thought—all because this was not supposed to be happening.

But that was over now.

Later in life, Sophia would look back on her relationship with

Abraham and think it hadn't been real; it was just a dream that she had met a man named Abraham, whom she crept to meet in the night, have long talks with, and love. The combination of the remoteness of the village, the brief time she had spent with him, and how abruptly their relationship had ended made the images in her mind surreal. The reality became a fantasy that she replayed often, a collection of memories that began to stray from the truth. The entire trip to Albania felt unreal, because it hadn't been with her father, had turned out to be entirely different from the way it had been planned. Her thoughts kept returning to Abraham, the schoolhouse, and the last time they had met at the pond, when he told her he was going to fight in Kosovo. Only the events that occurred in the Balkans, which were again to have their place in European history, compelled her to believe that the time she had spent with him was a reality that had come and gone.

Sophia was unaware that Old Man Arseni knew of her relationship with Abraham, that he had known since the first time they met by the pond. She thought it was their secret, and thought she was clever in meeting Abraham late at night. But Old Man Arseni didn't tell her that he knew, and he never would have if she hadn't broached the subject on his porch one day. When she began telling Old Man Arseni about the relationship, he didn't act surprised, as she expected, because he already knew. Only later would she figure out how he'd known who she was the first time she visited him.

Sophia sat in her usual chair across from Old Man Arseni. He knew right away by the look on her face that something was bothering her. He went into his house to throw away the broken glass he held, and returned to talk with her. She faced him, her arms resting on her legs, her hands fumbling with one another. Hesitantly, she began confessing her relationship with Abraham, the whole story, pouring her heart out to this stranger whom she had befriended simply through his connection with her father. She told Old Man Arseni everything: why she was attracted to Abraham, that voice that she could have listened to forever; how they agreed to meet at the pond one night, and had continued to meet frequently thereafter. She told him how secretive they'd been, and that it tortured her, and she had no one to talk with, no one to help her understand the circumstances swirling around her. The days she spent in the village had become a burden on her emotions. She felt she should rid herself of the reminders that were what defined a village. And this meant that she believed her time was done here, too.

She told Arseni that she had known that Abraham was planning to leave for Kosovo, but didn't stop him, and felt that it was her failure, because she knew his thoughts and his dreams and the pain he felt, the restless anxiety, and the obstacles silently resting between them. All of this, she now said to Old Man Arseni, was her fault. She kept talking as Old Man Arseni listened, his hands clasped in his lap. She even divulged her relationship with William, how different her relationship with Abraham was, and all the excuses she used to keep herself from a normal relationship. She felt that she was finally open to life and love, and had found this with Abraham, a man from her father's village.

And now it was gone.

When at last Sophia became silent, Old Man Arseni looked down at the ground, hesitant to say anything.

"I'm sorry to bother you, Arseni, but I feel somehow that I can talk with you about this."

He asked her why she wasn't comfortable talking with Athina.

"I don't want to discuss this with Athina. I don't think she would understand. I just don't know what to do. Part of me knows that nothing could ever have come out of this relationship, and tells me to just move on, but another part tells me that what I'm feeling is right, and something good could have come of it." She paused for a moment. "It's too late, though, isn't it?"

He looked at her and shifted his legs. "It may be, because he's gone and you're going back to America soon. What do you want, Sophia? Tell me what an ideal situation would be. You're telling me how you feel, but not what you want."

The clarity of Old Man Arseni's question confused Sophia. She was too torn to answer.

During their nights in the schoolhouse there had been plenty of talk, their cultural differences surrendering to the confines of the room, diminishing in the candlelight. They talked about all the things young couples talk about, and looked at each other the way young couples should. He told her of his truths and lies, and she told him of hers. Abraham lay with his head resting on her, relishing the new closeness of her body, his hands on her stomach, on her hip. The first time he confessed his dreams to her, he wasn't looking at her face.

"Sophia," Old Man Arseni said, "you have spent a short while here, but more than most who visit. People were surprised that you stayed this long, but your reasons are clear now. Abraham will be back from Kosovo and he will come back to this village, I believe this. You have to make a decision if you want to find him again, and find him here. If you want something for the two of you, there are possibilities. You just need to give things a chance, let them take their course. Right now, there's nothing you can do. But you have to understand why he left to fight this war; you have to understand what he's thinking — but I think you do."

"And?"

"We have lived our lives in these mountains the way we can, as we like. Things don't always work out as we want, but we know what and who we are. There is a massive backlash in this country: people are very angry and resentful about things not being as they were promised."

Social conformity, mass production, and technology, Albania had none of it; Fascism, Nazism, communism, Marxism, a precarious newborn democracy juxtaposed with full-fledged corruption — the country had all of it. Sophia wondered how people could live in a country where minds became dulled because everyone knew what to expect, where their lives were already planned, and the lives of their children and their children's children. A people sealed off from the rest of the world to "preserve" them, a lost society, the illusion of a "peasant's paradise" existing in the shadows of lies, of someone's opportunity to fill his pockets just a little bit more.

Old Man Arseni continued: "As we became aware of the world beyond our borders, our sense of progress quickly dwindled to nothing. We realized how far behind we were, and how the rest of the world was moving forward, becoming modern, technological. The factories and stores, the goods sold all over the world, the ships docking at our ports with crates filled with things for us, all were owned and made and sold by others. We looked at these things with awe. And there were the investors too, eyeing the pristine coastline and the virgin beaches of the Adriatic, seeing the nearby shores of Corfu and the possibility of ships sailing to Italy. 'Europe's last untouched shore in the Mediterranean,' they would say. 'How nice would it be to build on this coast.'

"Illogical borders created by world powers who thought somehow that language and religion and a common history did not define a nation. Memory is one of the greatest gifts, but memories are more than fond mementos in the mind; they portray painful experience, a picture of things that have fallen, forever lost to war and conflict. Such memories force people to recall them, dragging their minds through the dirt, carrying the burdens.

"Those who must submit to tyranny are distanced from the simple notions of freedom. Tyranny thrives on pretense, appearing triumphant in public, but tragic in private. One of mankind's problems is our inability to acknowledge wrongdoing and own up to what we have done. When a nation goes down, Sophia, its name is often forgotten."

Old Man Arseni paused and looked out into the valley. He shifted himself in his chair, making his body a little more comfortable. Sophia stared at him as he looked at the valley, the mountains beyond, the village stretching to the left, and the invisible border that lay to his right. He sensed the great paradox of this village — its unusual location relative to the dynamics of this region. If someone were to step into this place at random, he would think it was just another isolated mountain village, but it was more: this village had a history that helped define the problems that always existed and continue to exist.

"Sometimes I feel like leaving and going someplace where history doesn't know me and I don't know it," Old Man Arseni said to her.

Sophia found herself in a world of extremes, torn by conflict and contradiction. Yes, she was right, the village existed in isolation, but not from strange influences, and this village echoed the problems happening throughout this part of the world. A cultural uniqueness endured in these mountains, a sober country but with vivid idiosyncrasies, and an integrated view of life and its obligations. A whole generation was sealed off in a quest for purity, and the world outside thought of Hoxha's regime as a social experiment. Sophia knew it was real because she could see its effects. She had come here to venture far from the familiar. Her life, if she wanted, could have a routine, a sort of structure, a bit of organization that would allow her to plan if she ever wanted to. She knew what to expect of the world and what to expect each day she awoke and got out of bed. The opportunities were lying idly in front of her. But it was different here. The emotions that these people experienced, and the political shifts and unexpected turns of the globe were so unfamiliar.

They did not know what it felt like to be bored.

"I think I already knew that," she said to him.

"You probably did," said Old Man Arseni.

"Come what may, Arseni?"

"Come what may," he repeated.

Sophia stayed at Old Man Arseni's house for a while and sipped coffee. She calmed herself by talking with him about other things, trying to free her mind of Abraham even if it was for a short time. The sun dipped behind the mountains and the day slowly became night. Sophia finished her coffee and flipped her cup on the saucer. She thanked Old Man Arseni for talking; his advice and opinion had become invaluable to her during this episode of her life. As she was about to leave, she asked him not to mention what they had discussed to anyone. He picked up the two saucers and, smiling, said, "Whom would I possibly tell?" and walked into his candlelit home.

Sophia was alone. She stepped off of the porch and walked away. The way her father had explained Chatista, the way she pictured it, was right in front of her. It had not changed since her father told of the images still in his memory the day he died. She understood why people here were so angry — Abraham's anger was nothing new.

"Mama, what ever happened to my father? Why isn't he living with us?"

"Your father is in Constantinople, Nonta. He left the village to find work when you were just two years old."

"Why Constantinople?"

"Because Constantinople used to be the central city of our world, the capital of the empire that used to stretch into these mountains."

"How far away is Pa?"

"Very far, I'm afraid."

He looked down at the ground. "Is my father ever coming home? Will I ever see him, Mama?"

"Yes, he will come home one of these days."

"When?"

"I don't know, my son."

"You don't have any idea, Mama?"

"I'm sorry, my dear, I just don't know. But I promise you he will be back soon enough. And then you will meet your father."

"I will wait for him."

She smiled at her son and held his chin in her hand, looking into his face. "You have your father's patience, Nonta. This is what I see in you."

Twenty-one

Abraham's mother sat at the table, hands clasping a coffee cup. The cup was small; it looked like part of a doll's China set. She looked around the kitchen, noting how it could have been transformed into any other room — a bedroom, a sitting room. Nothing concrete defined the room as a kitchen: there was no sink, no stove attached to the wall. She cooked for her family every night at the portable stove in the corner of the room. The cabinets that her husband built held all her utensils and plates; the cabinets were the only distinctive element here, something her husband had built that transformed the room into a kitchen.

How much longer would she cook for her family? Now that Abraham had left, what about her daughter? She would have to be married in the next few years, or at least promised to someone. Then it would be only her husband and herself. She would still have to cook, but to cook for just two, did she need all the pots and pans and utensils in the cabinets — these cabinets that her husband built for her, the family?

Her throat tightened at the thought. Abraham's leaving was just the beginning of the changes in her life. She was the one who was always left behind when her family went away. She always stayed, and took care of the house, made sure everything would be just as they had left it when they returned. Now Abraham had gone. Was their any justice in this world? Why was she always the one who had to carry this burden, to feel the pain, reawaken the happiness once again within her when they would return? Now that Abraham had gone to Kosovo, how was she supposed to handle all of this? When was it going to end for her?

And whom was she supposed to speak with about how she was feeling? Her husband? This was something he would not expect from her. He might look at her oddly and question why she was thinking this way. He would tell her that this was the life they were given and that she must adapt to what surrounded her. The momentum of life does not accommodate anyone. "God only gave you as much as you could handle," he would say to her. And she would try to believe him.

Her emotions overwhelmed her and she began to cry. Perhaps she would try to talk with her friend Penelope. Yes, she would go to Penelope's house tonight and confess her thoughts, and maybe Penelope would understand how she was feeling. She would sit and have coffee with her friend and ask what she thought about Abraham wanting to fight in someone else's war — her only son, gone.

She heard giggling outside on the porch, her daughter coming into the house with a friend. She wiped her face with the edge of her apron. She didn't want her baby to know how she was feeling — it would be too much for her. Her daughter walked into the kitchen, her friend following behind. She quickly put a smile on her face.

"Hello, love. Are you girls' hungry? Come sit down. Let me make you something to eat," she said, walking toward the cabinet and reaching for a pot.

After feeding the girls, and sitting with them and talking about the sweater her daughter's friend was knitting — the things young girls talk about around a mother — Abraham's mother decided to visit Penelope to release some of her anxiety. She walked quickly up the path toward Penelope's house, passing a village man who was walking down.

"Hello, Maria, and how are we today?" he asked, taking off his hat and holding it against his chest.

"Oh, I'm just fine," she replied, not stopping, forestalling inquiries about her son, adding "Thank you for your concern," as she continued up the path.

She knocked once and entered. Penelope was in the kitchen, slicing potatoes, when she heard her front door open.

"Penelope, are you home?" Maria called out from the living room. Penelope walked into the room, wiping her hands on her apron.

"Maria, I didn't know you were coming over. Is anything wrong? Are you all right?" she asked, looking at her friend.

"Everything's okay. I just needed to talk to you about everything—about Abraham. I just need to talk," she said, desperation in her voice.

Penelope took her friend by the hand and sat her on the couch. "I'll be back in a minute. Let me make us some coffee and we'll talk."

Alone in the bedroom, Sophia could have a few moments to become the other person she was. From what the village knew of her, she was the American girl visiting relatives who had lived here in these mountains forever. She was the one who had come to Albania, the first relative from the States to do so, and they liked her just for this simple reason. She was the curious one, the adventurous one who wanted to know her kin.

But Sophia needed time alone to be herself, the American girl who had her studies and her social life and her private life. They would never see this side of her, wouldn't understand it. Telling her aunt that she was going to take a nap, she would close the bedroom door behind her and lie in bed, eyes wide open, staring at the cracks in the ceiling and noticing how they had gotten longer and more elaborate since the previous week. She would lie there and allow her body to collect itself for a few moments, look around the room, and suddenly realize how far away from her world she really was. The strangeness of the furniture, how everything was positioned in the room, as if someone had placed the lamp, the beds, the small table in the corner with precision, a purpose. This made her uneasy, made her wonder what she was doing there, feeling trapped in a strange land and couldn't get out. In solitude, she would wonder whether her father had felt like this when he had first come to America.

When she forced away the strangeness she felt, these thoughts quickly faded from her mind. Relaxed, she got the moment of clarity she had hoped for when she closed the bedroom door. The worn feeling of the village, the conversations that surrounded her, the old smell in the air, and the certainty of mountain life that made her feel this way. But in the back of her mind there remained the thought that this was just a visit to her family. Her real life awaited her on the other side of the globe, the life that she was born into and lived. She reminded herself that this was a journey into the unknown, a familiarization with things that were unfamiliar.

Sophia went back into her own world, back to a time when she was with William, near the end of their relationship. On his bookshelf he had placed a new photograph of a recent ski trip with a few friends. He stood at one end of the group of men, all arm in arm, smiling for the camera. *He never mentioned to the class that he'd gone away for the weekend.* She looked at the photo. Standing at the end was typical of William. He never wanted to be the center of anything, but wanted to be a part of it — an observer. This was his shyness, the aloofness that had once intrigued her. He had his friends, his life, but he always seemed to be enjoying his solitude. Had his wife been there with him? Was it a couples' weekend, and someone suggested that just the men be in this photo?

The photograph typified the parts of his life they never discussed. Sophia didn't ask him simple questions like "How was your weekend?" She was afraid of hearing something she might not want to know. Her knowledge of William was limited, which helped keep her curiosity alive. She would only learn about his ski trips from photographs that suddenly appeared in his office, like seeds that had been blown from a tree and begun to grow unexpectedly.

That there were no attachments between the two of them made him want her more. He knew he could say what was on his mind and she would understand that it was just for the moment. What he said to her while they were together had no lasting meaning, no intimation of what could be. There was nothing to look ahead to, nothing beyond the words that fell from his lips, no potential permanence, no strings, no promises, no expectations.

Though he helped define it, William never probed into Sophia's personal life, perhaps because he didn't want her to ask any questions of him. She accepted that this was how their relationship would be. Anything they were to find out about each other would come from observations, perceptions, and newly placed photographs around the office. He noticed her looking at them from the corner of her eye as she talked about her thesis, but he never offered any explanations. He would distract her by walking toward her and kissing her neck, crawling on top of her.

On her bed in the village, Sophia would doze for a while, falling asleep on her back and waking up on her stomach, the smell of sheets that had been in a trunk for a long time against her face. She would look around the room, wonder where she was for a moment, then roll over on her back and look again at the cracks on the ceiling. She fixated on these cracks; she could have sworn that they were getting longer every time she looked at them, that just moments ago, before she had closed her eyes and fallen asleep, they had been a bit smaller.

She gave her body some time to wake from her nap, lying on her back for a few minutes. She heard voices in the living room—her aunt and a woman who was upset and crying, talking quickly and gasping for breath between long streams of words.

Sophia walked to the door and put her ear against it, listening.

"I remember when Abraham's father took him out in the field and taught him to ride a horse. He must have been about eight years old the first time he got on a horse's back and held on to its mane. I was washing clothes near the garden and watched them walk in circles at first, his father holding the rope around the horse's neck and then letting go and Abraham riding all by himself, his little legs dangling at the animal's sides, his feet keeping his balance.

"I remember the look on my son's face. Although he was a young boy, he had a look of determination, like he wanted to learn how to ride the horse, like he *needed* to learn how. This seriousness was bunched up in his face; his eyes focused on the task at hand, taking quick looks at his father to see whether he approved of his riding. And when his father believed Abraham was ready to ride alone, he let go the rope. That expression on Abraham's face, trusting that if his father believed he was ready to ride alone, then he must be, and he rode with such confidence and grace, like a warrior.

"I knew my son was growing up to be a responsible boy, one you could count on to get something done. He helped his father with the farming and even helped me around the house sometimes, which is very unusual — you know this, Penelope. It didn't embarrass him to hang the wash on the line to dry. All that mattered to him was that it needed to get done and I needed some help. He was a charming boy. Our friends, Penelope, would ask what had come over my son, and joke with me that he was from another world when they saw him helping me around the house. They would ask me what I was feeding him, wanted my recipes to see if I cooked anything differently that made him so unusual. And I would tell them that he was just born this way, that I fed him nothing more or less than what they fed their sons. They never believed me.

"Abraham was an imaginative boy, too. He always had stories in his head, and ideas that most people would never in their lives think of. I don't know where he got this restless mind that was always wandering with new thoughts and visions. He would come up with the strangest ideas, and some of the kids would make fun of him for thinking of such things. One summer he made charts for how many times and how long he peed each day. I'm not lying to you, Penelope; this is true. The chart had a row across for the number of times each day and columns for how long he peed that time. Each chart was for one day and he would keep them together by weeks. When he showed these charts to the boys here in the village, they thought he was weird and that a spirit had got into him. He didn't know that this was unusual until the boys started laughing at him. I think his mind was just too smart for its own good. He got bored and wanted to analyze something, I guess. Needless to say, the pee reports began and ended that summer.

"It was very difficult for my son to come back to the village when he went for work in Ioannia. He came back as a broken young man, Penelope. He felt defeated. He didn't know how the outside world thought of Albania. I think we realized this after the fall of our government, what people said about us, how far behind we were as a nation. When the world was allowed into the country for the first time in decades, we realized that we needed a lot of work, but I didn't know and I still don't know. This is what my husband tells me when he comes back from the city. And I never told my son these things my husband told me. I let him learn of them on his own.

"I raised my son to be a strong man, and to be a source of strength for others, yet sensitive to their needs. I wanted him to understand people's desires and to respect those around him. My husband and I imposed this more when our eldest son passed away. We put a lot of responsibility on Abraham. We expected both of our sons to be strong, but more so when Niko died. But I never in my entire life believed Abraham would think to fight in someone else's war. A war that doesn't even make a difference to him, and he wants to go to fight among men he doesn't even know. What does this war have to do with our village? Can you find an answer, Penelope? I certainly can't. What is my son thinking? What have I done to deserve this?

"And I'm upset that Abraham spoke of this with his father and didn't want me to be there when he told him. It hurts me that he couldn't trust me in this way, that he thought I would get too emotional. I'm his mother! He knew I would try to change his mind. That's probably it. He knew that if he spoke with me first, I could have changed his mind. But he's gone now, to fight someone else's war. Does he even know this is someone else's war? Will they ask him why is he there to fight? My son Abraham was a strong son, a good son. He did a lot for his father and me. And for his little sister — you should have seen him with her, Penelope, he was gentle and kind and sweet to her — he protected her.

"I hope he was okay. I hope he had enough warm clothes, extra socks. I hope they fed him enough. Abraham had a good appetite. Yes, Abraham was a good son. He always did the right thing in his life. My son always knew right from wrong, always.

"Oh, Lord, Penelope!" Maria gasped, her hand over her heart. "I just realized that I'm speaking about my son as if he were forever gone."

Penelope put her arm around Maria's shoulder. "Oh, Maria, what are we to do? There's nothing we can do, only pray."

"I pray all the time, Penelope. I don't know what else to do." She looked around the room, taking a deep breath. "My son is gone. My last son."

"Don't talk like that, Maria. You'll see him again. Watch, he'll be home before you know it and he'll be fine, you'll see," Penelope said, trying to reassure her friend.

"I hope so, Penelope, I hope so."

They sat silently. The sipping of coffee and the tiny clink of cups returning to their saucers, the slight scrape of a saucer on the wooden table were the only sounds in the room. Sophia leaned her weight against the bedroom door, resting her head on the rough wood, allowing her mind and body a moment's ease. After a while, the women's voices jolted her out of her trance. They were talking about other things now, not about Abraham.

Sophia thought it might be a good time to walk out of the bedroom. "Oh, hello, Maria. How are you today?" she said.

"I'm okay. Just living life, day by day, you know…" Maria said, her voice tapering off into the air.

Sophia smiled at Penelope, who gave her a slight smile back. An awkward feeling settled among them, as when two people abruptly end a private conversation because a third has entered the room, presumably with no idea of what was being discussed. Sophia had heard everything, but acted like she hadn't. She stood looking at the women and they at her. Maria fumbled with her napkin, took a couple of deep breaths, and tried to hold back her tears.

When she noticed Maria breaking again, wanting to let it out but not wanting to do it in front of her, Sophia said, "Penelope, I'm going to go find Athina. It was good to see you again, Maria. I'll see you soon."

Maria smiled at her and wiped her cheek as Sophia stepped out of the house.

Because there was nothing else to do, Sophia and Athina took a walk around the village. It had been quiet lately since Abraham and Yanni left. No one was the same anymore. It seemed like life had been sucked out of the world. People didn't know what to say, didn't know what to talk about when they went down to the plaza every evening to socialize—trying to bring a bit of normalcy into their lives.

Sophia would remember these moments when she would take a step back and observe her surroundings. How melancholy the village had become since the recent departure of two of its boys. It was clear. It made sense to her to acknowledge the fact that Abraham and Yanni leaving was everyone's concern. And it was disheartening because they were to define the village in the future. They were the ones to hold the village together, keep it in existence, allow life keep its momentum. Their young men leaving. What next? What would happen to their world if their young were leaving for *wars*? Was this how it was supposed to be at this moment? A changing event that was going to define them and their existence — did they know the significance?

These were the moments that Sophia would lock in her mind and keep in permanence.

Athina wanted to show Sophia the old schoolhouse. Coming to it, they walked inside. The few overturned desks still sat on the ground; the badly stained chalkboard still leaned against the wall underneath the window. The open space in the center of the room was unchanged, the space where Sophia and Abraham lay each time they met, the space they had created for themselves. The wax was still on the floor from the candles that were their source of light, along with the moon, creating a border around the blanket where they would lie down.

"I never showed you where I went to school," Athina said. "We all went to school here. We had one teacher for all of us. She taught math and history and grammar, and she was really smart, smart enough to teach us at all grade levels."

Sophia's emotions swept over her when she stood at the place where she had sat and talked with Abraham not long ago, but she pretended she had never been in this room before, looked around as if inspecting it for the first time.

There was nothing left.

They walked toward the pond, the tall grass scraping their legs. The sun was low in the sky as they reached the pond's edge.

"People still fish here. This is where we get most of our meals."

"Are there a lot of fish in there?"

"Enough to feed our whole village," said Athina.

Sophia turned and faced the village that rested on the edge of the mountain. The houses were falling apart, held together only by stones, mud, and a little cement. Athina told Sophia that not much had changed in Chatista for a long time. "Nothing changes here, really," she said. They sat near the pond and watched the sun sink behind the mountains. Finally, Athina asked the question that had been on her mind since Sophia's arrival in Albania.

"Sophia, I always wanted to ask you, what do Americans think of our country? What do they say about us?"

"Well, Athina, most Americans don't even know where Albania is; they couldn't even point to it on a map."

Athina looked up at Sophia in astonishment, unable to believe what she had just heard.

Old Man Arseni saw two figures sitting on the grass near the pond. He watched them for a moment, straining his eyes in the dim light to see who it was. He sat like this for a while. The figures blended into the night.

He thought of his wife, of how much he missed her. He thought of his old friend, how he had recently been given a new connection to him. An unexpected gift handed to him at this moment.

He was no longer the young man he had once been. A hardness surrounded his body, defending him from the elements that chase and taunt those who are vulnerable. He saw this as a gift from God, a necessary tool for him to survive. The character of a person that once was remains deep in the body. Occasionally, it tries to reemerge, and somehow Old Man Arseni could control this. He studied the world, studied the village, studied himself. He found ways to adjust to the world and how it presented itself to him. He knew no other way than this pattern that guided him through life.

He has seen in Sophia's face the pain he had felt so many years ago when he returned to the village from the capital. He recognized the pain and empathized with it, but he did not pity her.

She has released from herself what lurks within. She has given herself to all that was impossible, and she will continue to do so.

TWENTY-TWO

Like many movements, what begins as a political ideology ends up as an individual's obsession. His passion is awakened by the people's belief in him; that he can make a change for the nation, bring back its days of honor, dignity, and hope, and bring power to himself. Gradually, he distances himself from the people and strengthens his grip on his credo, breathing it, feeling it, absorbing it through his skin. He becomes a stranger to the people, an odd figure standing on the pillars of an ideology that is already gone and bellowing the rhetoric of hope, change, and prosperity — security. The people don't know he is not one of them, or if they do, they say nothing, and force themselves to believe in his words, which penetrate the air and enthrall those who are desperate for this hope that he talks about.

When this leader goes home and lies in his bed, he tries to invent new ways to beguile the people even more. He needs them to catapult his passion to the next level. He twists and turns in his bed, becoming more zealous as he dreams up new schemes. He pulls his hair and stretches his legs to the edge his bed, all the while painting a devious smile across his face.

He continues his charade of compassion and self-determination for the people, and instills hope into them. He will make them his — he knows this. With these thoughts in mind, his obsession grows and strangles him. All the while, the people believe in him, grabbing onto hope.

They will become his.

Such a leader's obsession perverts the way the political ideology is defined. The terms change; the rhetoric becomes slightly more self-serving. The people begin to look at each other, seeking reassurance from one another that what they are thinking is not bizarre, that others are thinking it as well. But no one is speaking aloud; the people put smiles on their faces, and have hope, and yearn for the security their leader is talking about. They ponder and wait for the changes that were promised. They don't give up on the ideology or the man, knowing that anything is better than what they have now. But now the people define the ideology much differently than their leader does, as if two completely different ideologies exist simultaneously.

This leader has now become a dictator and begun to play by his own laws, his own beliefs, his own agenda. He has captured the people—they have become his. No longer do they control their minds, their destiny; perhaps they never have. He has instilled his beliefs in them, believing this is best for them, for the nation, and for himself. He believes that he and the nation are one and the same.

The people become resentful and hold onto hope carelessly. The expressions on their faces become more worn and more overt. Their hearts and souls become heavy and exhausted. Gradually, they begin to talk to each other, their minds slowly opening. They realize that what they have been feeling, and their confusing thoughts, are communal, agreeable, strengthening.

The people question the dictator, not openly, but in the privacy of their homes. They talk openly with each other and begin to remember the political ideology, and what it still means to them. They realize, at last, that the principles they embraced, that they loved and hoped for, have taken on a different meaning, a different existence. The dictator senses that something isn't right with the people, but reassures himself that everything will be all right and makes certain that his officers are still by his side, believing in him. Though uneasy and somewhat tense, he hides this side of himself from the people; he does not let on that he has begun to descend into paranoia. All is well.

The dictator knows he must maintain order now, must not allow the people to move against him. He begins to tighten his grip on the nation, the land, the people. He senses that he may lose control. He massages his obsession as he hardens his will. *I will not be destroyed. I will not be overpowered.* And his obsession begins to control how he thinks and eats and sleeps and hears what people are saying—the lingering talk in the night. He orders those who begin to speak out against him killed, and he questions if his officers are still loyal to him. His circle becomes smaller and smaller as his paranoia grows. He orders an officer, the questionable one, executed, to instill fear in those around him, to show he's still in control. He justifies his actions by calling this officer an enemy of the state. And he does all this with a smile on his face.

But when the people begin to talk out loud, a dictator has lost everything. Their hope is gone now, their faith in their government is gone, and their anger sets in. He has already lost at this point. His mind becomes chaotic: *What will happen to me, my ideology, my land?* He thinks about his mission, his obsession—what he must do to preserve his power and control.

There may come a time when the people win the battle against the dictator and redefine their political beliefs, and everything that they wanted can be had as they first adopted this ideology. The dictator's words become gibberish in their ears, and the sound of angry voices fills their hearts. The people take up their hope once again. All is well.

"With everything that happened yesterday with our Paul, we apologize for forgetting our manners, neglecting to offer you *buke e kripe e zemer* — bread, salt, and heart — we never asked you last night, where are you boys from?"

"We're from the south."

"Gjirokastra?"

"Farther, about an hour south of Gjirokastra."

"That's pretty far from here. Are you boys from Epirus?" he began to probe.

"Yes. We're from a village just on the border, the southernmost village before the border."

The man said something to his uncle in Albanian, in the Gheg dialect. Abraham and Yanni couldn't understand, as they were familiar with only the Tosk dialect.

"What are you doing out this way?" the man asked, returning to the Tosk dialect. "Are you trying to find someone?"

"We're going to Kosovo to fight in the war. Do you know where the KLA camp is from here?" said Yanni.

"You two are going to fight in Kosovo?"

"Yes."

"Why? If you don't mind me asking."

"Because we want to fight for the Albanians who live there. We want to help."

Again the man said something in the Gheg dialect. His uncle responded and nodded his head.

"After we have breakfast, we can take you to the camp. But first, we must have breakfast, as you are our guests," the man said.

"Thank you, sir," said Abraham.

"Yes, thank you very much. You've been very kind to us strangers," Yanni added.

"As you are our guests," the man repeated.

The survival of a people depends not on cultural superiority, but on awareness of the common good. So, when the fighting stops for a time, and the people's will to fight is drained, they can sit and reflect on what has happened and what they have won. Sadly, when the older generation become physically exhausted, they pass on the hatred and prejudice to the younger, so there might never be a time when two fighting peoples can say, they've had enough, and really mean it, and pass on this resolve to their children. This calm, when it permeates a soul, can persist indefinitely, soothe people's ruthless passions so they can reflect on the cruelties they have inflicted, and wonder why it must be this way. *Is the soil we fight over really worth the blood spilled on it?*

If this serenity might exist, even for a moment, the region would come to a utopian tranquillity, but this could never happen in this part of the world — there are too many differences; too many demands that the enemy, the other, will not meet. To settle demeans and dishonors the significance of their beliefs, their actions.

But if remorse were to overtake the urge of retribution, and empathy run freely for a while, then perhaps both peoples could regret all that has been lost in their battles, and that might compel them to feel and act differently. And the young could learn from this, breathing it, absorbing it through their skin, touching it with their fingertips. The world could be flooded by empathy, and compassion could flourish and pass on to future generations, lingering in the air, a collective inheritance, and "Where the sword is, there is religion" might be heard no more.

To renounce violence, a person must at one point have been part of the violence. One who has made the transformation and adjusted to a more tranquil life is someone who has carried out terror in the past. To dehumanize others through ceaseless interrogation can only be perpetrated by the permanently damaged. The conversion that takes place is a cry for redemption.

Some live a solitary life in the mountains, trying to diminish the memory of the atrocities they have committed. Others are forced into exile, or leave the country willingly, knowing what could happen to them were they to remain. Very few step forward to acknowledge their sins and simply beg forgiveness. Those who have done so have stepped out of their bodies for a moment and observed their deeds from another perspective.

The current war was an extension of the region's past. There was a different road now, yet it took the people to the same destination. The distant government had governed them, unaware of the demographics of Kosovo. But the people wanted their rights at any cost, and they fought for their rights, for acknowledgment of what they were. They had nothing to lose, anyway—their world had gotten worse than they ever imagined it might.

The population in Kosovo had increased. Women bore more children because of the expected loss of their sons during war. It was the family's duty to carry on its name; the Kanun had told them they must honor this. The government called this "ethnic genocide," and would see to it that an end would come of it.

The mothers of sons who went to fight the war gave up hope as soon as their sons walked out the door to fight for the people, because it was their duty, their honor. A mother would give her son a memento from their home so he would not forget the family, a part of his history, because it would become history. She would neatly fold a babushka and place it in his shirt pocket, or give him a charm that would help ward off evil spirits. And he would kiss his mother and tell her not to worry; he would be back as soon as the fighting was over. And everything would then be all right.

During the beginning of the war, refugees poured through the Albanian, Macedonian, and Montenegrin borders. People who were too old to fight, or those who had fought previous wars, knew what was to happen to their homes. Soldiers organized the mass exodus with methodical precision. Trains awaited the refugees, pointed outward, like an explosion from the nexus of the universe. The soldiers were ordered to get them out, but their officers were never given orders to make sure families stayed together during the evacuation. Humanity was lost along the way during this war.

Men and women were separated when the soldiers invaded a village. Gunshots were heard throughout villages, adding to the fear. The men were massacred, lined up against a wall in a deserted home, begging for mercy. The women suffered slow, humiliating deaths, ravaged continuously, many murdered thereafter. The soldiers gave other women the opportunity to live, thus further deteriorating family unity: a man leaves his wife if she has been raped — though alive and breathing, she is now one of the walking dead.

Sophia was tired of those who supported war. She couldn't understand a person's will to fight and kill for a piece of land, something she has never seen before. Previously, she had thought that people's will to hold onto their land was a noble and dignified expression of the heart, but things around her were becoming surreal and she no longer knew what to think. All that she experienced and witnessed and heard was too much. She knew that other motives fueled this war. Terror was the first thought that came to mind. Terror in a village in this part of the world was like smoking a cigarette — everyone would experience it eventually.

She remembered reading about war in history class. How distant and clear and safe war seemed from a book. How remote the atrocities were, the sounds of fear, the foreboding silence in the night, the unexpected and the unknown.

The sound of birds flying through a village after it has been deserted.

The ideas and discussions Sophia was experiencing now confused her. No longer was there the structured text, the precisely formed sentences and paragraphs that expounded the meaning of a war for a history course. War isn't that organized; war climbs all over, unaware of its strength and effects.

Sophia rested her head on the pillow and tried to nap. The bed was small and its springs old, but she liked this bed because it seemed to hug her; it comforted her, wrapped itself around her body. She felt protected. She thought of Abraham again, wished for him. He was gone forever, she knew. She hadn't the strength to let her mind wander to the moments she had shared with him—she would have been consumed.

The setting sun was about to dip behind the mountains. Everyone had gone down to the plaza to talk, leaving Sophia alone in the house. She looked up at the ceiling and noticed that the cracks had grown more, had now spread themselves out like a spider web. If someone were to softly touch the paint, several pieces of it would fall to the floor, leaving the ceiling entirely bare and vulnerable.

Only men who are dead see the end of war.

"You like to be left alone, don't you, Arseni?"

"I don't think people leave me alone, Sophia. I think I leave people alone."

"Why do you enjoy the solitude so much?"

"I don't feel like I'm alone. The thoughts in my head keep me company. I can have a conversation anytime I want with whomever I want, and I can choose any subject I want, creating the dialog as I see fit."

"But you have conversations with me."

"Our conversations are different. You don't live in the village. You don't have permanence. You're like the wind—the only thing in my world that is invisible yet real. Dialog is always better among strangers. You can paint the picture however you like. You can allow yourself to be perceived in the way you feel is best for you, comfortable for you."

"People here would disagree when you say the wind is the only thing that's invisible yet real. You don't think of God when you say this, Arseni?"

"You are the only thing—person—whom I see as invisible yet real."

"How can I be invisible if you can see me?"

"You are leaving soon, and you will be invisible to me, gone like the wind. You will be in my memory only."

"Should I say good-bye to you?"

"That isn't necessary. You should never say good-bye to me. I'll have you in my memory," he said smiling.

"How often do strangers come to Chatista?"

"Not often."

"Is this how you knew who I was when I first came by to visit you?"

Old Man Arseni looked at her.

"No."

"How did you know who I was?"

"I just knew someone. I knew you were my old friend's daughter," he said quietly.

"You have a lot of secrets, don't you?"

"No more than anyone else."

"But your secrets are much more complex, aren't they?"

"My story is complex, like everyone's who lives in Albania; everyone's who has left Albania."

His mind seemed heavy with the thoughts that never left him alone. Sophia wondered if he ever forced them to stop and, perhaps, go away. It was such a burden on him. He had the sadness of someone who has lost something that defines him. He missed his wife. He had to have been pretty lonely to think it's all right to be in company with just his thoughts. Memories have consumed him for so long time that his imagination and reality have meshed into one. The two have become a constant, no filter between them, like an open door that swung freely back and forth, allowing him to transfigure everything into a single vision.

As she stood still and waited for the days to pass by, knowing the time to go home was nearing, Sophia reflected on the life she had witnessed and the life she wanted to go back to for the sake of going back to a life, another life, her life.

Twenty-three

thina carried the two buckets filled with cow's milk slowly up the hill. Until a few years ago she hadn't been able to carry two buckets without losing her balance and spilling milk, but carrying two instead of one made her job a lot quicker and less burdensome. It wasn't that she loathed making two trips from the field to her home, carrying the milk through the house to the kitchen where her mother would then boil and pour it into containers. She didn't mind that—she could have made as many trips necessary. It was because it was so early in the morning that she found this chore difficult. But soon enough, when her little brother became old enough and strong enough, she would pass on this responsibility to him. She had already resolved this and mentioned it to Sophia.

Athina noticed that Sophia had been acting strange of late, a little distant and much less talkative than usual. It had always been Sophia who wanted to sit down in the evening and have a chat about anything. "Hey, cousin, let's make some coffee and talk," she would say, out of nowhere. And Athina would always make the coffee and sit with her on the couch or on the front porch. But over the last couple of weeks Sophia rarely greeted her this way—the two had coffee together only once. Some evenings, Sophia would go into the bedroom and lie down and look up at the ceiling. She had done that from time to time, but more often lately. Seeing Sophia staring at the ceiling, Athina felt compelled to ask what she was looking at, or thinking, but she never did. Athina knew that her cousin liked to be left alone sometimes, even if she had never said so. And it was on such evenings as these that Athina really missed Sophia, because she was leaving soon. She had grown used to her cousin living with them in the village, even if it was only for a short time. She liked having Sophia around, someone to talk with, someone she could spend time with. Although they had little in common, mutual curiosity made them capable of long talks together. Sophia always wanted to know more about Athina than Athina had ever dreamed of asking her why, but she did once.

"You always ask a lot of questions, Sophia, but aren't you bored with what I tell you? There's not a lot going on here in the village. You must have so much more where you come from, so much you've seen in your life. How can you be interested in what I can say about Chatista? Tell me more about America, what it looks like and how the people are and what you do for fun. Tell me, Sophia. I want to know what your life is like there."

This was when Sophia became self-conscious about asking Athina so many questions, poking around in her cousin's life as if she were a specimen, a science experiment that needed more research. So Sophia told Athina a little more about America and herself, but again their conversation turned around and she found herself asking Athina about the village and the family.

Here, Sophia felt like she had shed a layer of skin and allowed herself to breathe for the first time. Something inside her had just awoken to the realization that her life in America was mundane, that it left out many people and places and ways of life. She had never known the village lifestyle before; she had read about it, and listened to her father talk about it, but had never actually seen it, experienced it, tasted it. It was all new to her, livelier and more entertaining and heartwarming. The people were more interesting. They had stories to tell, memories to unfold, and their faces told the stories locked in their heads, showing her the world through their eyes. She would look into their eyes and they would look back, saying nothing with their voices, but their eyes looked as if they were trying to get their stories out, but didn't know how or to whom. And here they had found someone who was asking them questions, interested in their world.

Athina didn't know what to expect from her cousin who was coming from America to visit. She was nervous before Sophia's arrival, thinking that village life might scare her, that she'd want to leave as soon as she got there. But this didn't happen, and Athina appreciated that, and it made Athina love her cousin more. "I love you dearly," Athina would say to her. "I'm so happy that you're here, that you came to visit us. You don't understand what this means to me. I love you dearly, Sophia," Athina would say.

She wondered what had prompted Sophia to come now, and alone. She never asked, but the question was always in the back of her mind. There was more to the story, something that wasn't being unfolded for her. Maybe one day she would ask, one day when, perhaps, Sophia would come back to Chatista and visit again.

Athina had already been spoken for, to a young man with whom her family was very close. He was one of the few who hadn't left Chatista after the country's borders opened, so Kosta and Penelope had a slim selection from which to choose. Not that they would have chosen otherwise — they knew he would be able to take care of her. Kosta and Penelope sat down one evening with the young man's parents to discuss the arrangement and what was expected of either family. All went smoothly for them, but Athina confessed to Sophia that it was awkward after her parents told her that they had arranged for her to marry George, because she had known him since they were kids, and they had watched each other grow up. George was several years older than Athina, and this fact alone intimidated her. Yet they were to be married in two years, when Athina was at the "appropriate" age to start having children. When she found out George was going to be her husband, she felt differently around him, a formality and maturity that she felt she needed to present to him, to her family, and to his. There was no more playfulness; that was forever gone. She was going to be his wife, and she needed to behave like a wife—responsible, loyal, maternal. An enormous sense of responsibility swept over Athina, and there was no turning back. Most girls in Chatista felt this way. Responsibility was simply handed to them—there was no gradual transition to being a wife and mother. Whenever it was decided for daughters to marry, their carefree lives as they had known them were abruptly over. The comfort they felt living under their parents' roofs, in the homes where they had always lived, was gone. They were forced onto another family, and were not prepared for it.

Sophia wondered whether it was already arranged for Abraham to be married to a girl in Chatista or a neighboring village. He would have never confessed this to her even if she asked; people didn't talk about such things in the open—it was considered bad luck to talk about something that was supposed to happen in the future. One day, when they were talking about Athina's anticipated marriage, Sophia asked her if Abraham was arranged.

"Abraham? No way! There never was an arrangement for him. People think he moves around too much, he's an adventurous one. A girl's parents want stability, consistency. In most people's eyes, Abraham doesn't have these traits." She paused for a moment. "Why do you ask?"

"Uh, well, like you said, I can't see him being married. I was just asking because he's Stavro's close friend."

Abraham tried to open himself to the world and to his ideas, avoiding the confined track of a peasant's life. When he failed in his attempts to create something different, away from farming and shepherding, he was thought of as unstable. But he had never wanted to exclude himself from the world, and this desire within him was misunderstood by everyone. He wanted to be a part of the world, if only in a small way. If Abraham's name was mentioned as a prospective husband for their daughters, fathers would ask themselves, *What would become of my daughter?* But Sophia knew him in another way, and she defined his character differently. She admired his unwillingness to let his mind slow down, that he wanted to try something new, to break away from the confines to which he had been born. These facts were precisely why she loved him. She decided that Abraham had been born into the wrong environment; he just wasn't in his element, and she knew that he too realized this about himself.

Athina knew she wouldn't be ready when Sophia was to go. It was going to break her that Sophia was going to leave for only God knew how long. When would she return? People always say they're coming back, but rarely do. Sometimes it's really difficult to be left behind, with nothing to look forward to.

The next morning, Sophia packed her things to go home. The bus that normally came once a week had been broken down in the village for the past several weeks. The bus driver went to Gjirokastra to get the necessary parts and had not been back since. Maybe he was still waiting for the parts, or had abandoned his job and gone into some other kind of work. Regardless, Sophia absolutely refused to risk her life taking a bus out of the village. She believed that if she rode on it, death would follow her. She imagined the bus falling over a mountain cliff and tumbling down until it reached the valley floor below. So, Kosta was to journey with her in his friend's truck, out of the mountains, through immigration at the Border Control and then to Ioannia. A reverse, an unwinding of the trip that had brought her here.

"Do you have to leave, Sophia?" Athina asked as she sat on the bed watching Sophia stuff her clothes into her backpack.

"Yeah. I have to go back to start school. But I'll be back one day, you'll see."

"You promise?"

"I promise. Maybe you can come to America and visit me. Would you want to?"

Athina laughed. "How am I supposed to get there?"

"By plane —"

"Of course by plane, but how? I can't afford to come to America. Besides, I can't fly out of the airport in Tirana. I'd have to go to Greece and fly from there."

"Then fly from Greece."

"Sophia, why do you make everything sound so easy? It's not that easy for us just to leave and fly to America."

"I'm not saying it's easy, but you can do it. Have your father take you to Tirana and get you a visa," said Sophia, this time finding a solution to the obstacle. "You can come and visit me next year."

"If I got the chance to go to America, I might never come back to Chatista."

"Maybe not."

Athina began to cry.

She asked Sophia not to go, and then asked her to promise once more that she would come back and not forget them. Sophia grabbed Athina by the shoulders and told her not to worry — she would come back. She gave Athina her word that she would.

Kosta, Penelope, and Vangelli were sitting on the front porch waiting for Stavro to come and say goodbye to Sophia. Penelope put the spinach pies she had baked that morning on the table for Kosta and Sophia to take along with them on their trip.

Sophia thought of Old Man Arseni as she packed her backpack and was about to make her way out the door, away from the village, out of the country. She thought of his manner, his solemn looks, his understanding and compassion. How everyone had thought him crazy ever since he'd lost his wife long ago, but he let the world perform while he watched the show. He was along for the ride, didn't want to be a part of it because his wife wasn't there to live it with him. Sophia remembered the day when he told her things that only her father would have said; gave her advice that was invaluable and timeless. She knew now why her father felt close to Arseni, remembered him while living in America, and still considered him a friend after so many years apart. And never seeing each other again. A person didn't forget someone like Old Man Arseni, a man who had been true to his heart and soul his entire life.

She thought of the calm that enveloped Old Man Arseni. So much had happened in this country during his lifetime, and he experienced it in his own way, letting others to be the characters in the nation's play as he observed the world around him, searching for the answers that everyone else was searching for as well. He was bound by nothing, yet spellbound by the memory of his wife. He had lived an exhausting life, yet he still had all the courage, compassion, and love that a person could ever desire.

When she spoke with Old Man Arseni, Sophia saw her father, not a resemblance, but a true portrait of him. When she opened up to Old Man Arseni and told him about Abraham, the kindness he showed her made her feel the comfort and vulnerability she had known when her father was alive. The last time she visited at his house, Sophia wished Old Man Arseni well and told him she'd see him again. He smiled at her and said the same, thinking that the next time he saw her, he might see his old friend as well.

Sophia walked out to the front porch, where she said goodbye to her family and thanked them for all that they done for her. Kosta carried her backpack down the path toward the plaza where he would find the friend who was to take them to the border. Sophia started to cry because they were crying, her relatives, who had never met her before and had taken her into their home and treated her with great kindness. Her family's generosity to others, to guests, to strangers, to family, made her feel at that moment that her life prior to this trip had been filled with superfluous things and that only now was she realizing what was important. She was all of these. Sophia finished her good-byes to everyone and walked toward Kosta. He was talking to his friend, smoking a cigarette.

"Don't cry, Sophia. We know we'll see you again soon," Kosta said, as she approached the truck. He put his arm around her.

"Yeah, I know we will. I know."

They got into the truck and waved to everyone sitting in the plaza. The family walked to the end of the path to watch her leave. Athina and Stavro ran past everyone and up to the truck.

"Don't forget about us, okay?" Stavro said to Sophia, holding on to the door as the truck started moving.

"I won't forget about you, any of you. I'll be back. One day, I'll be back," she said, and touched his hand as he let go of the truck. Athina and Stavro stood and watched the truck move slowly down the rocky road that would lead them through the mountains.

Sophia wondered how long it would be until Vangelli found the pocket watch. She thought he might like it—knowing that the watch belonged here.

Sophia had discovered how love was supposed to feel. Her relationship with Abraham opened her spirit to life and love. She could think about him anytime she liked, and her memories of him gave her hope for what might come in the future. She was content. She felt that she had found herself, that she could experience the depth of love, penetrating beyond its surface. She had found the strength to have loved and, perhaps, to have lost.

She had no regrets. No shame for allowing her heart to be taken by a restless and adventurous person. And the risk had someone seen the two of them quietly walk out of the schoolhouse in the night and kiss each other one last time before they parted and crept back to their houses? After leaving Abraham, Sophia would say to herself before falling asleep, "This is how love is supposed to feel." And it would have been worth it all—the wandering eyes of the men, the continual gossip of the women, the hard stares of the vil-lage folk — to feel this way.

And this was locked in her memory.

Yet Sophia knew she had to let go of Abraham. He was living a new episode in his life, and she too was about to begin a new one. Perhaps their paths would cross again, though she didn't know when. Inner release enfolded her, a sense of resignation that comforted her as she yielded to the pain. It slowly drifted away, and Sophia let all of it go.

She stretched out her wings and floated toward the purple moun-taintops that surrounded Chatista, chasing the westward-moving sun.

Vangelli came in for the evening after playing football with his friends. He walked into the house and washed his face and brushed his teeth in the bucket his mother prepared for him every evening. He said goodnight to his father and mother, and went to his room to draw. He opened the top drawer of his nightstand and found the pocket watch. A folded note with his name written on the front was underneath. He opened it and read.

Vangelli,

Hey, this is your long-lost cousin Sophia. When you find this I'll probably already be gone — I planned it that way. This is something I want you to have, for more reasons than I can get into this little letter. Maybe one day soon I'll tell you all of them.

This watch used to be my grandfather's, your great-grandfather's. My father gave it to me several years ago; his mother gave it to him right before he left Albania. I don't know how long it's been passed on in our family, but it's yours now, and when you get older, you can pass it on to whomever you'd like.

I thought it best if the watch was back in Albania, in the village it came from; that's why I'm giving it to you now. And of course I thought you might like it, like it so much that you'd want to wear it. But please don't. Keep it in a safe place, but remember where you put it!

I'll see you again——you can count on it. As they say in your part of the world, you have my besa.

Love,

Your cousin, Sophia

After breakfast, Abraham and Yanni packed their bags and put them in the back of their truck and knocked on the door of the *zenana* and waited for the women to come out of their quarters. They said goodbye to the women of the house, and then met with the man and his uncle in front of the truck.

"I've never seen houses like this——all stone with high walls and no windows on the first floor. Why is your home built like this?" Abraham asked.

"For protection from other clans."

"Oh," was all Abraham could think of.

"Are you ready? Do you have everything?"

"I think so. We didn't bring much with us," Yanni said, shrugging.

"Okay, then. We'll take you to the KLA camp, is that where you'd like to go?" the uncle asked.

Abraham took out his cigarettes and offered them to everyone. "Yes, that's where we'd like to go. Do you know where we could leave our truck when we're gone, someplace we could leave it by the camp?"

"You could leave your truck by the camp. I think there's a place where men leave their cars. It's near the refugee camp, right?" the uncle asked his nephew, lighting his cigarette.

"Yes, you're right. We could all go together in your truck and then we'll find a ride back to our house. It won't be a problem at all. Is that all right with you two?"

"Fine. I guess we're ready," said Yanni.

"Let's go, then," said the uncle.

The man and his uncle put their rifles next to their bags in the back of the truck. "We always bring our rifles with us. It is the glory of our being," he smiled, answering Abraham's stare.

Abraham and Yanni waved to the women as they drove away from their home, and the women waved back and shouted, "May God be with you." The truck moved off, headed toward the KLA training camp.

They drove to the refugee camp in Kukes, which was near the KLA training camp. It looked like it had been there for years, stretching out forever, beyond what anyone could see. Countless families had made temporary homes there after being pushed out of their villages in Kosovo. Thousands of men, women, and children were living in flimsy tents, wondering what to do next, waiting to see whether anyone in this world was going to help them, and how.

Yanni drove the truck to the edge of the camp and slowed. "You should pull over there, a little to the side," the uncle said, pointing left. Yanni stopped where the uncle had told him to, and they all got out of the truck. The man and his uncle grabbed their rifles. Abraham and Yanni got their bags out of the back and looked around.

"Oh, God," Abraham said as he scanned the camp. "Can you believe this, Yanni?"

"No. No, I can't."

"Should we leave you boys here? The KLA training camp is just on the other side of this camp. If you walk this way just a little way," he said, pointing to the left, "you'll find the training camp up ahead. Ask around if you can't find it."

"We'll be fine here. And we want to thank you again for everything," Abraham yelled over the noise of the camp. "You've been very hospitable and kind and generous. We can't thank you enough."

"Yes, we can never thank you enough," said Yanni.

"As you are our guests," said the man.

The uncle smiled. "May God protect you from bearded women and barefaced men," he said, rubbing his cheek.

"Huh?" said Yanni, looking at their faces.

"It's an old saying here in the north, to give you protection on the journey you are about to begin," the uncle explained.

Abraham and Yanni looked at each other, confused, but brushed aside what he said.

"Maybe we'll see you again when we return? We'll stop by your home and say hello," said Abraham.

"If you like," the uncle replied.

"We will," said Yanni. He and Abraham said goodbye to both men and picked up their bags.

The man and his uncle stared at Abraham and Yanni.

"You are no longer our guests," said the man.

Abraham and Yanni looked at him and said nothing.

"You are no longer our guests," he repeated.

"We are no longer your guests," Abraham and Yanni said, looking at the man, not knowing what else to say.

The man lifted his rifle and shot Abraham and Yanni in the head as his uncle, smoking his cigarette, looked on.

"Orthodox fucking Greeks," the man said, spitting on the ground between them.

A crowd quickly turned to look when they heard the man's rifle go off twice. Women screamed, grabbed their children, and ran into the camp. Men stood confused, not knowing what was happening Two policemen ran over, guns drawn and ready to fire. They looked at Abraham and Yanni on the ground, already dead.

"It's okay, officers, it's okay!" the uncle yelled over the noise. "Don't shoot! Don't worry!"

"What's going on here?" one of the officers shouted.

"They're Orthodox, Greeks from southern Albania. They said

they came here to fight with the KLA," the uncle said.

"Orthodox?" one of the officers asked.

"Orthodox," said the man.

The officer raised his hand in approval, smiled, and turned around. He and his partner walked back to the camp and told the refugees who the dead were and where they had come from. The refugees cheered and clapped, holding up their hands to the uncle and the man who had shot Abraham and Yanni. Celebration swept over the camp, like a wave coming ashore.

There is a saying in the north: "It is evil to boast self-righteousness, denying the good in others." How different things could be if the world remembered this saying. And there is another one: "It is only what man believes he has found that divides the world's religions. It is the still-unfound, for which we all search, that makes mankind one."

Twenty-four

A month after Sophia returned to the States, she left for the West Coast for a six-year program of graduate work in European history. Years later, immersed in her life, her world, she would still remember her time with Abraham in Chatista. She wrote everything down — on the advice of her old friend, Vanessa, whom she had bumped into in Cambridge a couple of years earlier. When she wrote, her thoughts poured onto the paper as if her mind had sprung a leak. Vanessa had been right, it was therapeutic. Perhaps one day Sophia would sit and read what she had written, but not until years from now. She was certain.

She surrendered to the fact that the trip to Albania was just another episode in her unstructured life. There had never been a logical progression to the choices she made; things seemed to come about when they saw fit. Sophia's goals had always been ephemeral; she simply moved on to something different when she felt mired in a routine. She detested going through the motions, gradually becoming less aware of her surroundings, and tried to evade the simple notions of comfort and routine expectations. Though she had always wanted this unrestricted lifestyle, experiencing it in the moment sometimes saddened her. With no anchor to keep her anywhere for a long time, Sophia tended to float away to someplace new, like a raft aimlessly adrift in a large sea, allowing the wind to direct it.

Come what may.

The solitary hours she spent writing history papers about Eastern Europe, as the books defined it, would bring her back to the moments she had known in a Balkan village. Sophia marveled at how much was missing from those history books, written by scholars who had never left the manicured campuses at which they lectured and wrote, or hadn't revisited the Balkans in years and seen how different a place it had become.

She found herself thinking of Abraham as she researched and wrote. She was reading about a world he was in, yet was not a part of. The history books never talked about people like Abraham and how they lived and felt and thought. She would think of these things as she studied in her off-campus apartment that overlooked the street that ran past the school. She would look around her room and see her world, her comforts, her sturdy bed, her color TV, and her soft, comfortable couch — all these things that were hers and hers alone.

Her love of history had always kept her mind alive. It was the only part of her that was continually progressing. This was when it didn't matter to her where she was or what she was doing; she had this security, this constant. Sophia was doing something that made her tick and that grounded her unrestrained spirit.

Her friends thought her an eccentric who did and said things that seemed bizarre. They would laugh these off, but wonder afterward: *Does she really think about these kinds of things? Who would ever come up with that idea?* Sophia remembered one time when she was with a group of friends and mentioned casually that she would love to isolate herself from the rest of the world for a time and just read books. She said she was growing tired of the "social responsibility of life," as she referred to it. Feeling obliged to partake in society sometimes made her uneasy. Her friends didn't know how to take that — a weird recluse, perhaps, was what they thought of Sophia.

She had chosen a graduate school in California because she wanted to start over, yet she wasn't searching for a place to hide from her past. Rather, it was self-exploration, a challenge to adjust to something new. Her friends envied her for putting her roots elsewhere in the world. Even when she felt lonely in a different place, she knew that her friends were thinking how fortunate she was to have the opportunity to escape and be somewhere else. They believed that she was happy. An adventure is always intriguing to those who are left behind. Relishing the whole idea of "getting away from here" is human nature. Sophia delighted in it.

She couldn't help wondering how her life would change if ever Abraham could come to America and live with her, how different his life would be living in an American city and indulging himself in America's culture, opportunities, comforts. She would have loved the chance to make things the way they should have been, the way she wanted them.

A new bus is leaving Chatista in ten minutes. Abraham is standing next to it saying goodbye to his family and friends. Everyone is excited for him as he promises to write when he gets to America. His mother looks at him, hiding the tears of worry, yet she is happy for her son; his father gives him a strong pat on the back, telling him he is proud. The bus leaves the village and makes its way to the border, where he'll take a second bus after he gets his passport stamped at the Border Control station on the south side of the road. He arrives in a city that he's been to before, worked in. He feels a slight nervousness as he looks around the familiar surroundings that are Ioannia; the painful memories consume him for a moment. His throat tightens slightly. He shakes his head to wipe the thoughts away.

Abraham spends the next couple of hours at one of the town plazas, reading before stepping onto another bus, which stops in Larissa before arriving in Athens. The bus leaves him at the airport, where he finds the plane ticket that awaits him at the Olympic Airways desk. He checks in at the gate and waits for his flight to depart, eating spinach pie and drinking cola before he hears the boarding call. He shows the flight attendant his ticket and passport one last time before he walks outside and gets on another bus that leads him to the airplane sitting on the runway.

As the plane takes off for London, Abraham looks at a map in the seat pocket in front of him and is amazed by how far he's traveling from where he began his trip. It makes him feel both small and excited. When the plane lands at Heathrow Airport, he goes through Immigration, gets his passport stamped, and walks around the airport for a few hours before his next flight departs. He is mesmerized by the hugeness of Heathrow — the few hours are not enough time for him to absorb everything. Yet he checks in at the gate, walks through the corridor that leads him directly to the plane, and finds his seat. The plane's cleanliness, hospitality, and sophistication comfort him, make him feel important and accepted. He quickly finds the map in the seat pocket, and is anxious about how large the Atlantic Ocean is and how far around the world he will be. He studies the map and realizes that he will have flown halfway around the world to the great big continent that is North America, the land that he will fly over until he lands at its western edge at a place called San Francisco, where his new home will be. "San Francisco, San Francisco," Abraham whispers to himself. He likes the sound of the name. *How did America get a Spanish city? Do people speak Spanish in San Francisco?* Suddenly, a screen light up on the back of the seat in front of him, and a movie about a lovesick young couple on a sinking ship is shown. He notices that some of the actors in the movie have the same accents as those who are on this plane.

The plane arrives in San Francisco, and Abraham is awakened by a flight attendant gently shaking his shoulder and speaking to him. He can't understand her, and he feels like he's in a dream as he watches her mouth move and she smiles at him, her hand on his shoulder. He looks around trying to get a sense of where he is and what he is doing. He sees that everyone is making their way off the plane, so he smiles at the flight attendant, not saying a word, and grabs his bag from the bin above him and follows the other passengers.

He walks through the airport and goes through Customs and Immigration for the final time, has his passport stamped again, and walks down another hall that leads to the waiting area, where families and friends have gathered, waiting excitedly for their loved ones to emerge. Sophia notices him right away — his messy hair and Levi's and knitted sweater. A big smile lights her face and she tries to make her way through the crowd and get to him before he walks off. When she gets to the front of the crowd, he sees her, smiles, drops his bag to the floor, and walks to her and hugs and kisses her. They walk down the hall and down the stairs to Baggage Claim to pick up his suitcase, all the while holding each other. They find his suitcase and go to the parking garage, put his luggage in the trunk of her car, and drive out of the parking garage. They drive the freeway over the bridge to Berkeley, and along the street that leads to her apartment right off campus. Sophia parks her car in front of her building and walks up the steps to her home.

He follows her.

Sophia was jolted out of her thoughts by the ringing phone on the coffee table next to the couch. She looked around the room and saw and heard the things that were so familiar to her — the sounds outside, the students walking down the street, the comforts surrounding her. She let the voice mail take the call. Her apartment became quiet again, the noises from outside muffled after she closed the windows. She looked at her monitor and went back to her writing, finishing the sentence she had left incomplete a moment ago.

Twenty-five

As it moves across the landscape, a chameleon adjusts its skin to adapt to the background. It escapes attack by changing the color of its being. This gift allows it to roam freely in the world, feeling secure. Sensing danger, the chameleon can hide in the grass or sand and lie undetected until the enemy gives up and moves off to find other prey. The chameleon can sense danger readily and keenly. The ability to change color and to detect danger is one of its secrets.

There are chameleons living in the Balkans. They roam the countryside as if they were invincible. They crawl through the mountains and observe their surroundings, at the same time blending into the landscape. If they get tired of a particular area, they travel to another that is more appealing to their eyes.

Other animals living in the desert prey on the chameleons, and it becomes their obsession. The predators move throughout the land in search of them, but most of the time the chameleons are too clever, or perhaps just too lucky. A predator may waste its whole life searching for a chameleon and never succeed in its perpetual chase.

There are moments when a chameleon is very close to being caught; nearly having to surrender its soul to the predator, and moments when a chameleon has been captured, but escapes before its soul reaches the heavens. It escapes with wounds to its skin, tail, and legs, and maybe its mind, but in time, it always heals itself and moves on with its life. And it never forgets what has happened, making certain that it will persevere throughout the rest of its life, undetected, observant, hopeful.

Its capacity for adaptation, resistance, and perseverance allows the chameleon to survive in the Balkans. No matter what the chameleons encounter, they always finds a way to survive. They bring other chameleons into the world, and they in turn learn how to adjust to the ways of the Balkans. The chameleon will never fall out of existence; it will always continue its habits of adaptation and teach its young the ways of their world — an oral folk tale of a sort, passed from one generation to the next.

One finds the most resilient chameleons in the Balkans. Their ability to outsmart predators and survive in the tumultuous region speaks well for these creatures. But adaptation to the landscape, the change of skin color, was forced upon them for mere survival. It is amazing what the chameleon, an evolved being, will do to live in a particular land. No matter how much they are preyed upon, they always find ways to stay in the region. Their inner strength, their resilience, and their adaptability prove their passion for the land.

Few understand the chameleon. Some understand only its reasoning but not its passion. Most do not understand how it could want to live in such an unstable place, a precarious state that fumes with violence. They will never understand what the landscape means to the chameleon, the love it has for its home. The chameleon is fervent about its land because it defines its existence, its soul.

Each region has its own idiosyncrasies that create the foundation of a particular culture or mix of cultures. Some chameleons form bands and help one another to survive. In time, these bands create different thoughts, different ideas, different minds — different ideologies. They form a loyalty to each other, a bond that is never broken. They become willing to fight for each other, and fight against the other as if it were completely different, as if they had never been the same.

They fight for their ideas, for their cause, for their right to the land. And they define this as glorious — a courageous act, a destiny, a duty to their brethren, to their band, never reminding themselves that they were, in fact, one and the same at some point in time.

And what was the predator is not a danger any longer. The bands of chameleons have come to prey upon themselves — at once predators and prey. They know each other very well: their secrets, their skills, and their hiding places. Changing the color of their skin no longer provides a great sense of security; their art of war nullifies it.

Despite the evolution of their ideas and beliefs, all the diverse bands of chameleons are still chameleons. The fragmented region they live in creates leaders and followers. Some leaders will collapse, while other chameleons will lead many chameleons with their ideology. Life in the Balkans has become so divided and so intense that the beliefs of these chameleons have become part of their existence; violence has become a part of their existence.

But, as always, the chameleon will continue to adapt to its surroundings and evolve its being.

These mountains are alluring, but they can be deceitful. Their beauty and magnitude never cease to fascinate me. They present themselves with warmth and generosity, extending an invitation to explore the valleys and paths within them. Their presence is limitless, an expanse that reaches the horizons, the country's borders. One might be moved to venture into their heights and find the spirits that lurk in their protection, spirits that have seen no restrictions, no boundaries; spirits that have the power to lure a stranger. The mountains can captivate, and have captivated me. I've never felt so alive, so pure, as in these mountains. A calm comes over me, and I have seen and felt what others mean when they tell me they have been beyond the common experience.

These mountains have a healing effect. They ease my mind and enchant my soul. Their gentle presence is easily seen at dawn, when the morning fog rolls over and hugs the ground, softening their rugged appearance, evoking a sense of surrealism. These mountains mesmerize me; they have taken hold of me and pulled me toward their strength. I will not be able to leave this land completely—I have left part of myself behind.

These mountains bring out a person's character and distinct peculiarities. They distinguish the people who live here from others. Villagers define themselves with these mountains, which have become part of their being, their perpetual phenomenon. Though a villager may leave for a time, he will always come back to these mountains. *He knows who he is; he knows where he is from.*

Yet I've seen these mountains behave maliciously, and have heard stories of how cruelly they have molded people. I've seen in a man's eyes the pain he feels when he thinks of his how his wife was burned to death in these mountains. I've seen these mountains help a young girl kill herself because of something that was growing inside of her, hiding her from view in their depths. I've heard these mountains have no mercy for a villager as he is shot in the head, along with his friend, in wartime.

But I've been told that these mountains helped four people escape from communism, hiding them in a cave while soldiers looked for them, rifles aimed. Waiting.

My mountains. They raised Abraham, and taught him everything he knows and understands. They are part of him. The valley defined him; it possessed his soul. The mountains drove Abraham to honor and love his land.

I am a warrior and will fight for the cause. I come from this land and I will follow its rules and they will guide me. I will not back down from the enemy. I will live up to my ancestors' vision, the dream the Illyrians dreamed.

I will give my strength to the people, and hope they are willing to embrace it. I cannot go back, I cannot stand still. I must be a part of this tradition, a part of my land's history. I face the burden of my culture's ridicule and my land's shame. I face my religion's rhetoric and my government's religion. I face my people's hope. I must not fail.

The ideology I embrace, the vision I see, cannot be tainted by the weak or manipulated by those with strength. I must overcome the burdens I face. I must conquer the obstacles ahead of me. I will not be empowered by that which I do not believe.

My hope will carry me, and I will be loyal to it. I will fight ceaselessly and wield my sword swiftly. My ancestors will watch me from the heavens and they will guide me. They will not lead me through the forest blindly, but will hold my hand forever.

I must live up to the honor for which I seek.

Helen Dean Brewer is a freelance writer in marketing for various companies throughout the nation. She has a Bachelors degree in History and English from Elmhurst College and a Masters degree in American Literature from Harvard University. She lives in Chicago with her husband. *Gypsy of the Sea* is her first novel.